Death of a Matador

An Inspector Ruiz Mystery

DEATH OF A MATADOR

James García Woods

LUME BOOKS

LUME BOOKS

Published in 2021 by Lume Books
30 Great Guildford Street,
Borough, SE1 0HS

ISBN 978-1-83901-271-6

Typeset using Atomik ePublisher from Easypress Technologies

www.lumebooks.co.uk

This is for Eric, my dad.
and also for:
Collette, my sister, and Steve, her husband, who have given him
a wonderful home.

Author's Foreword

I've never written a foreword before, but there were a number of things I wanted to say which I couldn't see fitting in anywhere else, so here goes.

I know from emails I've been sent (and reviews I've read), that a fair number of my readers would like more background, so I have included a Notes section at the back of the book. It is an idiosyncratic collection of facts, comments and reminiscences. There are some readers, I suspect, who will find this unnecessary (and even pretentious), but hey, it's an extra, and you don't have to read it.

Following the same reasoning, I have also included a list of some of the books I have used as a source for this novel. A couple of them at weighty academic tomes, but most are easy, enjoyable reading.

You might like to know that Paco Ruiz appears in six more books. Three of them are published by Lume (and are also available as an omnibus). The others, all published by Severn House under the name Sally Spencer (a.k.a. me), are *The Butcher Beyond* – a DCI Woodend mystery, and *Echoes of the Dead* and *Death's Dark Shadow* – which are DCI Paniatowski mysteries and also feature Charlie Woodend.

Most of the characters in this book are fictional. The three exceptions are César the barman, my wife Lanna, and me. César is there because he owned the Cabo de Peñas bar. We are there because we drank (sometimes too much!) in the bar, and because we have allowed Paco and Cindy to occupy the apartment we rented forty years later. Even so, I haven't gone wild. We are all three background characters, and when I'm eventually allowed to speak, it's only to say how bad I am at playing German whist.

This is the first Paco Ruiz book I have written for over twenty years, I was surprised by just how much I enjoyed writing it. I hope you get as much pleasure out of reading it.

J.G.W., Calpe, Alicante, November 2020

Prologue

Saturday 15 May 1937

Once he sees the sword – *his* sword – aimed squarely at his chest, he freezes.

It is not fear that has paralysed him. He has faced death too many times in the bullring to be afraid of that. No, he stays rooted to the spot simply because he can't think of anything else to do – any other action he could possibly take.

His eyes are fixed steadfastly on the portrait of the Virgen de la Paloma – her skin so pale, her eyes so agonised, her hands clasped as though in stoic acceptance of what must be – but he is not actually seeing her.

With the eyes in his head, he is not really seeing anything at all in the chapel.

Ah, but in his *mind's* eye, he is seeing a great deal – there, he is picturing an entire world.

A bright blazing fire set in the middle of a sea – an ocean – of darkness. And around that fire – drawn to it as moths are drawn to candlelight – are people. Most of them squat, comfortably enough, on their haunches. Some of them are smoking, some are eating corn on the cob, and some are quite content to save their hands just for clapping.

And there is much clapping to be done, because the three handsome young women dancing against the light of the flickering fire – their black hair oiled and pinned up tightly at the backs of their heads, their long flowing dresses almost brushing the ground – make the earth tremble when they stamp their heels, and the air swirl when they turn their bodies.

He can not only see all this – he can hear it, too.

The *clack-clack-clack* of the castanets.

The cries of *olé*.

The music that breaks free of the guitars, music which – it seems to him now, if it did not then – has the power to drag the very devil himself from hell, and force him to dance on hot coals until his cloven hooves melt.

And there are the smells.

Oh yes.

The unmistakeable scent of burning olive wood.

The odour of roasting garlic.

And the sweat – a sweat so different from that which he smells in the city, a sweat that belongs to a people who are wild and free.

He cannot say definitely that this was the last time he was completely happy, though he suspects it was. And what he does know for certain is that he wishes he were there now.

And this is the last thought he has before the sword – his sword! – passes between his ribs and punctures his heart.

Chapter One

Thursday 12 May 1977 – morning

It was a little less than five hundred kilometres from Calpe to Madrid. The journey time would depend on the vehicle used – and who was driving it. The average family man, with the average family car, would usually take around six hours. The young men, who favoured dark glasses even when there was no sun – and who equated speed with masculinity – claimed that they could make the trip in under four. But if you drove a Seat 600, as Paco did, then you made an early start if you wanted to reach your destination in time to do more than just flop into bed.

And so it was that Paco Ruiz, ex-inspector in the Madrid Homicide Squad, and Charlie Woodend, ex-detective chief inspector in the Central Lancs CID, hit the road just after the sun had risen.

Woodend considered Paco's tiny car to be little more than a boxed-in motor mower, though he was wise enough not to say that aloud, since it was obvious that Paco was fond of the vehicle.

In fact, when Paco absent-mindedly addressed the Seat aloud, he called it *Rocinante* ('Come on Rocinante, you can make this hill.' 'I'm going to let this truck pass us, Rocinante, because he's much bigger

11

than you are.'), which Woodend, being well-read for an ex-bobby, knew was the name of Don Quixote's horse. And sometimes, it seemed to him, Paco held the steering wheel almost as if he were holding the reins of a broken-down old nag.

So if he saw the car as Rocinante, did he also see himself as Don Quixote, the romantic idealist who clung to the ideal of chivalry, long after chivalry itself had ceased to exist?

And if that was the case, did it also mean that he saw his travelling companion as Quixote's squire, Sancho Panza – stolid, down-to-earth and dependable? If he did, well, there were worse things to be thought of than stolid, down-to-earth and dependable.

So there they were, Woodend thought – Paco Quixote and Charlie Panza – setting off on their quest. He had no idea what the quest involved, but he did know that it was very important to Paco to go to Madrid, and to have his friend accompany him – and that was good enough for him.

Joan Woodend and Cindy Walker Ruiz stood on the terrace of the Woodends' villa, and watched in silence as the car carrying their husbands slowly made its way down the hill, towards the main road. Then, when the little Seat's rear lights disappeared around a bend, Joan turned to Cindy and said, 'Do you fancy a cup of tea, love?'

'I'd prefer coffee,' Cindy replied, and then, realising she might have put Joan in an awkward position, she added, almost apologetically, 'if you have it, that is.'

Joan grinned. 'Your Paco is round here every other day – so of course I have coffee.'

The Woodends' kitchen was quite unlike the one they'd left behind in Whitebridge where – instead of this view of the calm, beautiful blue sea, the panorama had been of rough, savage (though still oddly

12

beautiful) moorland – but there was enough of Lancashire about it to remind Joan of home.

As she brewed the tea and made the coffee, she glanced across at Cindy, who was sitting at the large wooden table that Joan had used for her baking for over 30 years, and had insisted (at some expense) on bringing with her.

Cindy was in her middle seventies, she guessed. Her long hair was as white as freshly fallen snow, and she was as slim now as she must have been when Paco first met her.

I was slim once, too, she thought, but now I'm what they call 'broad across the beam'.

Still, she supposed everybody ended up looking as they were supposed to, and Charlie was comfortable enough with her the way she was.

She took the two cups and the teapot across to the table.

'So, the two of them are off on a lads' adventure,' she said lightly.

'Yes,' Cindy agreed, unconvincingly.

Joan looked her in the eye. '*Isn't* it an adventure?' she asked.

'It's more than that for Paco,' Cindy said awkwardly.

'In what way?' Joan worried.

Cindy shrugged. 'It's complicated.'

'Well, you've got plenty of time to go into complications, and I'm a good listener,' Joan said.

'Yes, you are, aren't you,' Cindy agreed. She took a deep breath. 'When Franco's army rolled into Madrid in 1939, the killing started immediately. Thousands of people were tried and executed by firing squad.' She laughed bitterly. 'The trials often took less time than the executions. In the end, even the men in charge of it were sickened by all the death. They went to see Franco, and asked him if they could bring it to a halt. He refused that request, but just to show how

13

merciful he could be, he said that of the hundreds condemned to death every day, one man in ten could have his sentence commuted to thirty years hard labour.'

'What had all these people done?' Joan asked, horrified.

'They had fought against Franco, or else assisted those who were fighting against him,'

'But that's what happens in war,' Joan said. 'And anyway, they'd been on the side of the legitimate government.'

'In war, legitimate and illegitimate, right and wrong, do not matter,' Cindy said. 'There are only two sides, the winners and the losers, and we were with the losers, so we sat there, awaiting our fate.'

'You didn't think of running away?'

'I did, though I didn't call it that, of course. I begged Paco to go to America with me, but he refused to budge. He said he had fought the Fascists for three years, and he was not about to show them his heels now.' She smiled. 'He is a kind man and a loving one. He loves me, and wants what is best for me.'

'I know he does.'

'He is also a stubborn man and a proud man.' Cindy shrugged. 'But since that's the man I fell in love in love with, I suppose I have no cause to complain.'

'What happened in the end?' Joan asked, dreading the answer.

'It was never his plan to surrender. He intended to die with a gun in his hand. He hoped he could take a couple of the bastards with him.' Cindy grinned, unexpectedly. 'I have more faith in him than that. I think he could have taken three or four with him. But he didn't have the chance,' she continued, growing more serious again. 'They came for him early in the morning. He was in the bedroom, and I was in the living room. If there'd been a gun battle, I would have been caught in the crossfire. And so he surrendered.'

14

'Did they arrest you, too?'

'No. I still had an American passport in those days, and the Fascists were being very careful not to piss off the USA.' She shrugged for a second time. 'Of course, if they'd believed they could get away with it, they'd probably have shot me on the spot.'

'What happened to Paco?'

'Most of the time, the Fascists didn't publish lists of those they had killed – I suppose they thought it wasn't worth their effort – but there was an underground grapevine of sorts, and we learned many of the names of those executed through that. Paco's was not one of those names. It didn't necessarily mean he hadn't been killed, but at least there was still some hope, so I sat and waited.'

'For how long?' Joan asked, in awe of the other woman.

'It was five years before I heard anything. I was working as a translator when I was summoned to the hospital. Paco's left leg and some of his ribs had been broken in what they said was an accident. He had been in the hospital for a few weeks, but he was far from mended. The doctor told me they needed his bed for a more serious case, and asked if I was willing to take him. I couldn't get him out of that place quickly enough. I took him home. I carried him up the steps that led to our apartment – all ninety-bloody-two of them. He wasn't very heavy, because he was half-starved, but when I'd put him into our bed, it felt as if I'd broken my back.'

'Did you nurse him yourself?'

'Yes, I'd no formal training, but I'd worked as a nurse during the war. When he was well enough to walk, we took what little money I'd been able to save and moved to the coast. We've been here ever since, and the only time we've ever been apart was the three days he went north with your Charlie, when the two of them were helping to solve one of Charlie's old sergeant's cases for her.'

15

'So have I got this straight?' Joan asked, incredulously. 'You're saying you've only been apart for three days in the last thirty-two years?'

'That's right. When you've lost someone once, you make damn sure you don't lose them again.'

'And now he's gone to Madrid,' Joan said, regretting the words the moment they'd left her mouth.

'Yes,' Cindy said. 'I've tried to persuade him to go many times – I said I'd go with him – but he's always refused, and I understood, because I knew how hard it would be for him to face the past.'

'Look, I'm sorry if Charlie ...' Joan began.

'Don't apologise,' Cindy interrupted her. 'I am not jealous of Charlie. I'm glad that going with him gives Paco the strength to do what he feels he needs to do. I think one of the reasons is that they are very much alike.'

'You're spot on there,' Joan said. 'They're both stubborn as buggery, and absolutely convinced they're right.'

'And most of the time, they *are* right,' Cindy replied.

'True enough,' Joan agreed, philosophically.

Chapter Two

Thursday 12 May 1977 – late afternoon

Charlie Woodend and Paco Ruiz stretched their necks and gazed at the top floor of the old four-storey building on the Calle de Hortaleza.

'That was where we had our apartment, Cindy and me,' Paco said nostalgically.

'Which window was it?' Woodend asked.

'None of the ones you can see,' Paco replied. 'We were at the rear. We were very happy in that apartment.' He shivered. 'At least, we were happy when circumstances allowed us to be.'

His mind had transported him back to the past, Woodend realised – back to the nightmare.

'Let's go and have a drink,' he suggested.

'Yes,' Paco agreed, in a voice which was almost robotic. 'Let's go and have a drink.'

The bar under Paco's old apartment was called the Cabo de Peñas, which even Woodend's basic Spanish could translate to 'the Cape of Peñas'. The barman was a middle-aged man, with black hair which

17

was turning grey at the temples. In the room beyond the bar, two small girls sat quietly doing their homework.

There were very few customers at that time of day. A man drinking at the bar had his cap resting on the counter next to him. It was peaked and rather grand. It could have belonged equally well to either to an army general or a postman – but Woodend was putting his money on the man being the latter.

A couple in their late twenties sat in the corner, playing cards. The man's brown hair, like the barman's black, was already showing early signs of turning white. The woman was a redhead – or was it a strawberry blonde? – which alone was enough to make her stand out in any crowd in Spain. They were obviously foreigners, and when Woodend heard the man say 'Whitebridge', even the mention of his home town was enough to make him want to rush across and embrace them both as long-lost family. Yet he restrained himself, because he knew that as pleasant as that might be, his Spanish friend needed him.

Paco ordered two white wines, and the barman gave them boquerones in vinegar as a free tapa. They were probably the best boquerones Paco had ever tasted, but despite that, he was starting to feel morose again.

'When I lived here, this bar was called the Cabo de Trafalgar,' Paco said. 'It is a cape in Andalucía.'

'Aye, they tell me there was a sea battle pretty close to there, once upon a time,' Woodend said dryly. 'That's probably the reason why we have a bloody big square in London called Trafalgar Square, with a massive column in the middle of it, atop which perches a feller with his hat on sideways.'

It had been an attempt to lighten the tone of the conversation, but it wasn't working.

'And the Cabo de Peñas is in the north, about as far as it could be from Trafalgar. Do you think that could be symbolic, Charlie?'

'Of what?' Woodend asked.

'Of the fact that Spain itself has been a country of extremes – communists and fascists, believers and atheists – and those extremes still exist, even here, right in the middle of everything.'

'Could be,' Woodend said. 'On the other hand, there could be a much simpler explanation.' He turned to the barman. 'Excuse me, lad, do you speak English?'

'A little.'

'Could you tell me why this place is called the Cabo de Peñas?'

'Because it is my bar, and I am from Asturias,' the barman said, in a voice which suggested that whilst he didn't want to be rude to a paying customer, this customer had asked a particularly stupid question.

Woodend turned back Paco. 'There you go,' he said. 'Too much thinking can give you a headache, you know. Why don't we have another glass of wine instead?'

'All right,' Paco agreed.

Woodend went to the counter to get the wines, and when he returned he saw that Paco had taken one of the paper serviettes from the dispenser, and had sketched out a rough map on it.

'I was trying to remember what the position of the two sides was in May 1937,' he explained. 'I think I've got it more or less right.'

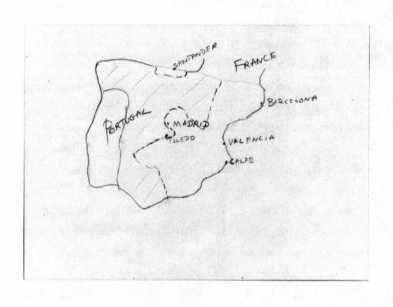

He handed the map over to Woodend. There was a line running down the centre of the country, but it was not a straight line, and it seemed to him as if the land on the left side of the line was fitted with a mouth which was gobbling up the land on the right side. Or maybe it didn't look that way at all – maybe he was just seeing it like that because he knew what happened in the end.

It was a bit of a shock, however, to see how close the dividing line was to Madrid. There was no scale on Paco's rough map, of course, but even allowing for that, the capital seemed very close to the fighting.

'Why did you draw this particular map?' he wondered.

He hadn't planned to ask that, but now he had, he recognised it for what it was – the kind of probing, exploratory question he would have asked back in the old days, during an interrogation.

'I don't know what you mean,' Paco said.

But he did! Woodend knew that he did.

'You could have drawn a map showing the position any time between 1936 and 1939, but you've specifically chosen May 1937,' he said. 'Why is that?'

Paco shrugged, awkwardly. 'I suppose it's because it was exactly forty years ago,' he said.

He was lying – or rather, he was not telling the complete truth, Woodend thought. And he realised something else – it hadn't just been important to Paco that they come to Madrid, it had had to be at precisely this time of year.

'What exactly happened in May 1937?' he asked.

Paco shrugged again – no more convincingly than the last time. 'The city was shelled by the Fascists, just as it had been shelled by them in April, and would be shelled by them in June.' He paused and looked around, as if searching for what to say next. 'I'll tell you what we'll do now,' he said decisively. 'We'll take a taxi to the place where, in the Siege of Madrid, the front line used to be.'

'Are there still signs of it left, after all this time?' Woodend wondered.

Paco shook his head. 'We might find the odd bullet hole or two in a wall, perhaps, but nothing more than that. General Franco was careful to eradicate all traces – he had no wish to keep anything which might remind him how heroic Madrid had been in its resistance – but even though the front line is no longer there, I will be able to see it.'

There were plenty of taxis going down Hortaleza, but it was a one-way street – the wrong way for their purposes.

So they walked the couple of hundred metres to the Gran Vía, where there was certain to be a whole stream of taxis.

While Paco lit a cigarette, Woodend – who had given up smoking at the start of his cancer treatment – checked his watch, and saw it was already a little after six o'clock.

'Isn't it a bit late for us to think of embarking on a new expedition, Paco?' he asked.

Paco smiled. 'How far do you think it is to the battle front?' he said.

Woodend shrugged. 'I don't know? Fifteen miles? Twenty miles?'

'Much less than that,' Paco told him, 'as you will soon see for yourself.'

Woodend saw an empty black taxi with a red blaze on its side approaching, but as he made a move to signal it, he felt Paco clamp his arm to his side.

'We do not want that one,' the Spaniard said.

'Why? What's wrong with it?'

'Black and red are the colours of the Fascists,' Paco told him. 'We will wait for a cab that does not make me want to puke.'

The next taxi which appeared was white with a red blaze across its body, and Paco waved it down.

'These are the new taxis,' he explained to Woodend, as they climbing in. 'They represent no ideology, and soon they will be the only ones around.' He turned to the driver. 'Parque del Oeste,' he said.

They drove down the Gran Via, passing all the cinemas which displayed huge, hand-painted posters to advertise their latest blockbuster films. They crossed the Plaza de España, and Paco pointed out to Woodend the statue of Don Quixote and Sancho Panza.

'It was the last thing we saw before we attacked the Montaña barracks,' he told Woodend. 'It seemed like madness to attack such a heavily fortified position, but Don Quixote's lance was pointing towards the barracks, as if urging us on, and so we did.'

'Only the Spanish would allow a statue to send them on a suicide mission,' Woodend said softly.

'What was that you said?' Paco asked.

'Nothing,' Woodend replied.

But he was thinking that if he had been there, caught up in the moment, he would probably have followed the statue's advice himself – so maybe there was a bit of Spanish blood in him, too.

The taxi stopped at the edge of the West Park.

'Have we arrived?' Woodend asked, surprised.

'We have arrived,' Paco confirmed.

They'd only been in the taxi for five or six minutes, Woodend thought, and if it hadn't been for the other traffic, they could have done the journey in four minutes easily.

Yet Paco said this was the front line!

Paco paid off the taxi driver.

'Let us go and see the pretty park,' he suggested.

Paco led the way with an assurance surprising in a man who had not set foot in the city for over thirty years.

The gardens were beautifully laid out. The trees were well cared for, the fountains soothing, the roses magnificent. It was so much better than the municipal park in Whitebridge, Woodend thought – and was instantly ashamed of himself for showing such disloyalty to his home town.

The park came to an end at a steep escarpment. Below them, they could see the River Manzanares, and on each of its banks there were several lanes of fast-flowing traffic.

'There were some roads there in 1937, but they were nothing like the size of these,' Paco said.

Beyond the roads was an area of parkland which stretched into the far distance. Within its bounds were a funfair, an amusement lake and large zoo, but even allowing for that, most of the parkland – which consisted mainly of hillocks and small pine tree woods – looked as if it had been totally untouched since the beginning of time.

'We're standing on your side of the front, and down there is the enemy's side,' Woodend guessed.

'You're mostly right, Charlie,' Paco said, enigmatically. 'Do you see that cable car?'

Woodend looked up, and saw a covered gondola on cables leaving the park. His eyes followed its journey, as it glided high over the river, and came to rest at its station in the Casa de Campo.

'Nice!' he said.

'And do you see the hillock near the station?'

'Yes.'

'That is Cerro Garabitas – Garabitas Hill. It is the highest point in the Casa de Campo, and it's where the Fascists put the big artillery guns they used to shell the city.'

'How far could the shells go?' Woodend wondered.

'You remember where we caught the taxi?'

'Yes.'

'They could go well beyond that point.'

Woodend whistled. 'So that whole area had to be evacuated, I expect.'

Paco smiled. 'Not at all,' he said. 'It was one of the busiest parts of the city throughout the siege.'

'Jesus!' Woodend said, almost to himself.

'The Casa de Campo was a maze of trenches, and so was this park. There was not a tree or a flower to be seen anywhere,' Paco continued. 'Franco had some of his best troops down there, including the Army of Africa.'

'The Army of Africa? What's that?'

'It was an army made up of soldiers whose only job was to pacify Morocco. Some of them were Moors. They were brave men, and though they could be brutal, there was a sort of savage nobility about them. The rest were the Spanish Foreign Legion. They called themselves the Bridegrooms of Death, and they would have fought their way into hell if there was any chance of rape and pillage once they got there.'

'So it's just as well that they were down there and you were up here,' Woodend said.

'Yes, and it would have been nice if it had stayed like that,' Paco said dryly. 'Could you manage a short walk?'

'Depends,' Woodend said cautious. 'What do you call "short"?'

'A little over two kilometres.'

'I'm sorry, lad, I'll get the hang of these metric measurements eventually, but for the moment, you'll have to translate for me.'

'A little over a mile,' Paco said.

'Aye, I could manage that, easily enough,' Woodend agreed.

They strolled through the pleasant university grounds before Paco brought them to a halt in front of a building that seemed to Woodend to be an attempt to combine the utilitarian modern – red brick and square – with the classical past – seven large pillars in front of the main entrance, holding up a roof which seemed to have no other function than to need seven large pillars to support it.

'This is the Faculty of Medicine,' Paco said. 'I choose this as an example because this was where I was nearly killed, but I could have selected any of a number of faculties.'

'So you're saying there was fighting here,' Woodend said.

'There were *battles* here,' Paco corrected him. 'Only small battles, it is true, but if you had taken part in one of them, you would not have called them anything else.'

'How did it happen?' Woodend asked.

'On the fifteenth of November, a division of Moorish troops managed to cross the river, and climb the hill. That moved the fighting away from the river and onto the university campus, and the enemy engineers were able to erect a temporary bridge, so more men and supplies could come across. The Fascists managed to take a number of buildings, but those of us in the Faculty of Medicine, and others in Pharmacology, were able to hold them off.'

'What was it like?' Woodend asked.

'It was the closest I have ever come to hell. The fighting was room to room. In one instance the enemy put a hand grenade in the elevator, so that when our lads opened the door, they were blown up.' Paco paused. 'Have you ever killed a man with a bayonet, Charlie?'

'Yes,' Woodend said.

'And do you ever think about it?'

'Sometimes, in the middle of the night, I can see the look in his eyes when he realised I'd killed him,' Woodend said. 'I think it's a dream – but I'm not sure.'

'I killed three men that way,' Paco said. He shook his head, as if to clear it of such thoughts. 'But eventually, when we were all too exhausted to go on, there was an unofficial truce, and we dug in. We had the buildings we had held, they had the buildings they'd captured, and there was no change from then to the end.'

This was not a case of the front line being just outside the city, Woodend thought – it was *in* the city, a couple of hundred yards from the bars and shops.

He wondered how long they could have held out against Franco's mighty military machine, backed as he was by Hitler and Mussolini.

A week? Ten days? Either of those would be heroic.

He was suddenly ashamed of how little Spanish history he knew, and resolved that when he got back to Calpe, he would study it in earnest.

'You're wondering how long the siege lasted, aren't you?' Paco asked.

'Yes, actually I was,' Woodend admitted, feeling guilty.

'We took up our position here on the nineteenth of November 1936,' Paco said weightily.

'Yes?'

'And when we abandoned the trenches, it was not because we had lost, but because the military commander of Madrid ordered us to surrender.'

'And when was that?'

'It was on the twenty-ninth of March 1939.'

Paco had suggested that instead of having a meal in a restaurant close to their modest hostel on Calle Infantas, they should bar-hop, and

Woodend agreed that it was a good idea. After sampling the tapas in several bars, they rounded off the evening in one called Das Meigas, which Paco explained was Galician for 'the witches'. Once inside, Paco insisted they order – and he pay for – a huge platter of seafood and a bottle of white wine.

'Did you come here in the old days?' Woodend asked, as he attacked a juicy *gamba* with relish.

'No,' Paco said. 'This place did not exist in the old days. There are only a few bars in the barrio which survive from when I was a policeman.'

Woodend chuckled, and helped himself to a clam.

'What have I said to amuse you so much?' Paco asked.

'It's not so much your words as your tone,' Woodend told him. 'You said, "*when* I was a policeman" – as if you'd ever stopped being a copper.'

'Funnily enough, I have the impression that I did stop,' Paco said. 'I know that I am getting old, and my mind has started playing tricks on me, but I think I remember that at one point I left the police and became a soldier.'

'You were never a soldier,' Woodend said. 'I'm not saying you didn't put on the uniform, and engage with the enemy. I'm not saying you weren't brave, because I know you were – I've done enough fighting myself to recognise a brave man when I see him.'

'Then what *are* you saying?' Paco wondered.

'That you were never really a soldier – not in your head. Oh, you did all the things that soldiers are supposed to do – and I'm sure you did them very well – but what you really were was a policeman acting the part of a soldier. Am I right?'

Paco smiled. 'Maybe,' he said.

'Once this police virus enters your blood, you can't get rid of it.

28

And I should know, because I suffer from the same disease myself,' Woodend said. 'Could I ask you a question?'

Paco shrugged. 'Why not?'

'First, you have to close your eyes,' Woodend told him, and when Paco had done as he asked, he continued, 'how many guests are there in this restaurant at the moment?'

Paco was silent for perhaps twenty seconds, then he said, 'I think there are thirty-four.'

'There are thirty-two,' Woodend told him. 'The reason I know that is because I've just counted them, but you did nothing so deliberate – you just automatically registered them. And do you think an ordinary member of the public would have done that?'

'Maybe not,' Paco conceded, opening his eyes.

'Close your eyes again,' Woodend told him.

'Haven't we finished your little test?'

'Oh no, we've only just started. That was in the nature of a warm up. Are you ready?'

'I suppose so.'

'Sitting at the table directly across from us are a man and woman. The man is somewhere around forty. He has big, hardened hands, and as far as I can see, he's one of the few people here who has chosen a steak instead of seafood. He's wearing a collar and tie, but he keeps reaching up and running his finger around the inside of his collar.'

'You are so much more observant than I could ever be,' Paco said.

Woodend grinned. 'Tell me about the woman sitting opposite the man,' he said.

'Is there a woman sitting opposite him?' Paco asked innocently. 'I hadn't noticed.'

'Yes, you had,' Woodend said.

29

'Yes, I had,' Paco agreed. 'Very well – she is in her late thirties. She's had her hair permed recently, and if her dress is not absolutely new, she's only worn it a few times. Conversation between her and the man is slightly awkward. This could be because they know each other so very well they can't think of anything new to say, but because of the hair and the dress, I think they hardly know each other at all, and are carefully feeling their way. I suspect that she's a widow, and this is their first date.'

'Maybe she's divorced or simply never married,' Woodend suggested.

'Unlikely,' Paco said. 'Divorce is still difficult to obtain in this country. And she seems too confident for a woman who has been condemned to spinsterhood until now – and in Spain, "condemned" is the right word. It is not illegal to be unmarried, but it might as well be.'

'Anything else?' Woodend asked, thoroughly enjoying himself.

'She wanted to eat the seafood platter – you can catch her glancing enviously at the other tables – but instead she ordered the steak, like the man.'

'And why did she do that?'

'The man is not used to eating out at restaurants like this one. He is a carpenter or a plumber …'

'Not a labourer?'

'No, not a labourer. The woman is obviously middle class, and though she might be prepared to lower her standards a little, and go out with a craftsman, she would never settle for a common labourer.'

'I see,' Woodend said. 'Go on.'

'He will be used to eating in the workmen's restaurants on Infantas or Chueca. He is not comfortable in a shirt and tie. He is afraid to order a seafood platter, because he doesn't know the rules for eating it …'

'I didn't think there were any rules,' Woodend interrupted.

'There aren't, but he doesn't know that, and he's afraid he'll make a fool of himself in front of the woman. So he orders a steak, and she – to save embarrassing him, orders one as well.' Paco opened his eyes. 'Have I said enough?'

'To prove my point? More than enough,' Woodend said with complacent amusement. He picked up a crab leg and explored it with the metal instrument provided. 'But you didn't quite give up *official* detecting, even in the army, did you?'

'No,' Paco agreed. 'As I think I've told you before, the Madrid High Command sent me down to Albacete to solve the murder of that International Brigade officer.'

'And that, you poor soul, was the last case you had a chance to investigate until you were rescued by the founding of the magnificent firm of Ruiz and Woodend, Private Eyes,' Woodend said, reaching for the wine.

'No, it wasn't actually,' Paco said, somewhat reluctantly.

'Really?'

'There was one more murder I investigated – not officially, but I did investigate it – and that was a few weeks after we returned from Albacete.'

Well, that was quite a bombshell to suddenly drop into the conversation, Woodend thought.

He and Paco had been friends long before they established *Ojos y Oídos*, their Calpe detective agency. They had spent countless evenings with a bottle of brandy between them, telling each other about all their old cases, but not once had there been even a hint of this particular investigation. And significantly, 'a few weeks after we returned from Albacete' would date the case somewhere around May 1937, which might offer a clue as to why Paco had wanted to be there at that particular time.

'If you'd rather not talk about it, I don't mind,' Woodend said, aware, even as he spoke, that the feeling of conviviality they had been sharing was quite gone, and in its place was a ... was a ... he didn't know quite *what* had taken its place.

'I suppose there are two reasons I haven't talked about it,' Paco said, answering a question that hadn't even been asked. 'The first is that the victim was a very old, very dear friend of mine, and even though we were living in a world where death was commonplace, I still took his killing very badly.'

'And what's the second reason?'

Paco took a long, reflective drink of his wine.

'The second reason is what my reaction was when I eventually tracked down the killer,' he said finally. 'I had expected to feel real anger – but I didn't. All I felt was sadness and pity.'

'Who did you feel the sadness and pity for?' Woodend wondered. 'Was it for the victim – or was it for the murderer?' And then, seeing Paco's blank response to both these suggestions, he dared to add, 'Or was it for yourself?'

'Perhaps it was for all of us,' Paco admitted – and it was clear that even after all those years, he did not know the answer.

'Look, if you want this conversation never to have happened, then it never happened, and I won't mention it again,' Woodend said.

'No, no, I want to talk about it to you, my friend and partner, but I cannot talk about it now,' Paco said. 'Perhaps it will get easier, the longer we are in Madrid. And if it does, I may tell you about it in stages – a little today, a little tomorrow – or maybe I will disgorge it at your feet all at once, like a dog emptying its stomach of some poison it has accidentally eaten.'

'Whichever it is, it's fine with me,' Woodend said. 'You know that.'

'Yes, I do,' Paco said.

His expression brightened somewhat, and he shouted something to a passing waiter which Woodend didn't quite understand.

'It is said they have a *hierbas* in this place that is so strong it will make a sober man drunk,' Paco said, 'and yet, by some mysterious means, it will also make a drunk man sober.'

'Which of those are we?' Woodend asked. 'Drunk or sober?'

'I don't know,' Paco confessed, 'but we will soon find out, because I've just ordered two double *hierbas*.'

Chapter Three

Paco and Cindy's tiny apartment could be found at the top of ninety-two wooden steps in an old building on the Calle de Hortaleza. It had a living room dominated by a large fireplace, and there was a small kitchen in one corner. The living room's only window looked out onto the internal well, whereas the window in the bedroom had a view over the rooftop of the building next door, which was perhaps a metre lower.

Twice the previous autumn, there had been rebel snipers on this roof – aiming at random targets below, destroying the lives of families they had never met.

On the first occasion, Paco had not arrived until it was all over, but the moment he saw the bodies of two men lying on the street – and the small group of weeping women knelling beside them – it was obvious what had happened.

'Where's the sniper now?' he asked a man standing close to the scene, who seemed on the verge of bursting into tears himself.

'Gone,' the man said mournfully.

'How can you be so sure?'

34

The man had shrugged. 'No one else is getting killed.'

On the second occasion, he had been in the apartment, and though he had heard what could have been shots, he had not known it was a sniper until Cindy had burst through the door and told him that a man and a child had been gunned down on the street.

He takes his gun from its holster, and squeezes through the small bedroom window, dropping down onto the ledge that runs around the sloping roof of the adjoining building.

He stays perfectly still, and listens.

Three times he hears the report of the sniper's rifle, which sounds more like a firework than a weapon of death – crack, crack, crack – but though he has now located his man's position, he cannot actually see him.

There are two ways to reach the man.

The first is via a narrow ledge which runs across the front of the building. If he chooses to follow that path, there will be nothing to protect him if he loses his balance – nothing to prevent him from hurtling down to the street.

But if he chooses the second route instead, which will involve climbing to the apex of the roof and then making his way along it, he will be a perfect target for the sniper.

He tells himself that if he chooses the ledge, and feels he is losing his balance as he makes his way along it, he can always twist slightly, and fling himself flat against the sloping roof. Do that, there is a good chance he can get a grip on the tiles – or some chance, anyway.

And if he fails – if he slides off the tiles and plummets towards the street – then at least his fate will have been in his own hands, not in those of a fanatic with a rifle.

There is the sound of three more shots – crack, crack, crack – followed by someone in the street below screaming. He begins to make his way cautiously along the ledge.

The sniper is on the next roof. He is near the edge of the building, which he has to be if he wants to be able to see down to the other side of the street.

He's a beginner at this, Paco thinks.

A more experienced man wouldn't still have been there, because he would have realised that most of his intended targets had now gone under cover – and that the longer he stayed, the more vulnerable he made himself.

A more experienced man wouldn't be so intent on watching the street, either – he would be continually checking his flanks and his rear.

And now it is too late for that.

'Drop your rifle,' Paco says – knowing that he won't.

The sniper swings round. He is young – seventeen or eighteen, or maybe even younger than that. There is fear in his eyes, and that again shows what an amateur he is, because a sniper shouldn't feel fear – a sniper shouldn't feel anything.

'Last chance,' Paco says.

The sniper turns towards Paco and raises his rifle. Paco waits until the boy's finger is just about to squeeze the trigger before he fires himself.

A red spot, like a bindi, appears on the sniper's forehead. He falls backwards, hits the edge of the sloping roof, and then rolls to the edge of the building. The slight incline of the ledge slows him down, and for a moment it looks as if he will stay there. Then gravity takes control, and he disappears over the lip, plunging down to the street.

'What, in God's name, did you think you were doing?' a voice screams.

Paco turns – though carefully, because there is always a chance he will follow the sniper, and unlike the sniper, he will know, in sickening detail, what will happen to him when he hits the ground.

Cindy is standing on the ledge outside their bedroom window.

'What, in God's name, did you think you were doing?' she repeats.

'Get back inside!' he says.

'Oh, I'll get back inside all right,' she tells him. 'And when you get back, I'll be waiting for you.'

The journey back somehow seems a great deal harder than the journey out had been, and twice he is quite surprised – and not a little relieved – that he is not suddenly finding himself dancing on air.

Cindy, as she signalled earlier, is in a rage.

'What the hell do you think you were playing at?' she demands, varying her theme slightly.

'There was a sniper out there,' he says. 'Someone had to stop him before he killed again, and I was the only one who could.'

'That isn't what I mean, and you know it,' Cindy says, pounding his chest with her bunched, angry fists.

'I've no idea what you're talking about,' he tells her.

And he hasn't.

'Do you really think that I didn't see the whole thing?' she asks.

'No, I … I hadn't thought about that.'

'Well, I did. I saw it all!'

'I still don't understand.'

'You had the drop on him, didn't you?'

'Yes.'

'You could have killed him without him even knowing you were there, couldn't you?'

'I suppose so.'

'But you didn't do that!' Cindy screams, beating his chest again – and now she is crying. 'You spoke to him! You just stood there while he turned his rifle towards you! Why did you do that?'

'Because I had to give him a chance to fight back.'

'So that's what you always do, is it – give them a chance to fight back?'

No, it wasn't. In Morocco, he had shot Moorish rebels at a distance, and only a few months earlier, he had taken out two Fascists in a machine-gun nest from under cover, in order to save the men they had pinned down.

'It isn't always possible to give them a chance,' he says.

'But when it is, you do?'

'Yes.'

Cindy sighs. 'What chance had that sniper given his victims?' she asks.

'None at all,' he admits.

'Then did he deserve a chance himself?'

'No.'

'So why did you give him one, you stupid bastard?'

'I didn't do it for him,' Paco says. 'I did it for me.'

For a few moments, Cindy is silent, then she unclenches her hands and starts to gently stroke his chin.

'I don't think I'll ever fully understand you,' she says softly, 'but there are moments when I really am quite proud of you.'

When Paco had returned from Albacete with his arm in a sling (and a hole in his shoulder previously occupied by a bullet), the doctor had cautioned him not to try to do too much, and Paco had assured him, through clenched teeth, there was absolutely no chance that he would.

'I don't mean now – at this very moment,' the doctor had said, a weariness in his voice suggesting he'd had this same conversation, with many men, many times before, 'I mean once you start to feel better. That's when you mustn't overdo things – small, careful steps are the order of the day.'

'I'll see to it that he's careful,' Cindy had said, making it sound more like a threat than a promise.

And so she had. For the first few days, he had walked no more than a block, and even that had seemed like an epic journey. Then, slowly and cautiously, he had begun to increase the length of his expeditions.

That morning, he was heading for the Puerta del Sol. A few weeks earlier that would have seemed impossible, but now he could accomplish it with ease, which meant, of course, that he would soon be fit enough to report for duty again.

He was dreading it, not because he might be killed – he had always believed he would not live to see his fortieth birthday – but because it involved leaving Cindy behind.

Cindy, Cindy, Cindy!

When he'd met her, less than a year earlier, she had been a farm girl, straight out of Kansas – the first member of her family to go to college – and had come to Madrid to improve on the Spanish she had learned during her studies. Since then she had been kidnapped by the rebels, almost killed by enemy agents, and been literally up to her elbows in blood as an auxiliary nurse on the front line. Yet she was still the wide-eyed country girl – her spirit uncrushed, her light undimmed – who had never lost hope that justice would triumph.

And she loved him! Incredible as it was, she loved him. He was the luckiest man in the world – and he knew it.

He reached Calle de Montera. A year earlier, it would have been bustling with all kinds of people at this time of day – maids out shopping; businessmen and minor government officials self-importantly moving along at a brisk pace with their briefcases under their arms; nuns – always in groups of at least three – observing this alien world with incomprehension (and perhaps a little envy); workmen, with their bags of tools, puffing energetically on Celtas cigarettes; and, of course, the whores, performing the difficult task of keeping in the shadows, where respectable people would not be offended by the sight of them, whilst also making themselves conspicuous to anyone in search of reasonably priced, joyless sex.

Now, the servants no longer ambled around, taking advantage of their limited freedom to sneak a little time with their friends. Instead they stood in long, slow-moving lines, queuing for whatever was available on the ration card. Now, there were no men in smart suits – sartorial elegance was taken as a sign of being an enemy of the Republic, and boiler suits or some kind of military gear were the only permissible clothing. There were still workers, of course, but now they tended to be older – men brought out of retirement – because the younger workers were all in the militias, and manning the barricades. There were no nuns at all, because the Catholic church was an avowed enemy of the Republic, and the nuns had fled, gone into hiding, or been killed, and even though he had witnessed none of the killings himself (and couldn't have prevented them even if he had) Paco still felt a burning personal shame that such a thing had happened in the city he called home.

And what about the whores? Well, there had always been whores – and there probably always would be.

The Puerta del Sol was not simply the heart of Spain – it was the heart of what had once been a vast empire. So, it was to Sol that visitors from Peru and Cuba, from Argentina and the Philippines, directed their feet, and once there, they would find themselves rubbing shoulders with pilgrims from closer at hand – peasant farmers from Andalucía, fishermen from Galicia, and potters from Teruel.

All distances in Spain were measured from this spot, so if a roadside stone in some distant, dusty province said four hundred and thirty kilometres, it meant four hundred and thirty kilometres from Sol.

It was also in Sol, on the thirty-first of December, that the ball dropped from the clock tower on top of the Real Casa de Correos, thus allowing the New Year to begin.

Sol was buzzing. Sol was exciting. Sol encapsulated the spirit of a modern Spain, though, by the standards of most of the rest of Europe, it was not really modern at all.

And the war had not put a stop to that – though, God knows, the Fascists had certainly tried.

A bomb, dropped from one of Hitler's planes, had blasted a huge crater near the metro station, and exposed part of the railway track, ten metres below. Shells, fired from the big guns in the Casa de Campo, had damaged the ornate frontage of several buildings.

Yet the square still lived. The trams were running, the lottery sellers were offering tickets, the shoe-shine boys were polishing shoes. People stepped around the craters without making a big production number out of it, and if they gazed up at the damaged buildings, they did so with a vague curiosity, rather than through horror or fear. It was almost, Paco thought, as if they regarded the damage as no more than the natural order of things, like a sudden rainstorm or an unexpected traffic jam.

As he passed one of the pavement cafés, he couldn't help smiling when he saw an empty table with a cup of milky coffee on it. The coffee had not been recently poured. In fact, mould had begun to form on its surface, and two dead flies bobbed up and down every time a passer-by nudged the edge of the table with his hip and made it vibrate.

Paco knew the story of why the coffee was there. The previous year, when Madrid seemed on the verge of falling, General Mola, one of the rebel leaders, had announced that he would be drinking coffee in the Puerta del Sol the very next day, and the café owner had put

41

out the coffee as a way of mocking the fact that he had not been able to live up to his promise. And it still sat there, a constant reminder that though the rebels had managed to overrun half of Spain, Madrid had said, 'They shall not pass' – and they hadn't!

Paco sat down at a table near the one with General Mola's coffee cup, and ordered a glass of wine. From where he was sitting, he got a clear view of new poster which was springing up everywhere. It showed a bear – the symbol of Madrid – eating a swastika – representing the Nazis and, by extension, the rebel army.

Paco's gaze shifted from the poster to Mola's coffee and back again. It was almost possible to believe, looking at that cup, that the Madrileño spirit would prevail, and that the rebels would be defeated.

Almost – but not quite.

The rebels had the backing of Nazi Germany and Fascist Italy, and those two powers had tied their own fates so closely to the fate of Spain that they would do whatever was necessary to ensure that Franco won.

'But at least we can go down fighting,' he said softly to himself.

As so many already had, he thought. He'd lost two close friends even before the war had got properly underway – Ramón, a clerk at one of the ministries, and Bernardo, a trades' union official. Ramón had been arrested by the anarchist militia just after the Montaña barracks fell, and had never been heard of again. Bernardo had been killed by a stray bullet as he manned one of the barricades in the battle for the University City.

Paco had known others who had died, too – Alfredo the shoe shine, and Pedro the street sweeper, both killed by General Castro's men in the mountains – and now, the only friend he had left was Fat Felipe, who had been his faithful sergeant in the old days.

And Cindy, of course – he did not know how he would survive without Cindy.

The tall, slim man who chose that moment to walk past his table looked vaguely familiar but perhaps it was just the graceful fluidity of his movements that reminded Paco of someone.

The man stopped, turned around, and, without making any attempt to be subtle, stared directly at him.

'Paco Ruiz!' the man said. 'Is that really you?'

Paco took a closer look at him. He was a handsome man of around his own age, and almost definitely a gypsy, which meant that there was a good chance he had been brought up in Andalucía, where Paco himself had spent part of his childhood.

'Faustino?' he said, tentatively. 'Faustino Vargas?'

The other man grinned, but at the same time raised a cautionary finger to his lips.

'Not so loud,' he whispered. 'I do not want to be recognised.'

Of course he didn't, Paco thought.

'Sit down,' he said, in a voice almost as low as Faustino's. 'Let me buy you a drink?'

'Thanks, I'll have a wine, too,' Faustino replied, and then, saying no more, he took a newspaper out of his pocket, opened it, and held it up in front of his face.

Faustino Vargas, Paco mused. They had first met when they were eight or nine years old. All the gypsies in the area were poor, but then so was everyone else, so it wasn't Faustino's poverty which had made Paco's friends single him out as an object of persecution. Perhaps, Paco thought at the time – or was it only in retrospect? – their lives were so desperate that they needed someone – anyone – to feel superior to, and Faustino's clear cultural differences made him the obvious candidate.

Whatever their reasons, Paco had wanted nothing to do with it, and if that meant losing all his long-time companions – which it did – then so be it.

He and Faustino became firm friends, and Paco was soon spending more time at the gypsy encampment than he did at home. The gypsies fascinated him. They were strange and mysterious, and he longed to learn what made them tick. But they did not remain of purely academic interest for long. In fact, they very rapidly became an important part of his life. Yes, they were different; they danced and sang flamenco by open fires, late into the night; and some of their eating habits – like their fondness for roasted hedgehogs – seemed both strange and revolting at first. Yet it was not long before he too was dancing, and tucking into the hedgehogs with relish.

In many ways, he became a gypsy himself.

In many ways, he still was one.

He and Faustino had swum together, raced together, and, in time, would no doubt have chased girls together. But it was not to be.

It is late afternoon. Manolo and Rosa, Faustino's parents, have been picking olives all day under a blistering sun, and have just been to the office – which is in the walled grounds of the landowner's finca – to receive the pittance they are owed. Now, they step through the finca's ornamental gates, and turn immediately to the left, following a path which will take them back to their encampment. Behind them, they hear the gates slam closed, a clear message – if they needed one – that they are only welcome when they can be exploited.

It is then that they see the wagon. It is coming down the hill at some speed, and shows no sign of slowing down. As it gets closer and closer, it becomes obvious that it will crash into the expensive metal gates.

Then, at the last moment, the driver swerves to the left, and now the wagon is heading straight at the two gypsies. There is no time to run, and though Manolo tries to push his wife out of the way, it is too late for that, too, and both of them are crushed against the wall.

Later

Though young Paco has already stopped believing in God, he attends Manolo and Rosa's funeral mass out of respect for them, and that is why he is in the gypsy encampment when the two guardia civil officers arrive.

The guardias never serve in their own region, because no one likes to break the head of a fellow Galician or Catalan, so it is much more efficient to have Galician policemen break Catalan heads, and Catalan policemen break Galician heads. They do not even live among the people they have been sent to police – perhaps through fear they might grow to like them – and so have their own barracks, which include schools for their children.

They are the law in the countryside, and they are justly feared. These two, though, seem quietly amenable, so perhaps even they have the decency to behave well at a wake.

'Who is the head of the Gypsy Council?' one of them asks.

'I am,' says an old man with a mouth full of gold teeth.

'And what is your name?'

'Borja.'

'Well, Borja, it's about the accident. We're here to discuss compensation.'

Borja nods. 'We have been talking about this in council. Manolo was a young man with many good years ahead of ...'

'Kindly do not speak until I have finished talking,' the guardia says, and there is a harsh edge to his voice now.

Borja looks down at the ground.

'I am sorry to have interrupted you, señor.'

'We will overlook it – this time,' the guardia says generously. 'But to

45

get back to the matter in hand – the two gypsies who were killed were drunk ...'

'They were not ...' Borja begins.

'They were drunk,' the guardia says firmly. 'The driver of the wagon – which, as you no doubt know, belongs to Don Alejandro – tried his best to avoid them, but the unfortunate result was that the truck crashed into the wall of Don Alejandro's finca. Both the truck and the wall were damaged. Now, as a matter of law, Don Alejandro has a good case for claiming compensation from the family of the two dead gypsies, but because he has a generous nature, he has decided, on this occasion, to waive his right. Is that clear?'

'Yes,' Borja says.

'Good. So am I to tell Don Alejandro that you wish me to express your gratitude to him?'

'Yes,' Borja says.

'Then our business here is done,' the guardia says, and the two policemen saunter away.

Everybody in the encampment knows the truth. Manolo and Rosa were not drunk. Gypsy women rarely drink, and though Manolo liked his wine, he would never indulge himself when he was working, because it is hard to earn enough even when you are sober. And though none of them saw the accident, they all know it did not happen the way the guardia said it did.

But what can they do? As well as owning most of the land, Don Alejandro is the cacique – the political boss – of the area, so the guardia civil and the magistrates will always be on his side.

Is it at this point that Paco's future is determined? Is it standing in this encampment that he tells himself that the role of policeman is too important to have anyone but an honest man filling it?

Looking back on it all later, he will tell himself it was.

The other gypsy families did not exactly adopt Faustino – they had no interest in complying with the legal arrangements laid down by the non-gypsy world – but they took care of him. The problem was that they were already struggling to get by, and having an extra mouth to feed made life even harder than it had been before the accident. Faustino grew thinner and thinner, as his clothes became more and more threadbare, and Paco – who donated a fair share of his own meagre rations to his friend – began to worry that one day Faustino would simply fade away.

And then, a miracle happened.

Despite his poor diet, the boy somehow still found the energy to play, and that morning, he and some other gypsy lads were practising bullfighting with Don Furioso – a mock bull they had constructed on the chassis of an abandoned perambulator – when something occurred which would change his life.

'It was Ignacio's turn to push Don Furioso, and mine to be the matador,' he explains to Paco later. *'Ignacio said that because he was the oldest, he shouldn't have to push it at all, but the others said he must.'*

'Ignacio always did think that he was better than everybody else,' Paco agrees.

'He came at me with Don Furioso, running faster than any of us would usually do, and at the last second, he ignored the cape and swerved towards me.'

'That's a dirty trick. No toro bravo *would ever have done that.'*

'No, but Ignacio wanted to punish me for taking my turn with the cape. He wanted to hurt me, but I did a magnificent pass which took him so much by surprise that he turned Don Furioso over, and fell himself.'

'He won't have liked that,' says Paco, chuckling.

'He didn't – but that is not the point of the story.'

'Then what is?'

'Somebody was clapping and shouting "olé!" I turned and saw that a man had been watching me.'

'Somebody from the village?'

Faustino laughs. 'No, he wasn't from the village – he was from another world. He was wearing a fine black silk suit, and a cape lined with blue velvet. And his boots, Paco – you should have seen his boots!'

'What about them?'

'They were not just made of leather – they were made of the softest cordovan leather.'

'And you know for a fact it was cordovan leather, do you?' Paco asks sceptically. 'How can you be so sure?'

'A gypsy just knows these things,' Faustino replies, enigmatically. 'Anyway,' he continues, growing more enthusiastic with every word, 'he told me his name was Enrique Gómez …'

'So he had the same name as a famous matador,' Paco says.

'He _is_ the famous matador!' Faustino tells him, almost bursting with excitement. 'He said I had real talent, and if my parents would give their permission, he would take me away with him, and train me. I told him that I had no parents, and he said that if that was true, then he would adopt me.'

Up until this moment, Paco has been doing his best not to be envious of Faustino's adventure, but now he starts to get worried for his friend.

'I have heard of this before – men who pretend to be famous in order to win a young boy's confidence,' he says. He frowns with puzzlement. 'I do not know why they want to win the boy's confidence – only that they do.'

'But this really was Enrique Gómez,' Faustino insists.

'How can you be so sure?'

'I have seen paintings of him on bullfighting posters, haven't I? And once, at the cinema, he was on the newsreel.'

'Did you recognise him immediately? Or did you only think you recognised him when he told you who he was?'

'It was when he told me who he was,' Faustino admits. 'But the reason I didn't recognise him at first was because I wasn't expecting a famous man to appear in our village. And because ...'

'Yes?'

'Because he didn't look as ...' He gropes around for the right word. 'As magnificent in real life as he does on the newsreels. But it was *him*,' Faustino says defiantly, 'and I am *going with him*.'

And, just as Faustino had said it would happen, it did happen. Enrique Gómez talked to the Gypsy Council. He convinced them of his sincerity, and – though Borja told him it was not strictly necessary – he made a largish contribution to the council's funds.

Paco and Faustino said farewell, and since boys did not cry, they went to great efforts to hide their tears. Faustino promised that the next time he was in the area, he would visit Paco, but the years went by, and Faustino never appeared.

And the next time Paco got any news of his old friend, his source was a bull-fighting poster.

Paco waited until the waiter had served the wine, then said, 'If you're trying to look inconspicuous, you've made two basic errors.'

Faustino lowered the newspaper.

'Explain,' he said.

'Firstly, that newspaper is not only old, but it *looks* old – even from a distance. Next time, use that morning's paper.'

'What's the second thing?'

49

'And secondly, you were holding it so close to your face that it would be impossible to read it. Anyone looking at you would assume you were just using it to hide your face – which is exactly what you *were* doing.'

Faustino chuckled. 'You're a detective, aren't you,' he said. 'I remember now that someone told me that.'

'I used to be a detective,' Paco corrected him. 'But with the war, that's no longer possible, just as it's no longer possible for you to be a matador.'

'But I *am* still a matador,' Faustino countered. 'That's the only reason I'm in Madrid.'

'What are you talking about?' Paco wondered. 'There are no bull-fights anymore.'

'There will be one on Saturday,' Faustino said. 'The prime minister himself has ordered it. It is to raise the spirits of the Madrileños, and to show them that even though the government has moved to Valencia, they are not forgotten.'

'But the best fighting bulls are all raised behind enemy lines,' Paco pointed out.

'True,' Faustino agreed, 'and that is why I have been behind those same lines and come back with six *toros bravos*.'

'You were taking a hell of a chance,' Paco gasped.

'True again, but then I am a very brave man,' Faustino said, assuming a heroic pose. Then his face cracked into a grin. 'Actually, there was very little risk involved. The Fascists do not have half as much control over their front lines as they think they do. And even if they did have, a cunning gypsy like me would soon find ways to outfox them. Besides, I am admired as much on the other side as I am on this, and they would never think of shooting me.'

It would have sounded arrogant coming from the lips of almost any other man, but the plain fact was that he was speaking no less than the truth. Faustino Vargas *was* much admired. Hell, he was probably the most admired man in the whole of Spain.

'Is it true that you have faced more bulls than any other matador this century?' Paco asked.

'Not quite,' Faustino said. 'My father has killed more bulls than I have – though not many more – but it is not just a question of numbers, there is the matter of style to consider, and compared to him, I am a ham-fisted bungler.'

Did he really believe that, or was it just false modesty, Paco wondered. Whichever it was, he was wrong, because although Enrique Gómez was considered to be a great matador in many ways, most *aficionados* and experts agreed that his adopted son was better.

'I am glad I ran into you, Paco,' Faustino said, 'because it's always good to see an old friend.'

There was something in his tone which suggested that he wanted to say more, but was not sure if he should.

Paco decided to give him the opening he needed.

'That's not the only reason you're pleased to see me, is it?' he asked.

'No,' admitted Faustino. 'As a matter of fact, I really need the services of a detective.'

'I'm not a detective anymore,' Paco reminded him.

'But you still have the skills?' Faustino asked, anxiously.

'Yes, I still have the skills,' Paco agreed.

And he was thinking, 'Why does he sound afraid? What could have scared this man, who has faced hundreds of raging bulls, and has driven into enemy territory to collect even more?'

'Tell me about it,' he said.

'I have been getting death threats,' Faustino admitted.

'Do you have any idea who might have sent them?'

'No, I haven't, but they all say the same thing – if I attempt to fight the bulls next Saturday, I will die.'

'Then don't fight the bulls,' Paco suggested.

'One of the bulls I brought back with me from Extremadura is the noblest animal I have ever encountered,' Faustino said. 'He deserves to die at the hands of an artist who respects and honours him. I cannot allow some butcher who only *calls* himself a matador to hack away at him. Besides …'

'Yes?'

'We live in troubled times, old friend. Who knows when there will be another bullfight, or if I will be alive to take part in it?'

And suddenly Paco saw it all. 'You're not afraid of being killed,' he said. 'You're afraid of being killed *before* the bullfight.'

Faustino looked down at the table. 'It is something I have been working towards my whole life,' he said.

Another suspicion crossed Paco's mind. 'Was this meeting as accidental as it seemed?' he asked.

The other man grinned at him, and it was the sort of half-rueful, half-mischievous grin that the much younger Faustino might have bestowed on the much younger Paco.

'No, it wasn't an accident,' he admitted. And then he was suddenly serious again. 'I needed someone I could trust – and who better than you?'

A pimply-faced youth, walking past and smoking a cigarette, glanced casually at the table, then came to an abrupt halt as his jaw dropped.

'It's you!' he said, incredulously. 'You're *El Gitano*!'

'You're mistaken,' Faustino said. 'I know I look a little like him, but …'

'I saw you fight in Cordoba last year,' the boy burbled. 'I hitch-hiked down there – it took me three days – and I sold two pints of my blood to pay for the ticket.' A look of uncertainty, which was verging on despair, came to the lad's face. 'You are him, aren't you?' he pleaded.

Faustino sighed. 'Yes, I'm him,' he admitted. 'But please don't tell anyone …'

'Hey, everybody, look who's here!' the youth shouted excitedly. 'It's *El Gitano*!'

'Will you help me, Paco?' Faustino asked.

'Of course I will,' Paco agreed.

A small crowd had started to gather around the table, and several of the people were thrusting pieces of paper in front of Faustino.

'Could you give me your autograph?' one of them begged.

'Will you sign this?' another asked.

'Do you have a pencil, Paco?' Faustino asked.

'Yes,' Paco said, reaching into his pocket. 'A good detective always carries a notebook and a pencil.'

But you're not a detective anymore, a voice in his head screamed, as he handed the pencil over. That's what you've just told your old friend Faustino, and it's bloody true!

Yes, he supposed it was *literally* true, but he couldn't stop his brain from thinking like a detective's brain, or his hands from checking his pockets before he left the apartment, in order to make sure his notebook was there.

Paco watched as Faustino signed the first piece of paper. It seemed an over-long, over-careful process, and coming from a man who moved so elegantly, his signature was surprisingly awkward and clumsy.

The second person to hand him a scrap of paper was a woman. 'Will you please write, "To Maria"?' she asked.

'I will write my name, and no more,' Faustino told her.

'Please,' the woman implored. 'It would mean so much to me.'

'It is just my name or nothing at all,' Faustino said, with a new harshness in his voice. 'Which is it to be?'

'Your name,' the woman said, sounding crushed.

No one else asked for anything more than his signature, and as the signing continued, Faustino's mood improved.

Finally, they were alone again.

'I must leave before more people arrive,' Faustino said. 'Will you come and see me in my room at the Hotel Florida tonight?'

'I will,' Paco promised.

'At what time?'

'Shall we say seven-thirty?'

Cindy received the news that Paco had met a childhood friend with only mild interest, and the further news that he was a famous matador with clear disdain.

'I take it that you're against bullfighting,' Paco said.

'Well, of course I'm against it,' Cindy replied. 'It's a part of your barbaric past which, for reasons I fail to grasp, a few of your fellow countrymen are desperately keen to hold onto.'

Paco shook his head sorrowfully. 'If you ever want to understand the Spanish people, you must learn to accept their love of the bulls,' he said.

'So the price for getting to know Spain is to approve of the mindless slaughter of innocent animals?' Cindy countered bitterly.

'I never said that you had to approve of it,' Paco said evenly, 'only that you should accept it as part of the culture.'

'Culture!' Cindy sneered.

'I have never seen a ballet,' Paco told her, 'but the people who know about these things say that the matador is every bit as balletic in his movements as a dancer in Swan Lake.'

'Really?' Cindy said sceptically.

'Really,' Paco confirmed. 'The only difference is that the dancer does not have to perform his movements while being charged by a four hundred and sixty kilo killing machine.'

'What are you doing now? Blaming the bull for making the matador's life more difficult?' Cindy demanded.

'No, I don't blame the bull for anything. He is doing what he is supposed to do – what his nature compels him to do.'

'Oh yes, of course. And his anger has nothing at all to do with the fact that he has two small spears wedged in his neck, does it?'

'That doesn't help,' Paco conceded, 'but the *banderillas* are not meant to weaken the bull – that would make the whole thing pointless – only to lower his head. A good bull is naturally aggressive, and the chances are that before he enters the ring he has already injured – or even killed – other bulls.'

'Even so, once he's actually in the ring, the bull has no chance.'

'On the contrary. Since the sport began, over five hundred matadors have been killed, and countless others have been badly injured. Faustino's own adopted father – Enrique Gómez – was badly gored at the height of his career, and has never been able to fight since. And if a bull is judged to be especially brave, it is spared the sword and can spend the rest of its life eating sweet grass and mounting its concubines.'

'It's still torture,' Cindy persisted.

'You might call it that, but consider the alternative. A bull which is not a fighting bull is kept in a confined space and fed on a diet aimed at fattening it up. When it reaches around fifteen months old, it is slaughtered – and you eat it, don't you?'

'Sometimes,' Cindy said defensively.

'Often,' Paco countered.

'Get to the point!' Cindy told him.

'A fighting bull is raised on a diet of sweet grass, calculated to increase his muscle and strength. He virtually never sees a human being. Then, when he is four or five years old, he is chosen to appear in the arena. The *banderillas* cause him irritation – maybe they even hurt a little – but he wants to fight the matador, not because he is angry or desperate, but because that is his nature. And when death comes, it is with a single thrust of the sword, and is instantaneous. So who has the better life – the bull raised for meat, or the bull raised for fighting?'

'You can make black seem white when you want to,' Cindy said, with a kind of furious impotence.

'Or maybe,' Paco suggested mildly, 'I can just make it seem a light shade of grey.'

'What about the horses that the picadors are mounted on?' Cindy asked.

Ah yes, the horses.

He could say in defence of using horses that the horses in question had reached the end of their effective working lives, and that if they had not been selected for the ring, they would already have been dispatched to the abattoir, to be rendered down into glue. He could point out that since the Primo de Rivera dictatorship, all the horses must have padding with the thickness of a mattress strapped to their bellies, which gave them much more protection than any of the men in the ring had. But neither of these negated the fact that the horses, unlike the men, did not choose to be there, and that even with the padding, horses *were* killed in the ring.

'When you are in the bullring, and are swept up the grandeur and spectacle of the event, the welfare of the horses does not even enter your mind,' he said, honestly.

'But that's so callous and cruel,' Cindy protested.

'I did not say it wasn't,' Paco agreed. 'I am merely telling you what most people feel at a bullfight. And over the last few months,' he added, 'I have seen men be more callous and cruel to their fellow human beings than anyone has been to the horses in the ring.'

Chapter Four

Friday 13 May 1977

Paco and Woodend were sitting at an outside café on Callao Square, each with a cup of coffee and a glass of brandy within convenient reach. The sun was on the wane, but still pleasantly warm, and on the ground, sparrows hopped around, searching for crumbs.

'It was at this café that I sat drinking with Faustino, two days before the bullfight,' Paco said. 'Well, not *this* café,' he amended, in the interest of accuracy. 'That café and its employees are long gone, but it was a café occupying the same *space* as this one.'

'It seems uncomfortably close to the front line,' Woodend said.

'It *was* uncomfortably close,' Paco agreed, looking around him.

He's gone again, Woodend thought.

It had happened several times since they'd arrived in Madrid – what Paco was seeing was not things as they were, but rather, as they had been.

'Where we are sitting now, I remember seeing a large crater in the ground,' Paco said. 'The cobblestones around the edge of the hole were stained a rusty brown.'

'That would be blood,' Woodend said.

Paco nodded. 'It was the blood of three men who had been sitting there that very morning, enjoying their coffee, when a shell landed on them.'

'And yet the café was open again in the afternoon?' Woodend asked, surprised.

'Probably earlier,' Paco said. 'Possibly as soon as the bodies had been taken away and the debris cleared.' He chuckled. 'Death did not come as a surprise to anyone during the siege. It was normal, and it certainly wasn't enough to make you interrupt your routine, because life was hard enough without that.' He paused to light up a cigarette, and almost offered the packet to Woodend before he remembered he shouldn't. 'Of course, it wasn't routine for everyone,' he said. 'That's why we had tourists.'

'The people who came here weren't exactly tourists, were they?' Woodend asked. 'You wouldn't call a war correspondent or a mercenary a tourist. And you certainly wouldn't apply that term to an arms' dealer or a secret agent working for a foreign power.'

'Despite my Cindy's best efforts, my English is not always as precise as I might wish,' Paco replied. 'I shouldn't have said "tourists," I should have said "day trippers".'

'So where did these day trippers come from?' Woodend wondered.

'From the parts of Madrid that were out of range of the enemy guns,' Paco told him.

The man and the boy are standing in the middle of the Puerta del Sol, looking lost. The man is around thirty-five, the boy with him perhaps eight or nine. They are the sort of people, who, in normal times, would never have thought of coming into the centre of the city in anything other than their best clothes, and even though they have now dressed down in order to blend in, they cannot quite shrug off the aura of bourgeois respectability it has taken them so many years to cultivate.

Paco is wearing his uniform, and this, perhaps, is why he is the one who the man and boy choose to approach.

'Excuse me, captain,' he says, 'but when is the shelling due to start?'

'What?' Paco asks, not quite sure he has heard correctly.

'The shelling,' the man repeats. 'We were told this was the place to be, but we've been standing here for over an hour, and nothing has happened.'

'You want to see a shell land?' Paco asks, incredulously.

'At least one,' the man answers, 'but preferably more. We've come all the way down from Chamartin to see it.'

'And I want a shell fragment – a big one,' says the boy, speaking for the first time.

The father laughs indulgently. 'Ever since one of the boys in his class brought a shell fragment into school, Tomas has been agitating for one of his own. And, of course,' he laughs again, 'it has to be bigger than Jacobo's fragment.' He shakes his head, 'Boys! What can you do with them?'

'Well, for a start, you can keep them out of harm's way,' Paco says.

The man looks puzzled. 'I don't know what you mean,' he says.

'Shells are designed to kill people,' Paco tells him. 'And if you're in the way when one lands, you'll be the one to get killed.'

'Surely, all you need is a little common sense, and you'll be safe enough,' the man says. 'And we're both very sensible, aren't we, Tomas?'

'Very sensible,' the boy echoes.

It would take a superman to remain calm in this situation, and though Paco has many sterling qualities, superhumanity is not among them.

'You're right – a little common sense goes a long way,' he says. 'And you have something else in your favour.'

'And what's that?' the man asks.

'The shells are specially programmed so they don't land on people

60

from Chamartin, even if those people from Chamartin are complete arseholes.'

'I find that very offensive,' the man says.

'And I find it very offensive that you seem to think that all those who were killed by the shelling must be complete morons,' Paco countered. 'So keep on telling yourself you're too smart to be hit, and stick to that belief even when you're carrying what's left of your son back to Chamartin in a bucket.'

'Agreed, the man from Chamartin was stupid,' Woodend said, 'but you were pretty stupid yourself to drink in a bar so close to the front. Why couldn't you have chosen somewhere safer?'

'The reason Faustino chose this bar was because it was across the square from the hotel he was staying in,' Paco explained.

Woodend glanced across the square, and saw a large department store which went by the name of Galerias Preciados.

'Is that where it was?' he asked.

'Yes,' Paco confirmed. 'It was called the Hotel Florida, and it was quite famous in its day. It was close to the Telefonica Building, which you may have noticed when we were walking here …'

'That big white building?'

'Yes. All the foreign correspondents sent their reports from there, so many of them lived in the hotel. Famous writers, like Earnest Hemingway and John Dos Passos, stayed there, too.' He paused. 'You've heard of them, haven't you?'

'I've heard of them, but I can't honestly say I've ever read anything they wrote,' Woodend confessed. 'I'm a Charles Dickens man myself. He didn't stay there by any chance, did he?'

Paco chuckled again. 'It is highly unlikely, since it was not built until 1924. But what a magnificent building it was – seven storeys tall and faced with white marble! It had two hundred guest rooms and each of them had its own bathroom. Back in the 1930s, even some of the expensive hotels in London didn't have a bath for every guest,' he added, with a hitherto hidden touch of pride in his capital city.

'That's right, they didn't,' Woodend agreed.

He didn't know whether what he had just said was true or not – though he suspected that it wasn't – but if it gave his friend pleasure, he saw no reason to disabuse him.

'And those bathrooms were magnificent,' Paco said. 'Truly magnificent.'

'Oh, you saw one yourself, did you?'

'I did.'

'If it was as posh as you say it was, I'm surprised they even allowed riff-raff like you through the front door, let alone gave you the chance to poke around in the bathrooms,' Woodend teased.

'Who said anything about going through the front door?' Paco asked innocently.

'You did. You said you'd seen one of the bathrooms and ...' Woodend stopped himself, realising that Paco, in a game-playing mood, had laid a trap for him – and he'd walked right into it, 'But it's true you never said anything about going into the hotel,' he conceded.

'Well, then?' Paco asked, with a grin.

'You must have seen it from the street. Were any of the bedrooms on the ground floor?'

'No. There was a lounge, a dining room, and some offices, but not a single bedroom.'

'Then you went to one of the upper floors of a building on the other side of the square ...'

'I didn't do that, and even if I had, I would have been too far away to get a proper look at one of the bathrooms. You were right when you said that I saw it from the street.'

Woodend waited for Paco to explain, but it soon became clear that he was enjoying himself too much to do that.

So let's see if we can work it out, Woodend thought.

Paco didn't go inside; he didn't see the bathroom from across the square …

'The front of the building was blown off by a shell!' he exclaimed.

'Not the whole front – just part of the third floor,' Paco said. 'It left two bedrooms and a bathroom exposed to the street. The explosion had turned the bath on its end, and it was using the wall for support, a little like a drunken man might, but you could still see that it must have been a very fine thing to have a soak in.'

'So what happened then?'

'Well, the management decided it would be pointless to try and let the rooms again, and someone told me that the third floor chambermaid complained of all the extra work the explosion had caused her. And, of course, there was a change in the pricing structure.'

'What do you mean?'

'The rooms at the front had a view over the square, and the rooms at the back looked down on an alley, so naturally, the front rooms were much more expensive – until the shell hit the building. Then, of course, the pricing structure was reversed.

'Did the hotel at least patch up the front?' Woodend asked.

Paco shook his head. 'There was very little building material around, even if you were willing to pay over the odds for it. The management asked the first aid architects if they could spare some, but …'

'Hang about,' Woodend said. 'Who the bloody hell were the "first aid architects"?'

'What do they sound like? They were architects,' Paco replied.

Woodend sighed. 'Are you enjoying this little game of yours?' he asked.

'Very much,' Paco replied.

'There are times when I could strangle you,' Woodend said.

But his exasperation was all faked, and secretly he was relieved that Paco was feeling spirited enough to play this game, because, frankly, there had been a few occasions since they arrived in Madrid, when it had seemed as if his friend was about to drown in the dark pit of his own misery.

'"First aid architects" is a name I made up for them,' Paco said. 'They were architects, and they had a team of builders working with them. They would go to buildings that had been bombed or shelled, and decide whether or not they could be patched up. If they couldn't, they stripped the buildings of whatever material they could use elsewhere. Wood was especially precious, but by the time they got to a site, all wood had often been removed by either the ordinary people or the army.'

'Why did they want it?'

'The ordinary people wanted it for fuel – for heating and cooking. I can assure you that as unappetising as plain boiled rice is, it's much better than *uncooked* rice, so a simple plank of wood can make all the difference to how your food tastes.'

'And why did the army want the wood?' Woodend asked.

'It was mainly the doors that the army wanted – they used them to line the trenches on the front line. There was always a danger of the trenches collapsing, you see, and doors were quite good at preventing that.' Paco shuddered at what was obviously a memory of a trench that hadn't been lined in this manner. 'Anyway, to get back to the subject of the Hotel Florida – the architects told the management that they hadn't got the resources or the time to fix up the frontage, but no real structural damage had been done. So the management just carried on as normal, except that now they had two rooms fewer to rent out. In fact they ignored those rooms completely – they didn't even remove the bath.'

Woodend looked down at Paco's cigarette, and wished he could have one himself.

'So what did you and Faustino talk about that night?' he asked.

'I was just about to tell you that,' Paco replied.

Chapter Five

Thursday 13 May 1937

The shells – fired from the big guns in the Casa de Campo – had been flying over Callao Square for the previous twenty minutes. Everybody knew that a shell would land in the square itself eventually, and so it was almost a relief when one did, detonating with an angry, terrifying roar, and throwing a cascade of cobblestones into the air.

Paco, sheltering in a doorway at the edge of the square, raised his hands to protect his eyes. He didn't want his hand broken by a piece of flying stone, true, but better that than that the stone should enter his eye – and perhaps even find its way to his brain.

The sound of the explosion echoed round the square for what seemed an age, each echo lower and softer, until eventually it was gone. The dust, which had been swirling like a desert storm, tired of the effort, and drifted back to the ground.

Paco glanced around the square. There were people in all the doorways, waiting for the attack to come to an end. A few months earlier, their faces would have been ashen – drained – as the fear gnawed away at their innards. But fear, like any other emotion, cannot be sustained at a high level over a long period, and now they either looked indifferent, or impatient that the barrage was preventing them from going about their business.

It wasn't that they believed there was no chance of them being killed – unlike the sightseers from Chamartin, these people came across death on a regular basis – but they had come to accept that it was a matter of pure luck whether they lived or died, and since there was nothing they could do about it, there was no point in worrying about it, either.

Paco looked across the square at the Hotel Florida. It was still an impressive building, even with the shell damage, which had blown a hole in the facade on the third floor.

There was a pause in the shelling, and he chose this moment to sprint across the square. It was a particularly pointless thing to do, he told himself, since he was as likely to be running *into* the path of a shell as he was running *away* from it, but he kept up the pace anyway.

He crashed through the doors of the hotel, and almost collided with the hardwood reception desk, on which there was a brass nameplate which read *Sr. Ortiz, Concierge de Noche*.

Not 'porter' but 'concierge', Paco noted.

Well, this *was* the Hotel Florida.

The man behind the desk – presumably the Sr. Ortiz identified by nameplate – gave a slight bow.

'Welcome to the hotel, sir,' he said – as if Paco had sauntered in gracefully, rather than thrown himself through the door in order to avoid any passing shells.

That was the thing about places like the Florida, Paco thought – the world outside might change completely, but the hotel carried on pretty much as it always had.

'My name is Francisco Ruiz,' he said, 'and I'm here to see Don Faustino Vargas.'

67

'Is he expecting you, sir?'

'Yes, so if you could just tell me …'

'I've only just come on duty, so I need to check on what instructions I've been left,' the concierge interrupted.

He consulted a small pile of notes.

'Yes, it does appear that you were expected, sir. Don Faustino left instructions that you were to be shown up to his room.' He frowned. 'But you were not supposed to arrive for another half an hour.'

'Does it really matter that I'm early?' Paco asked.

'Probably not, but I'd better just check.' The concierge picked up the telephone on the desk. 'Connect me to room 513, switchboard,' he said, in the voice of man used to exercising absolute authority within the confines of his own little kingdom. 'Switchboard? Hello, switchboard …'

He slammed down the phone in exasperation.

'Isn't it working?' Paco asked, although it was already obvious to him that it wasn't.

'This happens at least once a week,' the concierge blustered. 'It's this damned war. How can we maintain the high standards we've set ourselves with all this bloody fighting going on?'

He suddenly seemed to realise that he was saying all this to a man who, although not a guest himself, was a guest's visitor.

'I'm terribly sorry, sir, I shouldn't have lost my temper like that.'

'That's quite all right,' Paco assured him. 'Since you can't contact Faustino, can I go straight up?'

The concierge looked a little dubious. 'Is he a close friend of yours?' he asked.

A good question, Paco thought. They had been very close friends once – but that had been twenty-five years ago.

'We've known each other since childhood,' he said, by way of a compromise.

The concierge looked somewhat relieved. 'In that case, I'll get one of the bellboys to …'

'No need,' Paco said. 'I can find my own way. Room 513, isn't it?'

'That's right,' the concierge agreed. 'But if I were you, I'd take the stairs, because if the power goes off when you're in the elevator, you could be stuck there for hours.'

'Good point,' Paco said.

Now that the shelling had stopped, there was no real indication on the first and second floors of the hotel that a war was going on outside. On the third floor, everything seemed perfectly normal except for the fact that instead of a wall at the end of the corridor, there was gaping hole, which offered a quick – and probably fatal – exit to the square below. And even here, the chambermaid, conscientiously cleaning the corridor carpet, managed to imbue the scene with something like normality.

When Paco knocked on the door of room 513, a voice from inside called out, 'I'm coming,' and then the door opened, and Faustino appeared.

He seemed quite surprised – almost shocked – to see Paco standing there.

'We agreed to meet at half past seven,' he said.

'True,' Paco agreed, 'but since the siege began, it's always wise to allow extra time for your journey, and sometimes, if nothing goes wrong, you get to where you're going before you needed to. That's what happened today – it was a fairly uneventful journey.'

As long as you count shells landing fifty metres from you as 'uneventful', he added mentally.

'The thing is, Paco, I'm not quite ready for you,' Faustino said, somewhat flustered.

And having caught the briefest glimpse of a blonde-haired woman sitting on the bed, Paco thought he understood just why that might be.

'Listen, I'm in no hurry, so why don't I wait for you downstairs?' he suggested.

Faustino nodded. 'Yes, that would be for the best. Go to the lounge. I won't be long.'

The lounge was all wicker furniture and potted plants. It reminded Paco of all those films set in the British colonies, in which gentlemen wore immaculate white uniforms and sat around drinking pink gins, and all the natives were either loyal simpletons or evil-looking villains who were just waiting for their opportunity to stab their benevolent masters in the back.

Faustino appeared five minutes later. When he'd answered his door of his room, it had been in his shirtsleeves, but now he was wearing a very sharp blue suit which, from its stylish cut, Paco guessed had been purchased from Ramón Areces' high class tailoring shop, which was just down the street from the hotel.

Faustino looked around the room, as if he was deciding where to sit, then shook his head and said, 'Let's go somewhere with a little more atmosphere. There's a bar just across the square that I rather like.'

They stepped out of the hotel and crossed the square. Though there was still the sound of shells whooshing overhead, Faustino moved with the air of a man taking an elegant stroll in a fashionable park.

He made no mention of the girl, and Paco resolved, then and there, that he wouldn't mention her either. After all, he told himself, it really was none of his business.

'It doesn't seem to me as if the Republic will win this particular conflict,' Faustino said, as another shell landed at the far end of the square, and sent an angry vibration rippling through the cobbles.

'No,' Paco agreed. 'It doesn't.'

They had reached the bar, and Faustino opened the door.

'After you, old friend,' he said.

As they entered the bar, all the customers turned to look at them, but though most nodded acknowledgement to Faustino, none of them approached them.

'This is my favourite bar,' Faustino explained, as they walked to the counter. 'All the regulars are willing to respect my privacy,' he grinned, boyishly, 'especially since they know that if they leave me alone, I will show my appreciation by standing them a couple of rounds of drinks.'

The barman was a large man with a tremendous belly and thick arms. He did not look as if he smiled very often, but he smiled now.

'What can I get you, Don Faustino?' he asked.

'Two wines, Diego,' the matador said. 'And do you have anything special to offer me today?'

The barman looked around conspiratorially, then nodded. 'Some *gambas*, fresh in from Valencia. A man came in an hour ago – a *big* man, with a thick cigar and a gold ring on almost every finger – and said that he had heard I had some prawns, and would like to buy them.'

'And what did you tell him?' Faustino asked, with an amused smile on his face.

'I told him I was saving them for a valued customer. He offered me fifteen duros for them – a fabulous sum – but I still said no.'

'I'd like to thank you for thinking of me,' Faustino said. 'And I will pay you the same fifteen duros he would have paid you.'

71

'No, no, Don Faustino,' the barman protested. 'I don't want to …'

'I will not see you losing out because of me,' Faustino interrupted. 'I will pay you the fifteen duros, and that is the end of the matter.'

'Thank you, Don Faustino,' the barman said meekly – or maybe just *mock* meekly, Paco thought.

Faustino had such a commanding presence about him, it was hard for Paco to reconcile the man he was seeing now with the skinny little kid he had once known.

And as for ordering seafood …!

There was a saying that had become popular in Madrid since the siege began; *Quien come marisco, come oro* – whoever eats seafood eats gold.

It had suddenly become expensive for a very obvious reason. Before the war, a special seafood train had run from the coast. On the single-track system, the seafood train had priority over all other locomotives, including the ones carrying first class passengers. Thus, however rich or privileged you were, it was more than possible that, at a certain time of day, your train would be shunted into the sidings, where you would sit and watch as the seafood train steamed past.

Then the fighting had started, and the trains had stopped running. Instead of one locomotive, seventy or eighty lorries began making the daily trip from Valencia. Now, nearly a year into the war, there was only one lorry a day, and even that did not always get through, so seafood really *had* become gold.

But fifteen duros for twelve prawns – that was very expensive gold indeed!

Paco's friend Ramón, who'd worked at one of the ministries, had once confided to him that he hoped one day to have his supervisor's job.

'*And how much do you think I'll be earning if I have the good fortune to achieve that promotion?*' he'd asked.

'*I've no idea,*' Paco had replied.

'*Sixty duros a month!*' Ramón had announced, with all the flourish of a magician producing a fat, complacent rabbit from his top hat.

So, if Ramón had succeeded in getting his dream job, he would have been paid per week what Faustino had just spent on the prawns.

'I think that barman must have seen you coming,' Paco said to Faustino.

'What do you mean by that?'

'That you're an easy mark – a juicy orange just asking to be squeezed. Do you really think that the man with a fat cigar, and a gold ring on every finger, actually exists – because I don't.'

Faustino shrugged. 'I expect you're right.'

'So what's most likely to be the case is that the barman invented him, in order to raise the price he could charge you for the prawns?'

'Yes, that may well be the case. And why shouldn't he try to soak me? He knows I can afford it.'

'For God's sake, Faustino!' Paco said, exasperated.

'Don't worry about how much it costs, Paco,' Faustino countered. 'It's just a drop in the ocean to me. I earn more from killing two bulls in a single afternoon than many people make in a whole year.'

He wasn't being boastful. Paco was sure of that. He was simply saying what he'd said because he really didn't want his friend to worry about the cost.

The prawns arrived. They were big and juicy and tasted of the sea, and since it would have been an insult to them to talk while savouring them, Faustino and Paco ate in silence.

When all that remained was their heads and shells, Paco said, 'So tell me about these threatening letters you've been getting.'

'I can do better than that,' Faustino replied. 'I can show them to you.'

He reached into his pocket, and produced several sheets of cheap writing paper. He smoothed them out on the counter, and handed them to Paco.

'Which one would you like me to look at first?' Paco asked.

'Does it matter?' Faustino replied, sounding suddenly uncomfortable.

'I don't know whether it does or not,' Paco admitted. 'But most men in your situation would want me to start with either the first one they received, or the one that disturbed them the most.'

'They're all the same,' Faustino said brusquely – but it was an artificial brusqueness, Paco was sure of it.

He looked at the letter on the top of the pile. It was in block capitals and written in thick pencil.

WARNING!!!
DOING ANYTHING TO GIVE THE ENEMY
COMFORT OR COURAGE IS AN ACT OF
TREACHERY. YOU MUST NOT APPEAR BEFORE
THIS GODLESS COMMUNIST RABBLE. IF YOU
DO, YOU WILL BE SHOT AS A TRAITOR.
STAY AWAY FROM VENTAS BULLRING IF YOU
WISH TO AVOID DEATH.
LONG LIVE THE KINGDOM OF SPAIN
LONG LIVE GENERAL FRANCO

Paco quickly checked the rest of the letters. They were all, more or less, in the same vein.

'You really do take this seriously, do you?' he asked – though he already knew that if Faustino had bothered to seek him out, he *must* be taking it seriously.

74

'It is well known that there are any number of Fascists in hiding in the barrio de Salamanca, and that is just a stone's throw – or perhaps I should say a pistol shot – from the bullring,' Faustino said.

'So if you think you're in danger, why don't you just do what they say?' Paco asked.

'Are you insulting me, now?' Faustino demanded angrily.

'No, I …' Paco said, knocked off balance by his sudden change of mood.

'Would you run away if you were threatened in this manner?' Faustino asked.

'Well, no,' Paco admitted. 'I don't suppose I would.'

'Then how dare you assume that I would? Do you think I'm afraid?' Faustino smashed his fist down on the bar. 'Some people say that gypsies have no pride – but I have as much as any other Spaniard.'

'I know you do,' Paco said, full of remorse. 'You have proved your courage many times over in the ring. Forgive me for suggesting what I did earlier. You must fight. You wouldn't be the man you are if you didn't.'

'I'm not a coward, but I'm not a fool, either,' Faustino said, somewhat mollified. 'I won't run, and I am quite willing to die if that is how things must be, but if you can find a way to prevent me dying by removing the threat, then I would be very grateful.'

'And how do you think I can remove it?' Paco wondered.

Faustino seemed puzzled by the question. 'I've given you the letters,' he said. 'Can't you track down the man who sent them?'

That was the trouble with the general public, Paco thought – they imagined that the police were almost superhuman in their detecting skills.

'It would be a miracle if I could track him down from this – and I don't know how to perform miracles,' he said.

'But you're the man who solved the case of the headless body in a trunk at Atocha railway station,' Faustino protested.

'Oh, you read about that in the newspapers, did you?' Paco asked.

'No, I …' Faustino began, unexpectedly stumbling on his words. 'Somebody told me about it.'

'That was when I had the resources of the entire police department at my disposal,' Paco said. 'If I'd been given these letters then, the first thing I would have done was send them to the lab. Then I would have dispatched teams of men to all the *papelerías* in Madrid, in order to discover where the paper had been bought, and who had bought it. And if one of those teams of detectives had turned up someone who was a suspect – or even a witness – I would have pulled that person in to police headquarters for questioning. But I can't do any of that now. I don't even have the authority to *interview* anyone.'

'No, I suppose not,' said Faustino, downcast. 'I hadn't thought of it that way before.'

'What I can do is to provide you with some protection in the stadium,' Paco promised. 'But that won't come cheap because the people I hire will be the best available.'

'And can they guarantee my safety?' Faustino asked.

Paco shook his head. 'The only way I can *guarantee* your safety is by persuading you to stay away from the bullring altogether.'

'I won't do that.'

'I know you won't.'

'But if hiring these men will improve my chances of surviving …'

'It will.'

'Then I will gladly pay whatever price they ask.' Faustino put his hand on Paco's shoulder. 'You're a good friend, Paquito,' he said.

'I try to be.'

'And when this is over, maybe we can find somewhere in this city

76

under siege that still somehow manages to serve fine food, so that I can buy you an expensive meal before I move to Mexico.'

'Before you move to Mexico?' Paco repeated. 'You're not being serious, are you?'

'I am being very serious. I've already started to make the necessary preparations. I have told my manager to make sure all my money is readily available ...'

'You told him *what*?'

'To make sure that all my money is readily available.'

'But why does *your manager* need to do that?' Paco wondered. 'Couldn't you do it yourself?'

'No, I wouldn't know how to.'

'Surely, all it takes is to look at your various bank accounts ...'

'I don't have various bank accounts. I don't have even *one* bank account. We gypsies don't trust banks. We keep our money hidden in the knot of a tree, or buried under a rock.' Faustino laughed. 'But I earn too much for either of those things, and so I give it to Álvaro to look after.'

Maybe they'd look into his financial arrangements in more detail later, Paco thought, but for the moment, it was the other matter he wanted to discuss.

'This move to Mexico – is it meant to be permanent?' he asked.

'Yes.'

'But why? You love Spain.'

'You're right, I do love Spain,' Faustino agreed. 'But there are other kinds of love, too. I went to fight the bulls in Mexico last year, and there I found one of those other kinds.'

'You fell in love?' Paco said.

'I have never known a feeling like it – never known anything that came anywhere near it.'

77

'And she's in Mexico now?'

'Yes, that is where my true love is.'

So, it looked like the blonde on the bed was no more than a temporary diversion, Paco thought. And though it was not for him to question the depth of Faustino's love for the girl in Mexico, he knew that if Cindy had been there, he would never have dreamed of being with another woman in Madrid.

'Tell me about this girl of yours,' he suggested.

'I don't want to talk about it anymore,' Faustino said abruptly.

With his old friend's rapid changes of mood, this conversation felt like walking through a minefield, Paco thought, and he had no idea how to avoid the mines because he didn't have a clue why they had even been put there. Yet for all that, he still liked Faustino – and not just the Faustino he fondly remembered from his childhood, but the one who was standing next to him now. What was more, he was certain that Faustino liked him.

'Who is this man, and what are you doing with him?' asked an angry voice just behind them.

They turned round to see a tall, thin, young man with a hand-some – though slightly gaunt – face.

'His name is Paco Ruiz, and he is an old friend of mine from Andalucía,' Faustino told the young man, 'and this,' turning back to Paco, 'is Luis, my leading banderillero.'

'Is that all he is?' the young man asked sceptically, as he glared at Paco. 'An old friend from Andalucía?'

'Yes, and now that you've been introduced, it's only proper that you shake hands,' Faustino said.

Luis said nothing, and his hands remained firmly by his sides.

'Do you *want* to be a matador one day, Luis?' Faustino asked, with a severe edge to his voice.

78

'Well, of course I do,' the young man replied, in a sulky fashion. 'It is all I've ever dreamed of. You know that.'

'And can you think of something you might do that could prevent your dream from coming true?' asked Faustino – very much in control, very much the senior partner in this conversation. 'Can you think of a word or action which, while it might have nothing at all to do with the skill you show in the ring, could destroy your career?'

Luis said nothing.

'Can you?' Faustino demanded.

'Yes,' Luis replied, looking down at the ground.

'Then, bearing that in mind, I think that the best thing you could do at this moment would be to shake hands with my friend Paco, and then leave us, so we can catch up on old times.'

Luis still did not move.

'I'm waiting,' Faustino said.

Stiffly and reluctantly, Luis raised his arm. 'It has been a pleasure to meet you, Señor Ruiz,' he said.

For a moment, Paco considered rejecting the hand which had been so unwillingly offered, then, for Faustino's sake, he took it.

'It's been a pleasure to meet you, too, Luis, and I look forward to seeing you perform in the ring on Saturday.'

The handshake was perfunctory, and when it was finished, Faustino said, 'Good night, Luis.'

'Will I … will I be seeing you later?' the boy asked.

'Perhaps,' Faustino said cautiously, 'but whether or not you do, now is the time for you to go.'

Luis nodded briefly to Paco, and stormed out of the bar.

He had hardly slammed the door behind him when Faustino said, 'I think perhaps that I had better go after him.'

'Might it not be better to give him time to cool off?' Paco wondered.

'Perhaps,' Faustino agreed. 'But I would hate it if he did or said anything that could harm him.' He took a wad of green five-peseta notes out of his pocket, and placed two of them on the bar. 'There is enough money there for you to have another drink or two if you would like to. Why not try a glass of the twenty year-old whisky that Diego keeps behind the bar for rich Americans?'

'Thank you,' Paco said, 'but I try not to drink alone.'

'We will meet again soon,' Faustino promised.

'Be careful how you go – because there's a good chance the threats are real,' Paco said.

'I am *sure* they are real,' Faustino told him. 'And I will be careful. But my matador's instinct tells me that if anyone is trying to kill me, they will wait until Saturday, at the bullring.'

Chapter Six

The two old Madrileños sat at a corner table in the Cabo de Trafalgar, slowly sipping their white wines. They were known locally – though never to their faces – as Bufón and Pícaro (Jester and Rogue). No one could remember why they should have been given these names, because Bufón was rarely amusing, and Pícaro, far from being dishonest, could be trusted with your wallet, (however fat it was, and however careless about money you were). Yet, flying in the face of logic, none of the other patrons of the bar would ever have considered calling them anything else, so that was that.

The two old men had been playing a furious game of dominos, but now they had abandoned it, and were arguing about what men always argue about – except that this time, talk of football soon became entangled in talk of politics.

Paco, who had only dropped in for one quick drink on his way home from the Hotel Florida, found himself gripped by the drama, even though – he strongly suspected – the old men were arguing less because they fundamentally disagreed than because it brought a little variety into their lives.

'We should have nothing to do with either Valencia or Barcelona,' Bufón opined.

'Why do you say that?' Pícaro asked.

'Isn't it obvious? It's because they're all sons-of-bitches there.'

'They're also our allies in the fight against fascism.'

'To hell with them as allies. We don't need them.'

'So you're suggesting that we should fight Franco all on our own, are you?' Pícaro asked.

'Why wouldn't we?' Bufón challenged.

'Because if we did, we'd lose.'

'Maybe we would, but at least, if we did, we'd lose standing on our own two feet.'

'You have a cousin who works on the docks in Valencia, don't you,' Pícaro recalled.

'Thank you so much for reminding me of him,' Bufón said, sarcastically.

'That time he came here to stay with you, he seemed such a nice man. Don't tell me you've turned against him.'

'Yes.'

'But why?'

'That's none of your business,' Bufón said.

'All right, if you don't want to tell me, don't tell,' Pícaro replied, folding his arms.

They sat there in silence for a long minute, and then Bufón said, 'All right, if you must know, it's all to do with the way they behaved when the war closed down the national football league.'

'I've no idea what you're talking about,' Pícaro said.

Bufón sighed with exasperation at his friend's obvious stupidity. 'What's the first thing the football clubs on the coast did when war broke out?' he asked.

82

'Well, they formed a new league –the Mediterranean League,' Pícaro replied.

'Exactly! And would they let Real Madrid join it?

'You shouldn't call it Real Madrid, anymore,' Pícaro said, scoring a point with toothless glee.

Paco grinned. The second old man was right, of course. Real Madrid – *Royal* Madrid – had changed its name to the Madrid Football Club when the king abdicated, back in '31, because how could you have a royal *anything* in a republic? But it must have been hard for an old man like Bufón to make the adjustment, after a lifetime of calling the club by its former name.

'All right,' Bufón said, with an exaggerated patience, 'why wouldn't they let *Madrid Football Club* join the Mediterranean League?'

Pícaro shrugged awkwardly. 'I don't know,' he admitted. 'Perhaps they thought that because it had once been called "royal", it might secretly be siding with the enemy.'

'How could anybody seriously think such a thing, when the club's president is Antonio Ortega, who is a communist, not to mention a colonel in the militia?' Bufón asked with relish, having baited his trap and now looking on with some satisfaction as his friend unwittingly walked right into it. 'Besides, Atlético Madrid was denied entry too – and that has never been associated with the king.'

'True, but …' Pícaro began.

And then he fell silent because there were clearly no 'buts' he could think of.

At the bar, Paco took a sip of his beer. Perhaps the old man was wrong about the reasons Madrid had been banned from the competition, but he, too, could think of no counter-argument. And even if there was one, it didn't really matter, because most Madrileños would never accept it. The problem was that Barcelona and Valencia had their own closely related cultures and languages, and had never really trusted the big, centralising city that was Madrid – and Madrid, in return had never really trusted them. And things were even more complicated than that – anarchists and socialists distrusted communists and each other, and everyone was wary of the liberals.

The Fascists had it much easier because they were ruled from the top down. If you disagreed with the Generalissimo, he didn't argue with you – he had you shot. And that, combined with all the support the rebels were getting from Nazi Germany and Fascist Italy – meant it was almost inevitable that they would win out in the end.

So only a fool would continue to hold out against them, Paco thought – which probably made him the biggest fool around.

Fat Felipe, Paco's loyal sergeant of yesteryear, practically engulfed the small chair he was sitting on in Ruiz and Cindy's apartment.

He had arrived five minutes earlier, and the first thing he had gasped when Paco opened the door to him had been, 'Do you know how many steps there are between this apartment and the street, *jefe?*'

'There are ninety-two,' Paco replied.

'Yes, there are ninety-two,' Cindy confirmed, remembering struggling up each and every one of them with a broken Paco in her arms.

'There are ninety-bloody-two,' Felipe agreed. 'Have you ever thought of moving to somewhere a little closer to the ground?'

Now, halfway down the generous glass of Fundador brandy which Cindy had provided, Felipe was back to his normal, easy-going self.

'So how are you both?' he asked.

It was not an idle question, as the slight edge of anxiety in his voice showed. The three of them had last been together at the International Brigade's base in Albacete, where one of the two murderers they'd been tracking down had attempted to kill Cindy – and had come close

84

enough to land her in a coma for two days – and the other murderer had put a bullet in Paco's shoulder.

'We're doing well,' Paco said. 'The doctor says I'll be fit enough to re-join my unit next week, and he's given Cindy permission to go back to nursing. How about you, Felipe?'

The fat man shrugged, and his many chins oscillated. 'They wouldn't have me back in the army. They said I was too big a target.'

'And what did you say in return?' Paco asked.

He didn't try to hide his amusement, because he and Felipe had known each other for so long that it was almost impossible for either of them to hide *anything* from the other.

'I said my size was a real advantage for them,' Felipe told him, 'because while the rebel scum were lining up to take a pot shot at me, the real soldiers could concentrate on the job of killing them.' He sighed. 'But the army wasn't buying it, so now I'm a civilian observer.'

'And what does that mean, exactly?' Cindy asked.

'It means that for twelve hours a day, I sit on my arse watching the enemy lines, so that if the rebels decide to attack, I can warn our soldiers.'

'It seems like a worthwhile job,' Cindy said encouragingly.

'It's a crap job,' Felipe told her. 'Do you know how we'll know if the enemy are coming? It won't be because some bloody useless observer has spotted them through his spy glass – I'll tell you that for nothing. What will tip us off – give us just a little hint – is the rumble of their tanks as they roll towards us, and the rattle of their machine guns as they fill us full of holes. So, like I said, I'd be doing more good as a soldier.' Felipe sighed again. 'And to add insult to injury, being an observer, I'm not entitled to army rations.'

And that was the crux of the problem for a man like Felipe, who loved his food, Paco thought, because while army rations, which he and Cindy received, were not very good, civilian rations were even worse.

'Do you know what we're allowed on the ration card for a whole week?' Felipe asked, and without waiting for them to reply, he continued. 'A hundred grams of lentils, a hundred grams of chickpeas, seventy-five grams of white beans, a hundred and fifty grams of rice *or* two hundred and fifty grams of potatoes and half a kilo of vegetables or fruit. That's nowhere near enough for a man with a healthy appetite like mine.'

'So what have you been doing about it?' Paco asked.

Because he was sure that Felipe had being doing *something*, and was *almost* sure that the sack Felipe had brought with him – and which, it seemed to Paco, had been twitching of its own volition – held part of the answer.

'My cousin has a motorbike that is so old and knackered that the government didn't bother to requisition it,' Felipe said, 'and when we can lay our hands on a couple of litres of petrol, we go out to one of the villages. There's still plenty of food in places like Torrejon and Azuqueca.'

Paco tried to picture Felipe's huge backside perched on the rear of a decrepit old motorbike, and decided it was an image that belonged more to a Mack Sennett silent comedy film than to real life.

'So you've been buying food from the villages?' Cindy said.

'Not buying – bartering,' Felipe told her. 'Peasants aren't interested in money – a lot of them simply don't trust it – but there are things they need that they can't produce themselves.'

'Like what?' said Cindy, intrigued.

'Soap,' Felipe began, counting the objects off on his fingers, 'caustic soda, rope-soled sandals, jewellery (the gaudier the better), salt, cigarettes (one cigarette equals one egg) and, of course, black cloth.'

'Black cloth?' repeated Cindy, who was beginning to appreciate that she still had much to learn about Spain. 'Why *black* cloth?'

'For mourning clothes,' Paco explained. 'In the villages, displaying signs of mourning is mainly the job of the women, so when a woman's father dies, she will wear black for several years.'

'But before her period of mourning is over, her mother will probably die,' Felipe said, 'so the whole process will be extended.'

'Her uncle or her aunt will die next,' Paco continued, 'then her cousin, and perhaps her brother. She will probably still be in black when her own husband dies – all of which means that once she's starting wearing mourning clothes, she's very unlikely to stop. And that takes a lot of black cloth.'

'And I thought my home town was backward,' Cindy said.

'There are two reasons I've come here today,' Felipe said, getting back on the subject. 'The first was to check that you are both fine, and the second was to give you this.'

He put the sack on its side, opened it up, and prodded the closed end. Out of the open end, a hen emerged. It looked rather confused.

'They asked me in the village if I wanted them to kill it before they handed it over,' Felipe explained. 'But I said no. I thought you would want it as fresh as possible, so you would kill it just before you were ready to eat it. So they gave me something to keep it quiet.'

'They *doped* a chicken!' Cindy exclaimed. 'How would they know how to do that?'

Felipe chuckled. 'You'd be surprised what they know up in the mountains. They have potions to make a woman pregnant, and potions to make a man *want* to make her pregnant. Quietening down a chicken must be a doddle for them.' He glanced down at his watch. 'I must be going. I'm on duty in half an hour, and if I'm not there, the Fascists may sneak into Madrid without anybody noticing.'

'Thanks for the chicken, Felipe,' Cindy said.

'You're very welcome,' the ex-policeman told her.

It was half an hour since Felipe had left, and as the effect of the doping wore off, the chicken became much more animated, and began to wander around the small living room, as if in search of some grit to scratch in.

'Let's make a deal,' Cindy suggested. 'You kill it, and I'll pluck it.'

Paco winced.

'What's the matter?' Cindy wondered. 'It's a very good deal from your point of view. You spend a minute slitting its throat, and I spend half an hour getting feathers up my nose.'

'I don't want to do it,' Paco admitted.

'Why not? You must have done it before.'

'As a matter of fact, I haven't.'

'But you were brought up on a farm, just like I was – and you should know, there's no room for soft-heartedness on a farm.'

'My father grew olives and green peppers,' Paco protested. 'We didn't have any livestock.'

'But you've killed men before now, haven't you?'

'You know I have – far too many.'

'So what's the difference?'

'I suppose there's none at all,' Paco said. 'And if the chicken decides to come at me with a knife, believe me, I'll kill it soon as look at it.'

Cindy sighed – heavily and theatrically. 'All right, Ruiz, if you can just hold the bird above the sink, I'll separate its head from its neck.'

As she went over to the drawer to get a sharp knife, the chicken suddenly squatted down on the floor.

'I think it's crapping,' Paco said, in disgust.

Cindy shook her head pityingly. 'You really don't know livestock, do you, Ruiz!'

The chicken stood up and walked away, leaving an egg behind it.

'Bird, you've just saved yourself,' Cindy said. She turned to Paco. 'Nip down to the hardware store and get a couple of metres of wire netting will you, please? Then pop round to the nearest stable and get some straw.'

'You're going to keep it?' Paco asked.

'That's right.'

'In here?'

'Where else do you suggest I keep her?'

'This is crazy,' Paco told her.

'You won't think that when you're the only person on this street having an egg for breakfast,' Cindy countered.

'All right,' Paco agreed, bowing to the inevitable. 'I'll go and get some wire netting.'

'I think I'll call her Eleanor Roosevelt,' Cindy said.

'A couple of minutes ago you were going to kill it – and now you're giving it a name,' Paco said.

'A couple of minutes ago, it was dinner – now it's a member of the family,' Cindy told him.

Chapter Seven

Friday 14 May 1937

Moncho Valverde was a very tall, very broad man, and people seeing him for the first time would often reflect that his only physical flaws were that he seemed to be a little lop-sided, and to walk in a slightly awkward way. Then they would hear the dull heavy sound that his left foot made whenever it touched the ground, and quickly realise that his *real* physical flaw was that his left leg below the knee was gone, and had been replaced by a roughly carved piece of wood.

He had been a formidable fighter before he lost his leg, Paco recalled, as he watched the other man clip-clonk across the Cabo de Trafalgar towards his table. More than formidable, he had been a force of nature – strong, resourceful, intelligent, and with total disregard for his own safety – the enemy's worst nightmare.

Paco remembered one particular bloody day during the battle for the university – a day which had been going so badly that a number of men might have turned and run, had they not feared Sergeant Valverde's disapproval.

* * *

The battle has moved to the faculty library. There are perhaps thirty Moors in there, and the same number of Republican soldiers. They are not in nice, neat lines, one side clearly delineated from the other. Instead, they are like the contents of the devil's stew pot, bubbling up and swirling around together in a cauldron of desperation.

They all have guns, but none of them dare fire, in case they hit their own comrades, so it is down to hand-to-hand fighting – knives and bayonets.

Paco is on the ground, with two large Moors towering over him. He does not pray in what he fully believes will be the last few seconds of his life – who, after all, would an atheist like him pray to? – but he does mourn the fact that he is leaving Cindy to cope with the world on her own.

And then – suddenly – one of the Moors is no longer there.

Instead, he is being held in the air – above head height – by Moncho's two massive arms.

Moncho looks around him. The library window has been barricaded from top to bottom with thick books – centuries of learning now serving no other purpose than to stop bullets.

But that does not deter Moncho. He hurls the struggling Moor at the window. The books slow the Moor's flight down, but are not enough to stop him. Some of the books disappear through the gap where there had once been glass – a cascade of knowledge falling to the earth outside – and the Moor inelegantly follows them.

Moncho sees his nothing of this. His attention has already turned to the other Moor. It has only taken a couple of seconds to dispatch the Moor's comrade, but even that would have cost him his life, had not Paco – his own personal artillery war going on in his head, and his whole body feeling as if it had just been fed through a threshing machine – made an almost superhuman effort to lash out with his leg and catch the Moor on the kneecap.

The Moor is in great pain, but he marshals his strength, and in a moment he will be ready to fight again. But he is not given that moment, because Moncho wraps his arm around the man's head, and breaks his neck.

Paco was planning to embrace the other man, but before he had the chance, Moncho held out his arm, and they formally shook hands.

'It's good to see you, Moncho,' Paco said, as Valverde sat down.

'It's good to see you, too, captain,' Moncho replied.

'Captain?' Paco said, with a laugh. 'What is this shit? Call me by name, for Christ's sake.'

'Very well,' Moncho agreed. 'It's good to see you again *Don Francisco*.'

'Is this a joke?' Paco wondered.

'No,' Moncho said seriously. 'You want to hire me, and as long as I'm working for you, you're my boss, and nothing more. Once the job is over, however, you and me will go out and get roaring drunk.' He grinned. 'That is provided, of course, that your beautiful *Yanqui* girlfriend will give you her permission.'

It was meant as a joke, but everyone who knew Paco *did* think he needed Cindy's permission before he did anything. And the truth was he did usually ask, not because he had to, but because he wanted to – because he thought that was the right thing to do. And if that made him henpecked – well, he simply didn't care.

'So, you mentioned a job, *jefe*,' Moncho said. 'Just what is it you want me and my lads to do?'

While Paco outlined the task, Moncho listened silently and intently, and, but for the fact that he nodded occasionally – at points at which was appropriate to nod – it would have been fair to assume that he was asleep with his eyes open.

92

Finally, when Paco had finished, he said, 'That's clear – now spell out the details.'

Paco explained that he wanted everyone entering the bullring searched, and anyone carrying a weapon to hand it over to the security team, who would hold it until the *corrida* was over.

'It'll slow things down,' Moncho said. 'It will slow things down *a lot*.'

'I know it will.'

'And have the management agreed to this?'

'I haven't actually asked them yet,' Paco admitted.

'Ah!' Moncho said.

'But when I do raise the matter with them, they will agree to my demands.'

'You sound very sure of yourself.'

'I am.'

'Why is that?'

'Because I'll tell them that if they don't agree to all my terms, I'll pull Faustino out of the event – and without *El Gitano* to entertain the crowd, they have nothing.'

'And would Faustino go along with that?' Moncho wondered.

Paco grinned. 'No – there's not a cat in hell's chance he would. But they won't know that.'

'You've said how you want the entrance gate handled. What arrangement do you want inside Las Ventas?'

'I want the corridor patrolled on a regular basis. And I want several of your men in the ringside seats.'

'Do you think there's really a chance they'll try to kill him once he's in the ring?'

'What do you think?' Paco asked.

'The government's propaganda machine paints all the Fascists as yellow-bellied cowards,' Moncho said thoughtfully, 'and there is no doubt that there are *some* cowards on their side, but – and I'm ashamed to admit this – we have our own cowards.'

'We have,' Paco agreed.

'And there are plenty of brave men, on their side, too – and we both know that, because we've fought against them ourselves.'

'Brave *and* honourable,' Paco said.

'So maybe one of those braver rebels will even be brave enough to go against his own nature and do the cowardly thing – shoot down an unarmed man.'

'The crowd would tear him apart if he did that,' Paco pointed out.

'He would expect them to. More than that, he would welcome it, because by turning it into a suicide mission, it would validate his own courage.'

You'd have to be crazy to think like that, Paco told himself, but it made perfect sense to him, so maybe he was crazy, too. Maybe everybody caught up in this war was at least a little crazy.

'In your professional opinion, what are the chances we can protect Faustino?' he asked.

Moncho thought about it. 'If the assassin is young or nervous, then we have a very good chance.'

'And if he is a hardened professional?'

'Then we have no chance at all.'

Paco was back in the Hotel Florida, and once again got the impression that the management and staff of the hotel regarded the war much as a respectable family might regard its one disreputable member – they kept it at arm's length and pretended it had nothing to do with them.

The feeling was only reinforced when he entered the lounge. Here, in addition to the pot plants and cane furniture he had seen the previous evening, there was now a string quartet playing particularly bland versions of songs which had been more than bland enough already.

It was as if you were enveloped by the ordinariness of everything here, Paco thought, and life outside this reassuringly boring bubble – the bomb craters, the whining of the shells as they flew through the air, the distant background rattle of machine-gun fire – seemed little more than an illusion.

The man he had come to see was sharing the far table with two other men and a bottle of brandy. The other two men were much older than Faustino. One of them was dark and wiry, and sat slightly awkwardly, as if he had a heavy weight pressing down on his left shoulder. The other was much rounder, and was puffing on a large cigar.

Even from a distance, it was possible to tell that this was not the friendliest of meetings, and Paco was about to return to the reception desk when Faustino spotted him, and gestured that he should join them.

'This is my old friend, Paco Ruiz,' the matador announced, 'and this is Enrique Gómez and Álvaro Muñoz.'

Gómez was the old bullfighter who was Faustino's adoptive father and mentor, and judging by his extravagant cigar, Muñoz was either the promoter or his manager.

'Sit down and pour yourself a drink, Paco,' Faustino said. 'We are talking business, but we will not be long.'

Well, if they were talking business, Muñoz must be the manager – the man Faustino had instructed to get all his money together – Paco thought, as he poured a slug of brandy.

'When I am in a city where I am due to fight, Álvaro, I expect to see wall posters announcing my arrival – and the bigger the city, the more posters there should be,' Faustino said to his manager. 'Yet what did I see when I was walking around Madrid this morning?'

'I don't know,' Álvaro Muñoz replied, awkwardly.

'Then I will enlighten you – I saw nothing!'

'Don't go blaming me,' Muñoz said. 'If there is anybody at fault here, it is the promoter. It is his job to advertise the *corrida*.'

'Yes, it's his job, but we always have our own posters, in addition to his – and you know that,' Faustino said, slamming his fist down on the table.

'Normally, we do, but this time it is simply not necessary,' Álvaro protested. 'Look, Faustino, everybody knows you are here in Madrid. The people know it, the donkeys know it, the dogs and cats know it – even the rats in the deep dark sewers know it. It is the biggest event of the year.'

Although possibly, it could be argued, being under siege from a rebel army might be just a tiny bit bigger, Paco thought, wryly.

'My posters have a quality that the promoter's posters do not,' Faustino said. 'They are collectors' items. You see them hanging on the walls of bars everywhere – and sometimes even in people's homes.'

'Yes, they are quality – that is probably why they are so expensive,' Álvaro Muñoz muttered, almost to himself.

'Expensive!' Faustino repeated. 'Expensive! Are you saying I cannot afford them?'

'No, of course not,' Muñoz replied hastily.

'But that is precisely what other people will think,' Faustino countered. 'They will say to themselves, "It is a pity about *El Gitano*. Once, he thought himself king of the world. Now he cannot even pay for a few miserable posters".'

'They will not say that,' Muñoz assured him. 'And even if they do, what does it matter? You are a star. You are an artist. You are above all that.'

'Perhaps it is not too late to get some posters printed,' Faustino mused, as if Muñoz had never spoken, 'If it is a rush job, it will cost a lot more, but what does that matter? Then we can hire some men to plaster the walls with them tonight. Most people will probably not see them before the *corrida*, but they will certainly see them afterwards, and know that *El Gitano* is no cheapskate.'

'Listen to me, Faustino,' Muñoz pleaded. 'I have been in this business a long time, Remember, Enrique and I used to be matadors ourselves.'

'*Joder!*' Enrique Gómez said, in obvious disgust.

'Is something troubling you, Enrique?' Muñoz asked, in a prickly tone.

'Enrique and I used to be matadors ourselves,' Gómez said, his voice a gross parody of the other man's. '*I* was a matador, Álvaro. Before this bloody war broke out, they were planning to put a bronze statue of me outside the *plaza de toros* in Ronda – the spiritual home of bullfighting – and once the war is finished that is exactly what they *will* do. But you – what did you ever do but fight in towns that were so poor that you were not even allowed to kill the bull, because they could not afford to replace it?'

For a moment, it looked as if Muñoz would deny it, then he changed his mind and said, 'Do you think it is easy to fight a bull which has been in the ring before, and knows its way around? They are much more dangerous than any of the bulls you had to face, which were only just beginning to work out what was happening to them when you killed them.'

'Now you are not just insulting me – you are insulting Faustino as well,' Enrique said angrily, 'because he, too, fights bulls which have never been in the ring before.'

The sudden look of horror on Muñoz's face showed that he realised he had just made a big mistake.

'Faustino …' he began, in a choked voice.

But Enrique had not reached the end of what he wanted to say. 'The bulls I fought then – and Faustino fights now – were brave and courageous,' he said. And with that, he opened his shirt to display a deep, angry scar just below his heart. 'Could any of the broken-down cattle you had to fight have done this?'

'Any bull – from a *toro bravo* to a farmer's stud bull – can do that,' Muñoz said dismissively. 'You do not measure a bullfighter's skill by the size of his wound. The truly skilful matador avoids getting gored at all.'

'You *hijo de puta*!' Enrique screamed.

Faustino raised his hands to indicate that he wanted – and expected – silence from both of them.

'You have each shown a lack of respect for the other which I am sure you will regret when you've had time to calm down,' he said. 'Any bull – whether it has been in the ring before or not – is dangerous. And you know that, don't you, father?'

'Yes, I know it,' Gómez said, looking down at the table.

'And there is no shame in a great matador being gored,' Faustino continued, 'and you know *that*, don't you, Álvaro?'

'Yes, I know it.'

'So now that has been cleared up, I would like you, Álvaro, to go and see if you can organise at least a few posters before the *corrida*,' Faustino said, and now his voice was soothing and persuasive. 'And I would like you, father, to listen to what I have to say to Paco, in case I miss anything out. Are we clear on that?'

The two men nodded, and Muñoz rose to his feet.

'Before you go,' Faustino said, 'Paco will need some money to pay the people he has hired to protect me. How much do you want, Paco?'

'It's too early to say exactly because I don't know who Moncho has recruited, or how much he's agreed to pay them, but sixty duros should cover it,' Paco said.

'Sixty duros! Three hundred pesetas!' Muñoz explained. 'Are you planning to hire the entire army?'

'No,' Paco said, 'only a few good men who really know their business.'

'Stop quibbling,' Faustino said. 'Just give him the money, Álvaro.'

'I don't carry that amount of cash around with me,' Muñoz said. 'It simply isn't safe in times like these.'

'Get it by tomorrow,' Faustino snapped.

'I'll do my best,' Muñoz promised. '*Hasta luego*, Señor Ruiz.'

'*Hasta luego,*' Paco said.

'Until then' – the all-purpose Spanish sign-off which promised there would be other encounters, but was vagueness itself in terms of when those encounters might be.

'*Hasta luego,* Enrique,' the manager said.

But the old bullfighter had turned his face to the wall, and said nothing.

'I will see you tomorrow, Faustino,' Muñoz said.

'God willing, that is true,' Faustino replied, with a smile which promised that whatever slight unpleasantness might have passed between them, it was now completely forgotten.

'God willing,' Paco repeated, when the manager had left. 'It's not very often you hear God's name invoked anymore – at least, not unless it's being used in a curse. Most people even avoid saying *adios* now.'

He had said the words without really thinking. It was a truism that since the war had broken out, the Republican side had been strongly anti-religion, so he had not meant to postulate anything

99

controversial, and was doing no more than creating a noise to fill the awkward silence that Enrique Gómez's hostility to Álvaro Muñoz had created. But it had been a mistake – he could see that by the expression on Faustino's face.

'God is important to me,' the gypsy said stonily. 'He protects me. I would not dare step into the bullring if he was not on my side.'

'I'm sorry,' Paco said. 'I never meant to offend you.'

The stern look on Faustino's face melted away, and he smiled. 'Of course you didn't,' he said. 'Let's talk about something else. From what you said to Álvaro, you seem to have the matter of my security well in hand.'

'Yes, I do,' Paco agreed. 'The man I have put in charge is about as good as they come – but that still doesn't ensure your safety. The only way you can positively guarantee it is by not entering the ring at all.'

'I have told him a hundred times that he should not fight that day,' Enrique Gómez said. 'Of course, his followers would be disappointed, but I still have a name in the bullfighting world, and if I were to take his place, their disappointment would perhaps be a little less.'

At first, Paco thought the old man was making some kind of joke, because it should have been obvious to anyone – even him – that he wouldn't last a minute in the ring. But then he realised that Gómez was being deadly serious, and really believed he could pull it off.

Faustino was desperately signalling Paco with his eyes, and what that signal said was, 'Please do not make fun of my father.'

And Paco's eyes flashed back, 'It honestly never crossed my mind for a second to do so.'

'Perhaps an assassin's bullet would find me, but what does that matter?' Enrique Gómez continued. 'I am old man, and would be dying in the place I love the most, in order to protect my son, who I love even more. What man could ask for better?'

'I am sure you're right, father,' Faustino said gently. 'The crowd would be delighted to see you. They would probably count themselves lucky that instead of watching me perform, they were being given one last chance to see the legendary Enrique Gómez in action. But,' he lowered his voice even more, 'I have given my word that I will appear, and if a man cannot keep his word, then what kind of man is he?'

'I do not want to see you die in the ring,' the old man said, almost pathetically.

'Then you should never have encouraged me to become a matador,' Faustino said, and now there was an edge of impatience to his voice, 'because every time I go into the bullring, there is a chance I will not walk out again.'

'You are right,' the old man said. 'It is all my fault.'

Faustino leaned forward, and put his hand on Enrique's shoulder. 'Nothing is your fault,' he said, and the softness had returned to his tone. 'I could not have wished for a better father than you.'

'I think I'd better be going,' Paco said.

Faustino gave him a brief nod. Enrique kept his watery eyes firmly fixed on his adopted son.

Paco thought it extremely unlikely that either of them noticed him stand up and walk to the door.

Chapter Eight

Friday 13 May 1977

He would never have described the bullring at Las Ventas as magnificent, Woodend thought, but with its tall stately towers, arched windows and doors, and ceramic incrustations, it was certainly impressive.

'It's not actually Moorish, is it?' he said to Paco, more to stop his friend drowning in a sea of introspection than because he wanted an answer.

'What?' Paco said, startled.

'I said, it's not actually Moorish, is it?'

'No, it isn't. It's what's known as Neo-Mudéjar, which means, I suppose, New Moorish. Many tourists assume it is ancient, but in fact it wasn't finished until late 1929, which makes it a little less than fifty years old.'

His voice sounded strained, and Woodend, who recognised the signs, knew that this could well lead to a fit of despondency.

Considering what unhappy memories this place held for Paco, it could be argued that he should never have come anywhere near Las Ventas. But he had insisted, and Woodend had not fought against it because he was increasingly coming round to the idea that these unpleasant encounters were what his friend needed to endure if he was ever to exorcise the demons which had been haunting him for nearly fifty years.

Still, there was no harm in distracting him a little, if that helped, now was there?

'I get the impression that the average Spaniard doesn't hold the Moors in much regard,' Woodend said casually, as if he hadn't noticed the change of mood, and was once more just expressing genuine curiosity.

'The average Spaniard doesn't,' Paco agreed, 'but he should. The Moors made Spain a centre of enlightenment and learning when the rest of Europe was wallowing in the Dark Ages. When they were thrown out, they left behind them a legacy of scholarship, land irrigation and architecture. They established baths and glass factories. They worked in leather and ceramics. Spanish culture after the expulsion only flourished because they had prepared the ground in which it was nurtured.'

'That sounds like a line you learned in school,' Woodend said.

'It is,' Paco confirmed, 'but that doesn't make it any less true.'

'So you obviously had a good teacher,' Woodend said.

'I had the best,' Paco told him.

Don Simón is little Paco's hero. He is tall, and intense, and knows everything there is to know about anything. And, in addition, he is kind and patient – qualities often lacking in the other priests who work in Paco's school.

It is said that the reason he is teaching in this backwater place – this quinto coño *– is that he is both brilliant and unorthodox, which is more than enough to unsettle the powers that be, and Paco passionately* *believes this to be true, even though he has no idea what it means.*

Don Simón says many things that will leave a permanent imprint on Paco's mind, but perhaps the most significant is what is said during the teacher's 'discussion' with Alfonso, Esteban and Iñigo – a discussion which Paco eavesdrops on from behind a bush outside the classroom window.

The three of them are the sons of peasants, just like Paco, and they have been told to report to Don Simón because someone (it is never revealed who) has seen them throwing stones at a small Moroccan boy who is travelling through the district with his father, a carpet salesman.

As far as they are concerned, they have done nothing wrong, but nevertheless, they expect a beating, because unfair beatings – whether dished out at school or at home – are a part of life.

But Don Simón does not beat them. Instead, he talks to them, and it doesn't take them long to decide that they would rather have the beating.

'It is wrong to throw stones at anyone,' Don Simón says, 'but what we are here to talk about is why you chose that particular victim.'

It seems to the boys to be a particularly stupid question.

'He's a Moor – a Muslim,' Esteban says.

'Top marks for observation,' Don Simón says.

And though he cannot see them from behind his bush, Paco can well imagine that Esteban – who has never got top marks for anything before – is smirking complacently.

'I still don't see why you picked on him,' says Don Simón, sounding genuinely puzzled.

'I'm a Christian,' Esteban says.

'Are you, indeed?' Don Simón asks mildly. 'Do you go to church regularly?'

'My mother does.'

'But what about you? And your father?'

'No, we don't go.'

That is way it is in Andalucía – most of the women attend church (many out of habit) and most of the men do not (mainly out of a vague atheism).

'So we've established that you're not a very good Christian,' Don Simón muses. 'Are you now saying that even a bad Christian should throw stones at Muslims?'

'Yes,' Esteban says. He pauses, to consider what he has just confessed to, then decides to stick to his position. 'Yes,' he repeats.

'And why is that?'

'Because when the Moors were in Spain, they tried to turn us all into Muslims.'

'On the contrary, the Moors tolerated Christians and Jews because they were children of the Book, as they were themselves. Of course, the Christians and Jews had to pay an extra tax, but if your faith isn't worth spending a little money on, then it is not much of a faith at all.'

At this point, Esteban should quit, but he has never been one to let his brain stand in the way of exercising his mouth.

'The Moors killed all the Christians,' he says.

'Are you referring to the Granada Massacre of 1066?' Don Simón asks.

'Yes,' Esteban says, though it is obvious he has no idea what he is agreeing to.

'But it was Jews, not Christians, who were killed by the Muslim mob, wasn't it?' Don Simón says.

'I suppose so,' Esteban agrees.

'And since the vizier – a Jew – was planning to sell the city to its traditional enemy in Almeria, the mob's actions, while never justifiable, were at least understandable, wouldn't you say?'

'The Muslims killed the Christians,' Esteban says stubbornly.

'We've already established that there were only isolated incidences of that happening, whereas if you want full-blown examples, you have only to look at the way the Christians massacred the Muslims – and the Jews. And whereas the Muslims allowed the Christians to continue practising their religion, the Christians insisted the Muslims convert immediately. And just to make sure they had, they insisted they ate pork and left their doors open on a Friday, to prevent them praying in secret.'

'Are you on their side?' Esteban asks, amazed.

'I am on the side of decency, honesty, and intelligence,' Don Simón says.

The "discussion" goes on for another hour, and when they leave, it is plain from the way the boys carry themselves that the harshest beating would have been preferable.

They all learn something from the experience.

Alfonso, Esteban and Iñigo learn that if they are to be bigots, they must be <u>covert</u> bigots, and it is a skill they very quickly develop, so that when Faustino, the little gypsy boy, joins the school, they can persecute him without Don Simón having an inkling of what is going on. It becomes so bad that Paco begs Faustino to allow him to tell the teacher about it, but Faustino will have none of that – his pride will simply not allow it – and instead he simply stops coming to school.

And Paco himself? When he is a soldier in Morocco, the other soldiers he's serving with have countless names for the enemy – Muslim scum, circumcised dogs, brown monkeys – but he subscribes to none of these. To him, the men he kills are simply people with guns who want to kill him.

'You were off with the fairies again, weren't you?' Woodend said.

'Yes,' Paco agreed, 'I suppose I was.'

'Well, look, that's another landmark in your past ticked off, what say we go and have a drink?' Woodend suggested.

'All right,' Paco agreed.

They turned and walked towards Plaza de Roma, but they had only gone a few metres when Paco stopped and turned around again.

He ran his eyes up and down the walls of the bullring.

'I'm sorry, Faustino,' he said, in a choked voice. 'I screwed up. I really screwed up.

Chapter Nine

Saturday 13 May 1937

At three o'clock, Paco finished oiling his pistol, and slid it into his shoulder holster. He reached for his jacket, and only then did he notice that Cindy already had her coat on, and was sitting by the door.

'Where are *you* going?' he asked.

'I'm going with you.'

'But I'm going to the *corrida*,' Paco pointed out.

'And so am I,' Cindy replied.

Paco laughed – although he should have learned by then that laughing at one of Cindy's statements of intent was always a mistake.

'The problem is,' he said, 'you'll need a ticket, and all the tickets will be sold out by now.'

'Then how have you managed to get one?'

'Faustino is providing one for me, and one for Felipe.'

'Now there's a coincidence,' Cindy said.

'What do you mean?'

'Faustino is providing me with a ticket, too.'

'You don't even know him.'

'No, but I wrote to him saying I was your floozy, and asking if I could have a ticket, and he sent me a note – although it was actually signed by someone called Nieves – to say it had all been arranged.'

'Even if you've got a ticket, are you sure you actually want to come?' Paco asked, discouragingly. 'I think it will horrify you. And if it doesn't do that, then it will bore you.'

'You said I could never understand the Spanish if I didn't understand the bullfight,' Cindy pointed out.

'That's a load of rubbish,' Paco replied.

'So why did you say it?'

Paco grinned, unconvincingly. 'I was losing the argument. I had to say *something*.'

'It's not at all like you to care so much about winning arguments,' Cindy said.

He shrugged, helplessly. 'So I had a moment of weakness.'

'Or could it be that you're worried about taking me somewhere there might be danger?' Cindy asked astutely.

'No, that's not it all.'

'So if I don't go with you, you're saying you'll be perfectly safe on your own?' Cindy asked, in a voice which would have made generations of Inquisition interrogators green with envy.

'Yes, that's right,' Paco agreed. And then, under her steady gaze, he had felt compelled to add, 'although, of course, no one is ever completely safe in a city under siege.'

'Well, that settles it,' Cindy had said, placing her hands firmly on her hips. 'I'm coming with you.'

'But why?'

'Because if it's safe, I'll at least get to spend time with you, even if it is at a dumb old bullfight, which any civilised person would steer well clear of.'

'And…?' he asked – because he knew there was an 'and'.

'And,' Cindy replied, her eyes moistening, 'if there *is* danger – and you end up getting killed – then I want to be with you when you die.'

He was going to give way to her, as he always did. His old friends would have been shocked that he had not firmly put his foot down as a *macho* Spanish man – the head of the household – was supposed to do. But then Cindy wasn't a compliant Spanish wife, she was a thoroughly independent American woman, and the fact that she had no intention of ever living under his benevolent dictatorship was one of the many reasons he loved her so much.

'Did you really say in your letter to Faustino that you were my floozy?' he asked.

'Yes!' Cindy said. 'Although,' she admitted, 'I might have phrased it a little more tactfully than that.

By four o'clock that afternoon, nearly twenty-five thousand men – and quite a few women – were descending on the bullring at Las Ventas, among them a former police inspector (almost recovered from taking a bullet in the shoulder), his gourmet, over-weight ex-sergeant, and his blonde American mistress/floozy (who he would have married in an instant, if this had been a country in which divorce was at all possible).

Moncho was standing by the main entrance. He was dressed in his old army uniform, which was mottled with pale spots where the bloodstains – his own and probably those of others – had been bleached out. His wooden leg gave him a nautical air, and it was easy enough to picture him as a blood-thirsty pirate. He was not the kind of man people normally argued with, and despite their obvious extreme annoyance at being held up and searched, none of the *aficionados* were arguing with him now.

Moncho saw Paco approaching, and signalled he should join him.

'*El Gitano* asked me to give you these tickets,' he said.

Paco took the tickets, and saw that – disappointingly – there was one for Cindy. He put them in his pocket.

'How's the operation going?' he asked.

'We've searched the entire stadium,' Moncho told him. 'If there's a bomb or a gun in there, then it must be bloody well hidden.'

It would have been much more reassuring if Moncho had said there were definitely *not* any hidden guns or bombs, Paco thought glumly, but he recognised that no search, however thorough, could guarantee that.

'And I'm absolutely certain that nobody's managed to smuggle a weapon into the stadium past my lads,' Moncho continued.

He would trust Moncho with his life, Paco thought – he *had* trusted him with his life half a dozen times in a matter of months – yet he could not quell the feeling in his stomach that Faustino was already as good as dead.

'One more thing,' Moncho said.

'Yes?'

'We still haven't been paid.'

No, they hadn't, because despite the fact that Faustino had instructed his business manager to hand over the money to Paco, Álvaro Muñoz had proved to be a very difficult man to track down.

And what would happen if he continued to be hard to track down once the bullfight was over, and Moncho and his men had completed the job they'd been contracted for?

'I'll get you the money one way or another, Moncho,' Paco promised.

'What does that mean?'

'It means that if I can't get it off Faustino's manager, I'll just have to rob a bank.'

Moncho grinned. 'I'd like to see that,' he said. 'In fact, let me know in advance, and I'll be there to clap you on.'

He would, too, Paco thought.

'Stay vigilant,' he said.

'I will,' Moncho promised.

When it came to considering what kind of ticket to buy, the bull-fighting *aficionado* was presented with several options. There were two covered sections at the top of the ring (which was where the president of the bullfight's box was located), but most true *aficionados* opted for a totally open-air seat, in either the *tendido bajo* or the *tendido alto*.

Each of these had its own particular advantages. In the *tendido alto* (the higher seats), the *aficionado* was presented with a panoramic view of the whole ring, and could clearly see how the various elements engaged in the fight – the picadors, the banderilleros, the matadors and, of course, the bulls – all formed part of the composite picture in which the drama of life and death was enacted. On the other hand, those in the *tendido bajo* (the lower seats), were *part* of that drama. They could hear the gasps of the matador, and the angry snorts of the bull, and could almost smell the man's sweat and the animal's rage. And when the blood gushed out of the man or the bull – an obscenely scarlet jet pumped through the air by a hysterical heart – it was as real and as vivid to them as if it were their own.

The tickets that Paco had asked for were in the shaded part of the *tendido bajo*. He had chosen these seats because they gave him the best possible view of the *callejón* – the narrow passageway between

112

the bright red fence which encircled the ring and the first line of seats. It would be in this *callejón* that Faustino would stand and observe, as the matadors who preceded him dispatching their bulls. And while everyone else would be watching the action in the bullring, Paco would be scanning the seats behind the *callejón* for any signs that a would-be assassin might be lurking there.

Behind him, he heard an *aficionado* say, 'You probably don't know this, but *El Gitano* has killed more *toros bravos* than any other matador in Spain.'

It was the way he said it that gave him away, Paco thought – not 'did you know?' but 'you probably don't know'. In other words, he was advancing the idea that he was better informed than his neighbour, and thus implying that this made him superior.

'What you're probably trying to say is that he's killed more *toros bravos* than any other matador in Spain *this century*,' the neighbour said.

'What do you mean?' the Knowledge King asked, and Paco chuckled as he pictured the look of uncertainty spread across his face.

'I mean that in the last century, both Miguel Diaz and *El Malagueño* killed more bulls than *El Gitano* has,' the Challenger said. 'You have heard of them, I take it,' he added scathingly.

Actually, on reflection, the Challenger was just as bad as the Knowledge King, Paco thought – maybe even worse. He was the sort of man who learned the times of all the trains to Barcelona, on the off chance he might have the opportunity to contradict someone who was actually planning to make the journey.

'Well, of course I have heard of Miguel Diaz and *El Malagueño*,' the Knowledge King said uneasily. 'What I meant was that he has killed more bulls than any other matador *this century*.'

'You're wrong about that, too,' the Challenger said, sounding so smug and complacent that Paco yearned to turn round and shake him so hard that he'd be playing castanet music with his teeth.

'What do you mean, I'm wrong about that, too?' the Knowledge King asked, and now he really did sound concerned.

'I mean that facts don't lie, and according to the facts, you are wrong,' said his opponent, the trivia gatherer. 'When *El Gitano* has killed his allotted *toros bravos* today, then – and only then – will he have killed more bulls than any other matador this century. Perhaps that was what you meant to say all along.'

The Knowledge King, having effectively been dethroned, said nothing. The Challenger whistled tunelessly to himself, which was as loud a cry of victory as he needed to make.

The pride of a Spaniard was both his greatest strength and his greatest weakness, Paco decided. At its best, it would lead to him to perform acts of selfless heroism. At its worst, it resulted in petty conversations like the one he had just heard, in which the only important thing was to come out on top. Maybe the Challenger was right about Miguel Diaz, *El Malagueño* and Faustino. Maybe he had made most of it up, just to win the argument. But true or false, did it really matter? And when you attempted to belittle other people, weren't you really just belittling yourself?

'What's on your mind, Ruiz?' Cindy asked.

'I was just wondering if we somehow managed to talk ourselves into this war,' Paco admitted.

'I shouldn't be at all surprised if that was exactly what you did,' Cindy said. 'After all, why should this war be different from every other war?'

'Get your snacks here! Get your snacks here!' called a voice.

Paco looked up. There were a number of vendors working their way around the ring, their trays hung around their necks. Before the siege

114

had begun, the trays would have been weighed down but all kinds of treats, but now all the vendors had to offer was bags of *pipas* – dried sunflower seeds – and beers which they swore were cold, but could only have been – at best – lukewarm.

Paco turned back to Cindy. 'Do you want anything?' he asked.

She glanced at the trays. 'Oh, how you spoil me, Sr. Ruiz,' she gasped, as if overwhelmed by the offer.

He smiled.

Fat Felipe signalled for a bag of *pipas*. He had never been particularly fond of them, but when there was nothing else available, they suddenly became as desirable as sirloin steak.

'Tell me, Felipe, how do you feel about bullfights?' Cindy asked, as he opened the bag with his chubby fingers.

Fat Felipe scowled. 'I strongly disapprove of them.'

'You see!' Cindy said to Paco, with a hint of triumph in her voice. 'I'm not the only one!'

Paco chuckled. 'Ask him *why* he disapproves,' he said.

Though she sensed that she was falling into a trap of her own making, Cindy saw no way out, and asked the question anyway.

'It is a waste of good grass,' Felipe said.

'Excuse me?'

'The best meat comes from cattle fed on good grass. Fighting bulls are fed the absolutely best grass. And what is the result? – the meat is very flavoursome, but is too full of muscle. Imagine then, what potentially wonderful meat is never produced because of this so-called spectacle.'

'Paco says it's artistic,' Cindy said, surprised to find herself apparently defending a position she didn't actually subscribe to.

Felipe shrugged his weighty shoulders. 'A good paella is a work of art, and so is a delicately prepared *riñones al jerez*,' he said. 'This is

115

merely a flashy show, put on by men in tight trousers who want to impress both other men and women of great beauty, and if I wasn't playing at being a policeman again, I wouldn't even be here.'

A sudden expectant silence fell over the ring, and all heads turned towards the president's box, which was located at the very top of the ring, on the west side. When the president entered the box, sat down, and waved his handkerchief, the crowd broke into applause. But if he'd turned up late, this same crowd would have booed and whistled, Paco thought, because even the president of the event did not have an automatic right to respect.

The same was true for the matadors – and for the bulls. If a matador fought well, or the bull was particularly brave, the crowd would drench them with cheers that verged on adoration – but if the matador fought badly, or the bull was deemed to be cowardly, the audience would hiss and throw their cushions into the ring as a sign of their contempt. And there were no exceptions made to the rule. A matador returning to the ring after recovering from a serious goring would be given no leeway while he regained his confidence – if he failed to deliver immediately, the crowd would be merciless in its scorn.

So maybe Cindy was right, and whole process was barbaric, Paco mused. Maybe it taught people to be less tolerant of weakness – and there was far too little tolerance of that in Spain already, which was why the country was falling apart.

There was a blast of the trumpet, and two men on horseback, dressed in the fashion of the 1560s, galloped across the ring to the president's box, doffed their caps, and bowed low in the saddle.

'Who are they?' Cindy asked.

'They're the bailiffs,' Paco told her. 'They execute the president's wishes. It's traditional.'

'Is it an old tradition?' Cindy wondered.

'Quite old, I suppose,' Paco said dryly. 'When it first began, for example, no one dreamed there would ever be a country called the United States of America.'

The band started to play a *pasodoble*, and the procession appeared at the *cuadrillas* gate. It was led by the three matadors, walking shoulder to shoulder, and behind them, in single file, came their teams of banderilleros.

Faustino looked calm, dignified and in total control of himself – the complete bullfighting hero.

The matador next to him was stolid, and gave the impression that while he would put on a more than satisfactory performance, no one should be expecting any real thrills.

It was the one on the end who was really interesting. He was the youngest of the three, and though he was doing his best to counterfeit Faustino's mannerisms, he was not quite making it. This was probably the first time he had fought in Madrid, Paco thought, and he would be fully aware that if he didn't make a decent showing in this, the most important bullring in the whole of Spain, his career would be over before it had ever really got started.

The procession came to a halt in front of the president's box, the three matadors removed their hats and bowed.

And even here, there was a difference between them, Paco thought. The youngest matador carried out the gesture with great reverence, almost as if there were something sacred about it. The middle matador went through the motion mechanically, recognising it as a necessary step he had to take, in order to earn his pay. But with Faustino, there was something mocking in the bow, as if he were saying, 'I am doing this because ritual requires it, but we both know which one of us is really important in this affair.'

The procession wheeled round, and returned to the part of the ring near the *cuadrillas* gate. Here, it divided, and all three teams took up their position in the *callejón*.

Once they were all in place, the two bailiffs rode back to the president's box, and one of them held out his cap. The president threw down a set of keys, and the bailiff caught it neatly in his hat.

'What happens if he misses?' Cindy asked.

'If who misses?' replied Paco, who was keeping his eyes focussed on Faustino, except when he was making a rapid sweep of the spectators behind the matador.

'The president,' Cindy said. 'When he throws the keys, what happens if he misjudges it.'

'That doesn't matter,' Paco told her, his gaze still fixed on Faustino. 'It's part of the ritual, but not an important part, and if he misses, one of the servants will pick the keys up and place them in the bailiff's hat.'

'There seems to be an awful lot of ritual – taking an awful lot of time,' Cindy said.

'A man should never rush into death, even if that death is not his own,' Paco said.

Although he'd seen enough of it in the previous few months to know that rushing into death was now almost the norm.

The bailiffs rode across his line of vision, and though he could not see it, he knew they would now be handing the keys to the old man who would open the gate and release the first bull of the afternoon.

He sensed a collective intake of breath, and understood that the bull had arrived.

Though he could not yet see it, he could picture it easily enough. It would be large and black, with wicked horns. It would be aggressive – because they were bred to be aggressive – and might already have killed another bull in the pasture which had been its home until a few days earlier. And it would be disorientated, because for the first four to five years of its life, it had rarely seen a human being – and the ones it had seen had never been on foot – and yet now here it was, in this vast arena, surrounded by thousands of these strange two-legged creatures.

Its instinct told it that the only way out of this situation would be to fight. That same instinct would drive it to familiarise itself with the battleground, and once it had done that, it would search out an enemy to attack.

In the *callejón*, Faustino was watching the proceedings with mild interest. There was nothing in his demeanour to indicate that he had any worries about being assassinated, but then of course, matadors were adept at hiding their fears, Paco thought.

By now, the young matador, having studied the way the bull reacted to be the banderilleros' cloaks, would have entered the ring, and would be using his own cloak to put the bull through a series of passes. This stage was not particularly dangerous for the matador, as he was taking no real chances, merely studying the animal's nature and approach to combat. Yet there was always a chance that he would make a wrong move, or that the bull, not yet weakened, would act unpredictably.

Paco fumbled in his pocket for his cigarettes, and from the corner of his eye, he caught sight of the picadors entering the ring. The bull would have noticed them too, and would be heading towards one of them.

Man and bull each had their own objective in this part of the ritual, and whatever the man, whatever the bull, this never varied.

The bull's aim was to get his head under the belly of the picador's horse and turn the animal over. The picador's job was to use his lance

119

to stab the bull's neck, thus forcing the animal to lower its head during the later stages of the fight.

Paco took a drag on his cigarette. He wondered what Faustino's girl in Mexico was like, and if he had made the right in choice in deciding to give up his life in Spain for her. He wondered if Faustino had told his girl in Madrid that she was nothing more than a stopgap.

Beside him, he heard Felipe say, 'These men are the banderilleros, Cindy.'

'I know that,' Cindy replied. 'And they're going to drive those little spears they're holding into the bull's neck and shoulder, aren't they?'

'That's right,' Felipe agreed.

'Hmm, seems to me like the odds are stacked against the bull right from the start,' Cindy said.

They were, Paco silently agreed – but that didn't mean that he always lost.

He scanned the crowd of people behind the *callejón*. Every one of them had their eyes on the bull. Not a single person was watching Faustino. So perhaps the letters had been nothing but a bluff. Or maybe the assassin, on seeing all the guards Paco had posted, had decided to give up the attempt.

Careful Paco, this is no time to lower your guard! he told himself.

They would have reached the final stage of the fight by now. The matador would have re-entered the ring, with a cape in one hand and his sword in the other. He would enact a number of passes – some simple, some complicated – and then he would try to manoeuvre the bull into a position where he could drive his sword through the animal's aorta or heart.

If there was going to be an assassination attempt, now would be the time for it, Paco thought, because everyone would be so absorbed by what was happening on the sand that even the people sitting next to the killer wouldn't notice what he was doing.

He checked his shoulder holster. It would only take him a second to free his pistol, but if the assassin knew his job, a second would already be too late.

There was a loud *olé* from the crowd. Perhaps the matador had executed a pass with great artistry, or perhaps it had only been particularly daring. Since this was a young matador, the chances were that it was the latter, because artistry comes with experience, but courage must be demonstrated right from the start. Timidity or caution often resulted in boos and thrown cushions, and some matadors who had been particularly disappointing had enraged the crowd so much that they needed a police escort to leave the ring.

There was still no one in the *tendido* showing the slightest interest in Faustino, and if the man himself was concerned, he was showing no signs of it.

The rapid series of *olés* told him all he needed to know about this particular matador – the man had clearly opted for the high-risk strategy of performing several dangerous passes in a row.

The sudden collective gasp told a different story, and Paco couldn't stop himself from turning to the ring.

What he saw there was enough to send shivers down the spine of any man. The bull was shaking its head from side to side. It was clearly an awkward movement, because the animal was somewhat restricted by the man who it had skewered on its right horn.

The bull shook its head again, and the man was flung free. He did a double somersault before hitting the sand, and once he had landed, he just lay there, showing no inclination at all to escape.

The matador's blood stained the sand in which he was lying, the stain growing larger as his body pumped out more blood through the hole in his chest. For a moment, it looked as if the bull would walk away, but then it seemed to decide that the man on the ground still had enough life in him to retain its interest, and it lowered its head and prodded him with both horns.

Members of the matador's team surrounded the bull, their capes fluttering in a provocative and challenging manner, and the animal turned its attention to this new disturbance.

Paco swung round to check on the *callejón*. There was no sign of Faustino, nor of his banderillero (and close friend?) Luis.

Paco vaulted over the fence and landed on the other side with a jarring thud. His wounded shoulder was almost healed, but it had not been expecting this, and screamed in protest.

'What are you doing, *jefe*?' Felipe called after him.

'Faustino … gone …' Paco gasped, all the breath temporarily driven out of him.

If he could have sprinted, he would have done. As it stood, he could manage no more than a jog, which would just have to do. He headed towards the *cuadrillas* gate, since that was the most likely place for Faustino to have gone. It took him longer than it should have to get there – everything was taking longer than it should have – because he had no choice but to make a wide arc around the circle of confusion made up of the angry bull, the fallen matador and the frantic banderilleros.

He was not sure where to go once he got beyond the gate. He knew that immediately inside was a small surgical operating theatre, and that opposite was the room where the bullfighters gathered before they walked out into the ring. He knew that there was a chapel, and beyond were the horses' stables and infirmary, but he could not see what could be important enough in any of these places to make Faustino defy ancient tradition and leave the ring.

The second he was inside, he saw Luis. The young banderillero was just standing there, his face unnaturally pale, and his whole body shaking.

'Where is he?' Paco demanded. 'Where's Faustino?'

With what seemed like an almost superhuman effort, the banderillero raised his arm and pointed to the chapel.

'What's he doing in there?' Paco asked.

But after all the effort of pointing, Luis seemed totally incapable of anything else.

'You're a woman!' a voice behind him said accusingly.

'Top marks for observation,' Paco heard Cindy replied.

'But women can't come in here – women don't come in here,' the man said, with an awkward mixture of outrage and disbelief.

Paco whirled round. The official was facing Cindy and blocking her way. Every time she moved slightly to the left, he moved slightly to the right. Every time she moved slightly to the right, he moved slightly to the left.

Under normal circumstances, Paco would have really enjoyed watching the confrontation play itself out – but this wasn't normal at all.

'She's with me!' he said.

The official had never seen him before, but it was obvious from Paco's tone that messing with him would not be a good idea. He stood aside, and let Cindy through.

Paco turned around again, and saw that Luis had vanished.

'Where's Faustino?' Cindy asked.

'I think he's in there,' Paco said, pointing towards the chapel.

'Well, shouldn't we go and see if he's all right?' Cindy asked.

'Yes, I suppose we should,' Paco agreed.

But after seeing the look on Luis's face, he really didn't want to.

There is a phrase in Spanish – *estar en capilla*. It can be literally translated as 'to be in the chapel', but it signifies so much more than that. Its real meaning is to commune in mind and soul with the Holy Spirit, thereby attaining the strength to face the challenging times ahead. And that was not just empty words to the men who fought in Las Ventas – it held real life-and-death meaning.

There had long been a strong vein of anti-clericalism running through Spanish society, and there was reason enough for this. Many of the priests in the countryside had allied themselves with the land-owners, rather than the peasants – even choosing to drink in the rich men's casinos, instead of the peasants' rustic bars. And when the landlords – or the *guardia civil* acting on their behalf – cheated one peasant out of some of his land, and beat another viciously to intimidate the rest, the clergy, like the priest and the Levite in the parable, tended to walk by on the other side of the road. And it was as bad – though rather different – in the towns and cities. Here, the priests would fawn over their rich parishioners, but not even bother to change into a clean shirt for a poor person's funeral mass. As a result, there had been a spate of church burnings even before the rebellion, and this had naturally increased when the rebels began to attack the Republic. All over Madrid, there were now the blackened skeletons of ecclesiastical buildings.

Yet even at the height of the frenzy, no one had suggested that the Las Ventas chapel should be desecrated, because this place was not about politics or privilege – it was about the bullfighters' need to become at one with the universe, before facing a force of nature intent on their destruction.

And so these matadors would stand before the altar, flanked on one side by a statue of Jesus weighed down by the cross he had been forced to carry, and on the other by a statue of the crucified Christ, once he had reached his destination at the top of that green hill. They would look up at the painting of the Virgen de la Paloma, who is the patron saint of Madrid, and they would pray. Some would pray that they would fight so well that the crowd would ask the president to grant them the singular honour of leaving the ring through the Grand Gate. Other matadors, with less ambition – or perhaps less confidence – would merely pray that they survived their encounter with the bull.

That was before the bullfight.

The ones who visited *after* the bullfight would be brought in on stretchers down the short corridor that connected the chapel with the operating theatre, and would have been aware of the fact – if they were aware of anything at all – that the doctors had given up on them, and they were being brought there for the last rites.

It was a place of calm and sanctity, of optimism and acceptance. It was also the place where Paco and Cindy found Faustino – lying on the chapel floor with his sword protruding from his chest.

Paco had seen enough homicides in his time to know that there was need to check for signs of life.

Faustino was about as dead as it was possible to be, he thought. A blade through the heart will do that every time.

Paco stood, perfectly still, in the chapel doorway. He wondered why he wasn't moving, and couldn't decide whether it was because he didn't want to, or because he was unable to.

'Paco?' Cindy said uneasily.

'Give me a minute,' he replied.

A minute?

Would that really be enough?

Then how about an hour? Or a week? Or a year? Or ten years?

Would any of those really make a difference?

Even if he was given all the time in the world, would he ever be completely at peace with himself again?

He knew he couldn't take the entire blame for this. Faustino must bear some of the responsibility because he had insisted on coming to the ring even after the death threats. A share of the blame must also go to the men Paco had hired to protect the matador, since they had somehow let the killer slip through.

Even so, he could not absolve himself anything like completely. He had allowed himself to be distracted when the matador was gored. If he hadn't, he would have seen Faustino leave the *callejón*, and by following immediately, he might perhaps have been able to prevent the murder.

From somewhere in the distance came the sound of thundering hooves, which meant that several cattle had been brought into the ring, and were being driven towards the bull. They would be manoeuvred into completely surrounding the killer, and then the whole bunch would be driven back through the *toriles* gate, beyond which the bull would be killed by a professional butcher who had no artistic aspirations at all.

The hoof beats died away, and were replaced by the noise of an excited exchange between men who had just entered through the *cuadrillas* gate.

'Should we take him to the infirmary?'

'No, it's too late for that. No doctor can help him now.'

'Well, then …?'

'We'd better take him to the chapel.'

'What's the point of that? You said yourself that he was dead – and even if he wasn't, there's not a single priest left in the whole of Madrid who can say a prayer over him.'

'It's all we can do for him now, isn't it? Perhaps once he's in there, the Virgin will take pity on him, even without a priest asking her to.'

Paco turned, and saw the matador's team – their smart uniforms darkly stained with the dead man's blood – carrying a canvas stretcher on which their fallen boss lay.

'Wouldn't it be disturbing the crime scene if they put him in there,' Cindy whispered.

Yes, it undoubtedly would.

But did that matter?

Not really!

'Even if the killer has left his fingerprints all over the chapel, there's no one around to lift them and compare them with the records anymore,' he told Cindy. 'Hell, there probably aren't even records left to compare them to.'

The same was true if the killer had left forensic clues. Even if he'd scattered them as liberally as a farmer scatters seeds, they would be useless without anyone to interpret them.

Crime detection had been set back 100 years – and that was taking a rosy view of it.

'Faustino is in there. He's dead,' he told the man at the front of the stretcher.

'Faustino? Do you mean *El Gitano*?'

'Yes.'

'How can he be dead? He hasn't even been in the ring yet.'

'See for yourself,' Paco said, finally finding the energy to step to one side.

The grisly cortège took a few steps forward, before stopping at the chapel door.

'He's … he's been murdered!' the lead stretcher-bearer gasped.

'Either that, or it's the cleverest case of suicide that I've ever seen,' Paco replied.

That was better, he thought. Now he was sounding less like Faustino's friend, who had let him down, and more like the cynical profession homicide investigator he had once been.

'So what do we do with Don Diego?' asked the other man, glancing back at the body on the stretcher.

'Oh, why not lay him down beside Faustino,' Paco suggested, 'then if – against all odds – there really *is* a Virgen de la Paloma, maybe she'll save herself some time by giving them both her blessing simultaneously.'

Chapter Ten

The noise of the crowd wafted through the *cuadrillas* gate and filled up the space in front of the chapel.

It was not at all like the customary roar of excitement, and though describing it as a roar of anger might be a little closer to the truth, even that would be somewhat overstating the case. Perhaps, then, it would be best to think of it as a roar of exasperation – and of impatience.

The dead matador has been removed from the ring and the bull has departed with his herd, the roar seemed to say. All the necessary procedures have been followed to clear up after the bloody debacle, and yet nothing new is happening, which leaves us staring at an empty circle of sand.

Of course, the crowd was sorry that Diego had been killed after putting on such a spirited display for them, but death was, after all, an occupational hazard – something which added an extra frisson to the whole proceeding – and the show must now go on.

That was the way it had always been – one matador is gored another matador kills his second bull.

But what would happen now, with two matadors lying dead? Paco wondered.

Would the remaining bullfighter – the workmanlike one – fight all the five remaining bulls? He might well, because business was business, and to be paid for killing five bulls was obviously better than being paid to kill two.

And would the crowd stand for that? Again, they might well, because any bullfighter was better than no bullfighter at all.

Moncho appeared at the end of the corridor. There was a pained expression on his face, and though he normally walked as if his wooden leg was no real impediment at all, his gait was now clumsy and laboured.

So I'm not the only one wracked with guilt at having screwed up, Paco thought.

Moncho was not alone. By his side was a grey-haired man in a colonel's uniform.

Paco made a rapid assessment of this new arrival. From his overall bearing, it was obvious that he wasn't just some lawyer or trade union official, who had led his own militia of enthusiastic amateurs, and then found his militia absorbed into the regular army. No, this man was a long-serving professional soldier, who, when Franco's rebel scum were issuing all their high-sounding proclamations, had remembered the oath that they had all sworn to protect the republic – and decided that he, at least, would stick to it.

The colonel came to a halt a metre away from Paco. He had grey eyes which nearly – but not quite – matched the grey of his hair. They were not eyes which suggested he had a particularly good brain, but they were perfect at signalling that when he issued an order, he expected it to be obeyed.

'I am Colonel Sanz, the area commander,' he said. 'I was in the president's box when Sergeant Valverde, here,' he nodded towards

Moncho, 'told me there was something I needed to see. I assume that, even though you are not in uniform, you are Captain Ruiz.'

'Sir!' Paco said, coming to attention and saluting.

'And this is the murdered man?' the colonel asked, looking through the door and into the chapel.

'Yes, sir,' Paco replied, although what he really wanted to reply was, 'Why should you assume that a man lying on the ground with a sword projecting from his chest is the one who's been murdered?'

'Sergeant Valverde here tells me *El Gitano* has received several death threats in the last few days. Is that correct?'

'Yes, sir.'

'From the rebels?'

'That's what the letters implied,' Paco said, cautiously.

'What do you mean by saying that they *implied* it?'

'Well, they ended with the words "Viva Franco!"' Paco said.

The colonel's nose twitched disdainfully. 'I trained with him in the Toledo Infantry College,' he said. 'He was a self-important little shit even then. Funny, isn't it, how some men seem to get all the promotions?'

There seemed to be no satisfactory answer to that, and anyway, Paco had other things on his mind. What he had told the colonel about the letters was quite true, but whether they were fake or whether they were genuine, he was beginning to doubt that they had anything to do with the murder. It was looking, to him, much more like a crime of opportunity than a coldly calculated political assassination.

'Well, then, it seems like a simple open and shut case,' he heard the colonel say.

What!

'I'm sorry, sir, I'm not sure I quite understand,' Paco said.

131

The colonel smiled. It was kindly smile which said that Paco should not worry – that colonels were quite used to mere captains not being as quick to follow things as they were.

'*El Gitano* was murdered by the Fascists,' he said, speaking slowly to give Paco more chance of comprehending. He turned to Moncho. 'You said you were in charge of security here, didn't you?'

'Yes, sir.'

'Has anyone left the ring since the crime was committed?'

'No, sir.'

'You're certain?'

'Absolutely certain.'

'So the killer is still here,' the colonel mused, 'but that doesn't really help us, because he could be any one of the thousands of *aficionados* out there.'

Or he could have been any of the dozens of people who worked behind the scenes, Paco thought, gloomily. And the problem was, he simply couldn't command enough skilled manpower to question them all, which meant that, as much as it pained him, he would have to take a back seat, and let the colonel's men conduct the investigation.

'Well, there we are,' the colonel said, with a laissez-faire tone that took Paco completely by surprise.

'There we are?' he repeated.

'Yes, it seems we'll never find out who killed him.'

'Aren't you going to investigate?' Paco demanded, and then added a belated, 'sir?'

The colonel's grey eyes flashed with something close to anger.

'Are you questioning my decision?' he asked.

He was a soldier, and the colonel out-ranked him, Paco reminded himself. But even if he'd been a civilian, it wouldn't have made any difference, because in this barrio, Sanz's word was law – and that law applied to everyone.

'No, I'm not questioning you, sir,' he said. 'I was merely seeking clarification as to exactly what your decision was.'

'Well, then, to be perfectly clear, I am not going to investigate,' the colonel said. 'In case you haven't noticed, Captain Ruiz, there is a war going on. Hundreds – sometimes thousands – of men are being killed every day, and yet you seem to expect me to devote some of my precious few resources to tracking down the killer of one man, do you?'

'No, sir,' Paco replied, because what the colonel had just said made perfect sense.

But the problem, as he saw it, was that if you were operating on the principle that one death didn't really matter, it was not long before ten deaths became of little importance, then a hundred, then a thousand.

'Will you give me your authorisation to investigate the murder myself, sir?' he asked.

The colonel scowled. 'Shouldn't you be on the front lines, fighting the enemy?'

'I was shot,' Paco explained. He touched his shoulder, though lightly. 'The doctors say I won't be fit for active duty for another week or so.'

'Ah!' said the colonel, softening now that he realised Paco carried with him the cachet of being a wounded warrior. 'But would you even know how to start investigating a murder?'

'Yes, sir,' Paco said.

'It's not as easy as you might think, you know.'

Oh God, here we go again, Paco thought, as he realised, with a heavy heart, it was confession time.

'I was a policeman before the war,' he admitted. 'I worked in the homicide squad.'

'Homicide squad,' the colonel repeated thoughtfully, 'Wait a minute. Ruiz … Ruiz … Weren't you …?'

Paco sighed. 'The detective who solved the case of the headless corpse in Atocha railway station?' he said. 'Yes, sir, that was me.'

'Well, you certainly should know what you're doing,' the colonel conceded, and in his mind, he was already telling his wife about his encounter with the famous detective. 'All right, captain, you go ahead.'

'Could I have something in writing, sir, to give me official status?' Paco asked.

The grey eyes hardened again, and now they were wary.

'I said, you had my permission to investigate,' he said. 'And so you have. But I made no mention of my authorisation. It's never wise to try and push me too far, Captain Ruiz.'

And so it went, Paco thought. Even when caught up in a struggle for survival, a great many men were never quite able to put their self-interest to one side. The colonel had given him permission, but not authorisation, which meant that if he succeeded in catching the killer, Sanz would claim his share of the glory, but if anything went wrong, well, it had absolutely nothing to do with the colonel.

'Could I ask you one favour, sir?' Paco asked.

'What?' the colonel asked, in a tone of voice which combined suspicion and irritation.

'I'd like you to ensure that *El Gitano* is given an autopsy.'

'Won't he get one anyway, as a matter of course?' the colonel asked.

Jesus, if he could think that, the man must really live in a bubble of his own self-importance, Paco told himself.

'They *might* conduct one, sir, but given all the pressure the doctors are already under, dealing with the wounded, they may decide it's something they can just let slip.'

'And isn't that a reasonable decision?'

'Perfectly reasonable from their viewpoint, but looking at it from *our* viewpoint, an autopsy may just provide the investigation with the vital information we need.' The grey eyes flickered, and Paco realised that the colonel was about to turn his request down. 'Of course,' he continued quickly, 'I realise that your authority may not stretch as far as the hospitals …'

'I have control over everything that happens in this barrio,' the colonel snapped. 'I will instruct the medical staff to conduct the autopsy as soon as they get their hands on the body.'

'Thank you, sir,' Paco said humbly.

'Well, I suppose it's time to get back to what's left of this bull-fight,' Sanz said. 'I wonder, Sergeant Valverde, did I ever thank you for saving my life, that day out on the sierra? You know the day I'm talking about – the one when you lost your leg.'

'Yes, I remember the day, and I was only doing my duty, sir,' Moncho replied.

Which was as good a way as any other of saying, 'No, you bloody well *didn't* thank me!' Paco thought.

'I'll tell you what, then, Valverde, why don't you come up to the president's box with me? I expect a glass of cava wouldn't go unappreciated, or if you don't like that, I've some very fine brandy.'

'That's really very gracious of you, sir, but given the situation, I think I'd better stay here,' Moncho replied.

'Maybe you didn't hear me properly,' Sanz said. 'I invited you, a common soldier, up to the *president's box*.'

'With the greatest respect, there are matters I need to deal with,' Moncho said, stubbornly.

'Hmm, there's gratitude for you,' the colonel snorted, before wheeling round and marching away.

'I'm so sorry that I let you down, Paco,' Moncho said.

'It was nothing we could have foreseen,' Paco told him.

'So what do we do now?'

What we do now is treat it as much like a real police investigation as is possible, given the circumstances, Paco thought.

'I want your men to question everyone down here – the servants, the grooms, the friends and managers of the matadors. I want to know where they were around the time Faustino was killed, and if they saw anything suspicious. And I want a list of all their names and addresses, so I can talk to them myself, when I can find the time to get round to it.'

It was like asking teams of road repairers to carry out brain surgery, he thought. Even if these men of Moncho's didn't miss obvious clues, they would be unlikely to pick up on the nuances, as a trained investigator would. But if all you had was rice and vegetables, then you made vegetable paella.

'What about the spectators?' Moncho asked.

'I don't think it was one of them,' Paco said.

Because if it was, if the killer had left his seat in one of the *tendidos*, made his way to the chapel, killed Faustino and returned to his seat, all without any of the bullring employees noticing him, then the colonel was right, and it was pointless looking for him – because they'd never bloody find him.

The Palace Hotel was a fine Art Nouveau building on Parliament Square. Until the previous year, it had been one of the best hotels in Madrid (if not the whole of Europe) and, with style and aplomb, had entertained foreign royals, North American industrial millionaires and South American cattle barons.

Its centrepiece was a magnificent rotunda with a stained-glass cupola. Paco had seen it before, because he had once come to the hotel to question one of its guests in connection with the murder of a high-class prostitute, and the man had insisted they take tea in the rotunda.

'This really isn't necessary,' Paco says, as they sit down.

The other man – Señor Pérez – waves his hand carelessly through the air.

'I know it's not necessary,' he says. 'But why shouldn't we spoil ourselves, once in a while?'

Except it's not once in a while for you, is it? Paco thinks. You're used to luxury. You're the man who can afford a hundred peseta a night whore.

The tea is a magnificent affair, overseen by a small army of waiters. There are an assortment of exotic beverages and a small mountain of expensive cakes. And as they are eating and drinking, Pérez explains that of course he visits prostitutes when he is away from home – what man doesn't? – but when he is back in Burgos, he is the most faithful husband in the world. And as for killing a prostitute …

How did she die, incidentally?

She specialised in clients who liked to play rough games, Paco explains and her client that night played it just a little too *rough. But surely Sr. Pérez knows that, because he is listed as one of her clients.*

He didn't do that sort of thing with her, Pérez says.

Then why did he ask for that particular whore, if he had no interest in her speciality? Paco wonders.

Pérez knows nothing of her speciality. To him, she was no more than a pretty girl who was pleasant to talk to, and that was why he asked for her.

When the bill comes, Pérez insists on paying it, but not before he has made sure Paco has seen just how much it is.

That's about a week's salary, Paco notes. I wonder if Pérez thinks he's bought my silence with that.

A few days later, after Paco has arrested Pérez, and escorted him discreetly through one of those doors that hotels like this install specifically to make such discretion possible, he returns to the rotunda, and hands the headwaiter an envelope.

'What's this?' the waiter asks.

'It's a tip,' Paco tells. 'I think you'll find it's exactly equal to half the cost of the tea I had with Señor Pérez.'

'But he paid for everything – and left a generous tip of his own,' the waiter says.

'That doesn't matter.'

'Look, you're not like the rich bastards we usually get in here – this is a lot of money to you.'

'You're right,' Paco says, because there's really no point in denying it.

'So take it back,' the waiter says, offering him the envelope. 'It's really not necessary.'

'But it is necessary,' Paco replies. 'I need to be able to look at myself in the mirror in the morning, because if I try shaving with my eyes closed, I'll probably cut my bloody throat.'

The Palace Hotel still had the rotunda, but it wasn't a tea room any more. Now that the hotel had become a hospital, its rotunda was an operating theatre, or – to be more accurate, a number of operating *areas*. Sometimes, only one or two operations were being carried out there, but when the fighting was particularly heavy – or the bombing and shelling particularly intense – there were so many surgeons operating, on so many patients, that they were practically touching elbows.

It was not the rotunda to which Paco was directed, but to a smaller operating theatre which – to judge by the white tiles on the walls – had once been part of the kitchen complex.

There was a surgical table in the centre of the room, and lying on it was a slab of meat and bones which had, until earlier in the day, been the greatest matador in Spain.

The doctor standing next to the table was a small man in his late fifties. He had an avuncular look about him which seemed to belong in a family surgery rather than a room in which autopsies were being carried out, but when he saw Paco standing there, he frowned, and any resemblance to a favourite uncle disappeared.

'Are you a doctor?' he asked, and the authority in his voice belied the mildness of his appearance and the diminutiveness of his stature.

'No, I'm not,' Paco admitted.

'Are you then a nurse – disguised as a man?' the doctor asked.

Paco grinned, though there was no evidence the doctor was attempting to be humorous.

'No, I'm not that, either,' he admitted.

'Then you have no business being here,' the doctor said firmly.

'Faustino Vargas was my friend ...' Paco began.

'I am sure Don Faustino had many friends, but that still does not entitle you to be here.'

'And, in addition, I was a homicide detective before the war.'

'Were you, indeed,' the doctor scoffed. And then, after a moment's pause, he added, 'Actually, your face does look vaguely familiar. Is your name Rodriguez?'

Paco shook his head. 'It's Ruiz – Paco Ruiz.'

'That's right,' the doctor agreed, as if he'd just decided to grant Paco his permission to use that name if he wanted to. 'Aren't you the man who tracked down the murderer of the headless corpse in ...?'

'That was me,' Paco interrupted him.

He had solved dozens of murders during his time with the Madrid police – maybe even scores of murders – and yet for the second time in an afternoon, someone was bringing up the bloody headless corpse.

He was sick of it happening, and imagined Salvador Dali would feel that way if the only question anybody ever asked him was, 'Aren't you the man who did the picture of the melting clocks?'

'I want you to know that though I was ordered by some petty bureaucrat to carry out this autopsy, I would never have agreed if there had been more useful work I could have done with the living,' the doctor said.

'So noted,' Paco replied gravely. 'You are a man of principle. I respect that. But, at the same time, Faustino was my friend, and I want to track down his killer, so I am glad you felt able to do something which will undoubtedly help me.'

The words seemed to take some of the wind out of the doctor's sails.

'Actually, I enjoyed doing it,' he confessed shamefacedly. 'It's what I trained to do, and what I'm best at. So what can I do for you, Inspector Ruiz?'

'Give me something I can use,' Paco said simply.

Finally, the doctor smiled. 'It seems an age since I last talked to a policeman about a cadaver. This is starting to feel like old times, isn't it?'

'Yes, it is,' Paco agreed.

'Faustino Vargas died as a result of his heart being pierced by a sharp blade,' the doctor said crisply. 'The weapon used for the attack was the sword you see over there, which they tell me was his own.'

'It was,' Paco agreed. 'Are you sure …'

The doctor held up his hand to silence the ex-policeman.

'Let me forestall you by answering the sorts of questions that any policeman worth his salt always asks,' he said. 'Am I sure that it was the wound to the heart which killed him – rather than there being some other cause? Yes I am. He wasn't strangled or poisoned prior to the attack. He was very much alive at the moment the sword pierced his heart, and dead a split second later. Am I sure that the initial wound was not made by something else, and the sword only inserted to disguise that fact? Yes, I am. The sword fits the wound like an expensive glove fits the hand of the man it was made for. Is there anything else you need to know?'

'Was it a clean thrust?'

'Very clean,' the doctor said. 'It passed between the ribs without so much as grazing the bone.'

'Does that mean the killer knew what he was doing? That he might have been – say – another matador or a banderillero?'

'Are you thinking of anyone in particular?' the doctor asked.

Yes, I am – I'm thinking of Luis, the banderillero that Faustino and I met in the bar opposite the Hotel Florida, Paco thought – the banderillero who was standing just outside the chapel when I arrived.

'No, I'm just talking in general terms,' he said aloud.

'Yes, it's possible the killer knew what he was doing. But it's just as likely to have been a lucky thrust, though, of course, it didn't turn to be very lucky for Faustino Vargas.'

'What was Faustino doing when he was attacked?' Paco asked.

'Doing?'

'Was he, for example, kneeling in prayer?'

'No,' the doctor replied. 'He was standing up.'

'And he was stabbed through the chest, not the back?'

'That is correct.'

'So he must have seen his attacker coming for him?'

'I suppose he couldn't really have missed seeing it.'

'Then why did he just stand there, offering an easy target? Why didn't he try to take some kind of evasive action?'

'Perhaps he was frozen with fear,' the doctor suggested. Then he shook his head. 'No, I'm talking absolute rubbish, aren't I? I've seen him perform in the ring. He was absolutely magnificent, and if a raging bull didn't make him freeze up, then a man with a sword certainly wouldn't.'

'So he just stood there and let it happen?'

'I can think of no other explanation.'

But why? Paco wondered. What could have led him to accept his fate without a struggle?

He remembered once being told the story of a Spanish commander in the army of El Cid. This man's company suddenly found itself surrounded by a Moorish army. He knew that terrible things lay in store for him if he fell into the hands of the enemy, and even worse, he was afraid that he might give away valuable secrets under torture. So he decided it was necessary for him to die. But there, he hit a problem. He could not kill himself, because suicide was a mortal sin in the eyes of his church. And so he handed his sword to his loyal lieutenant, and told him to do the deed.

Is that what might have happened here? Did Faustino ask Luis to kill him?

But why would Faustino *want* to die? He had found true love in Mexico, and was looking forward to going to see his girl.

'Perhaps if you could find out who actually killed him, you would find out why he acted as he did,' the doctor suggested.

'Well, that sounds simple enough, but in reality it's a hen and egg question,' Paco said.

'A hen and egg question?' the doctor repeated.

'Which came first – the hen or the egg?'

'Ah, yes, it must be the hen, because she is the one who lays the egg, but without there being an egg, the hen will not be born.'

'So I can find out why Faustino acted the way he did once I catch the killer, but the chances are that in order to be able to catch the killer, I need to know why Faustino acted as he did.'

'You have a problem,' the doctor said sagely.

'Bloody right I do,' Paco agreed.

Chapter Eleven

Saturday 13 May 1937

The Cabo de Trafalgar had been Paco's local bar ever since he had moved into Calle Hortaleza with Pilar, his wife. Pilar herself had never set foot in the bar. She disapproved of such places – and of her husband being in such places. She spent much of her time on her knees in the local church, and had the priest allowed it, she would probably have made up her bed in one of the pews and never left.

Well, now she had left not only that church, but also her husband, and gone back to Valladolid to live with her parents, who were probably strong supporters of General Franco. In her letters, she had begged him to embrace the church, and promised that if he did, she would return to him. She didn't want to go back to him, of course, any more than he wanted her to come back, but as a good Christian she thought she should. Paco thought that as a good Christian it was her duty to seek annulment of her marriage to this spawn of Satan, and if it helped things along, he was more than happy to appear in St Peter's Square carrying a trident and demanding the blood of virgins.

He had answered the first few letters, then, since he knew what they would say, he started to file her letters – unopened – in the nearest bin. It made no difference, because they still kept coming – Pilar no doubt considering herself a martyr in her persistence – and only stopped when the Fascists had overrun Valladolid. It annoyed Paco that he should feel grateful to Franco and his gang for *anything*, but he just couldn't help himself.

The bar had, until a few months earlier, been run by Nacho, a huge fat man – and a positive genius in the kitchen – who had seemed such a fixture that it was almost possible to believe that he had always been there, and the place had been built around him. And yet he too had left, and gone to serve as a cook for one of the early militia groups fighting in the mountains north of Madrid.

'I expect I'll be killed up there,' he'd told Paco before his departure. 'It's all right as long as we're advancing, but if we ever go into retreat, well, I'm too fat to run away, aren't I?'

His prediction had been proved accurate. He had indeed been killed, though not before he'd caved in the skulls of two rebel soldiers with the pan he used to make his delicious paellas.

After Nacho had gone, one of the unions had stepped in to take over the bar – as the unions had stepped to in to take over so many businesses after the breakdown of normal society – and it had installed a new barman called Eduardo. He was a pleasant enough man, Paco thought, though the bar would never be the same without Nacho. But then, he reminded himself, there was very little of the life he had known which would ever be the same again.

It was in the familiar and comforting Cabo de Trafalgar that Paco, Cindy and Felipe had agreed to meet. They arrived almost simultaneously, but since this was Paco's barrio, he was the one who went up to the bar and ordered three coffees and three brandies.

'This is real coffee, you, know, not the stuff made of acorns that they've started to serve in some other bars I could mention,' Eduardo said, as he was pouring the drinks.

It was true that some of the bars had started doing that, Paco thought. It was a foul drink, which only vaguely resembled the thing it was replacing, but people ordered it anyway, because drinking a coffee in a bar had been one of the cornerstones of their lives for so long that even filthy muck like that was better than nothing.

'Yes, it's real coffee,' Eduardo repeated, in case Paco had missed the point. 'I've got a source.'

And he winked.

Of course he had a source. He would have a cousin, who had a friend, who knew a girl who was going out with a man from one of the foreign embassies. The man at the embassy would give the girl the coffee because she was sleeping with him, she would give the friend some of the coffee because he was providing her with an alibi so her father wouldn't know she was sleeping with the man from the embassy, the friend would give some of his coffee to Eduardo's cousin because the cousin had helped him out in one way or another in the past, and Eduardo's cousin would pass some of it on to Eduardo because … well, because he was his cousin. That was the way it had always worked – it was known as having an *enchufe* or plug – and the siege of the city had only intensified the process.

As a policeman, the *enchufe* system had infuriated Paco, because it had so often got in the way of an investigation, but he had come to accept it as an inevitable part of the Spanish way of life. And Eduardo, to do him credit, had not used his *enchufe* for his own benefit, by selling the coffee on the already thriving black market, but instead had chosen to draw his customers into this minor web

146

of corruption by offering the coffee to them – and very good it smelled, too!

Paco took the tray back to the table.

'What do we know?' he asked.

The words were like the starter's gun at a race to Felipe – a signal that the investigation was now properly underway.

'We know that Faustino was killed, and that his own sword was used as a weapon,' the fat man said. 'That *is* right, isn't it?'

'It's right,' Paco agreed. 'The doctor confirmed it.'

Felipe reached into his pocket and produced a sheaf of papers. 'We also have these statements that Moncho's team took from the bullring staff.'

'Have you read them?'

'I've looked at a couple of them.'

'Do you think they'll be useful to us?'

'My grandmother would have done a better of job of questioning the witnesses,' Felipe said. He shuddered, involuntarily. 'But then, my grandmother was not the sort of woman you would ever think of lying to.'

He'd never had high hopes that the statements would lead anywhere, Paco thought.

What he really needed to do was interrogate all the staff himself, but there simply wasn't time. At best, he had a week to solve the murder, before he went back to the front line. At worst, he could be killed by a shell tomorrow, or the Fascists could break through Madrid's line of defences, and it would all be over.

Very well then, they would have to approach the case from another angle.

'Do we think the person who wrote the letters to Faustino was also the person who killed him?' he asked Felipe.

'I find it very hard to think *at all* without a plate full of cheeses and sausages to stimulate my brain cells,' Felipe said, piteously.

Paco grinned. 'Do your best.'

'Perhaps if I imagined it,' Felipe said.

'Yes, that might help,' Paco agreed.

Felipe gazed down at the table, and his eyes began to light up as a picture of the platter began to build in his mind.

'There's everything here,' he said, almost dreamily. 'There's Cabrales cheese from Asturias, chorizo from Pamplona, morcilla from Burgos, juicy butifarra from Catalonia …'

Half those things were no longer available, however much *enchufe* you had, because they were made in territory held by the enemy, Paco thought. And soon, it would probably be much more than half.

'Semi-cured Manchego cheese, mountain ham …'

'The letters, Felipe!' Paco interrupted. 'Tell me about the letters.'

'Ah yes, the letters,' Felipe replied, as his vision drained away. 'Was the killer the same man who wrote the letters? I don't think so, unless, of course, the letters were only there as a red herring.'

'What do you mean by that?' Paco asked, though his own mind was already running along similar lines.

'I mean this is a personal killing, not a political one,' Felipe said. 'So if the killer did write the letters, he was only trying to confuse us – using politics to mask his true motive.'

'How can you possibly know that?' Cindy asked wonderingly.

Paco and Felipe exchanged glances.

'Do you want to tell her, *jefe*?' Felipe asked.

'All right,' Paco agreed. 'If it had been a political assassination, the killer would not have used Faustino's own sword.'

'Why wouldn't he?' Cindy wondered.

'The assassin would not have relied on finding an appropriate weapon at the scene of the crime. Besides, there is nothing sportsmanlike – nothing *mano a mano* – about assassination. By using the sword, he would be giving his victim the chance to fight back – and that is a risk which no professional would have run.'

'So what would he have used?'

'He would have selected something which have given him an undoubted edge. A gun, maybe – or a bomb – or something else he could have hit his victim with before the victim even became aware that anything was happening.'

'Perhaps he did have a bomb or a gun, then he saw Moncho's security men on the gates, and realised he'd never be able to smuggle it through. So he abandoned the weapon he'd brought, and decided to improvise, which meant grabbing whatever weapon came to hand,' argued Cindy, reluctant to concede the point.

'A professional assassin would never take that chance,' Paco countered.

'Then maybe he wasn't a professional – maybe he was just a wide-eyed fanatic.'

'And do you think Faustino would just have stood there and let a wide-eyed fanatic stab him through the heart?' Paco asked.

'Maybe Faustino was just too scared to move,' Cindy suggested, just as the doctor had done earlier. And then, like the doctor, she realised what a stupid suggestion that was. 'He was a matador,' she continued. 'He was used to being charged by a huge bull. He wouldn't be intimidated by a man with a sword.'

'Exactly,' Paco agreed.

'Then why didn't he …?'

'Why didn't he try to fight back?'

'Yes.'

'He wasn't expecting whoever had the sword in his hand to kill him,' Felipe said, 'which makes it more than likely that he knew his killer, and perhaps even thought of him as a friend. It is also possible that the killer himself never intended to murder Faustino, and would not have done if the sword had not been conveniently lying there.'

Cindy looked at Paco, who merely nodded.

'You guys don't need to talk things through, do you?' she asked. 'You've got this weird mental telepathy action going on between you.'

'Sometimes,' Paco agreed. 'Especially in the early stages of an investigation, when everything is still so obvious.'

'Hmm, obvious to *you*, maybe,' Cindy said.

'Our main problem is that we don't know enough about Faustino yet to guess who the killer might be,' Paco said. He took a sip of his coffee, which, he was annoyed to discover, he had allowed to go cold. 'Though when I think about it, there are a couple of obvious suspects.'

'Who are they?'

'His banderillero, Luis, for a start. He seemed very angry with Faustino when he came across us together in that bar opposite the Hotel Florida. And just before I found Faustino's body, he was in the corridor outside. In fact, he was the one who pointed me towards the chapel.'

'But if he was the murderer, wouldn't he have left immediately?' Felipe asked.

'Maybe he did intend to do just that,' Paco said. 'Maybe he had just come out of the chapel – and was about to make his escape – when I arrived.'

'Good point,' Felipe agreed. 'Who is the other one?'

'When I went to up to Faustino's room in the hotel, there was a woman there, and they both looked as if I had interrupted something very important. If she was his mistress – and since she was in his room alone with him, I don't see what else she could have been …'

'She could have been a prostitute,' Felipe interrupted.

'She could,' Paco conceded, 'but Faustino didn't strike me as the kind of man who would use the services of a prostitute. Besides, there was something about the way he blocked me from seeing her, and almost pushed me down the corridor, which seemed very protective – almost chivalrous.'

'All right, let's assume then that she was his mistress, rather than a whore,' Felipe said.

'So he has the mistress in Spain, and she learns that he is abandoning her and moving to Mexico. How is she going to feel about that?'

'Hell hath no fury like a woman scorned,' Cindy said. 'But are you saying that the girl could have done it?'

'No,' Paco told her. 'But it might have been some relative of hers – a brother, or a father. It's a question of family honour. But these are only two starting suggestions. I'm a mild, inoffensive man myself …'

'Yes, you are,' Cindy said.

She was almost surprised to hear herself agree, but thinking about it, she supposed Paco was *indeed* a mild inoffensive man, unless you crossed him. But if you did cross him – then God help you.

'A mild, inoffensive man,' Paco repeated, 'but I have still managed to make a lot of people angry – and not all of them ended up behind bars, where they can do no more harm.'

Felipe, who had been doing some silent counting, nodded. 'You have at least enough enemies to form two football teams – and that still leaves some left over to do all the catering after the match.'

Cindy chuckled.

'What's funny?' Felipe asked.

'You are,' Cindy told him. 'You just made a joke.'

'Did I?' Felipe asked, looking puzzled.

'That thing about the two football teams,' Cindy said helplessly.

'But that *is* how many enemies the *jefe* has,' Felipe said, still mystified. 'Two football teams is twenty-two men, and the catering would need at least …' he began counting on his fingers, 'Yes, at least another five.'

'Is he joking *now*?' Cindy asked Paco, uncertainly.

Paco smiled enigmatically. 'I don't know.'

But that simply wasn't true, she thought. These two men were so close that each knew what the other was thinking practically all the time.

Paco loved her. And he would lay down his life for her if the need arose – he had proved that.

So how dumb was it to be jealous of his relationship with Felipe?

About as dumb as it could be.

But she was!

'The point I was trying to make was that Faustino, who was much more famous than me – and also more arrogant – will have had even *more* people who will have wished him harm,' Paco said.

'*Was* he more arrogant than you?' Cindy asked, and realised just how angry she was.

'He was a famous bullfighter,' Felipe said, as if it were a pointless question to ask. 'A matador does not get a reputation like Faustino's without believing that he is better than everyone else. If he started having doubts, he would soon either be booed out of the ring, or else end up hanging from the horn of a *toro bravo*.'

'My point is that we need to collect a great deal more information on Faustino before we can even begin to investigate properly,' Paco said. 'So we start tomorrow morning – talking to people who knew him, and building up a picture of what he was really like.'

'Just like we did in the old days,' Felipe said wistfully.

'Yes, just like we did in the old days,' Paco agreed.

'The problem is, *jefe*, that we're not policemen anymore,' Felipe pointed out, 'so what gives us the right to question people?'

'I'm a captain in the army – that gives me a certain amount of authority,' Paco said.

But nowhere near as much authority as if Colonel Sanz had been willing to put something in writing, he thought.

'And me?' Felipe asked plaintively. 'What about me? I'm just a civilian observer.'

'Nonsense!' Paco said. 'You're an inspector in the Observation Corps.'

'Am I?' Felipe asked, his chest swelling somewhat. 'Yes, I suppose I am.'

'Can I ask a question?' Cindy said.

'Of course,' Paco said, and if he was surprised at the edge in her voice, he gave no indication of it.

'I forget the name of the matador who was gored in the ring. Was it Diego?'

'Yes, it was. Is that the question?'

'No, the question is this – why did Faustino leave the ring immediately after Diego had been killed?'

'Maybe he was meeting someone.'

'But under normal circumstances, he couldn't have done that

without being noticed by twenty-five thousand spectators, could he?' Cindy asked.

'No.'

'And the only reason no one noticed him leave this time was because of what happened to Diego. But Faustino couldn't have known that Diego would be gored, could he? Or do you think that he did?'

'No, he couldn't have known,' Paco admitted. 'Perhaps he desperately wanted to see this person, but had persuaded himself he would have to wait. Then, when he saw his chance, the temptation was just too much.'

'Why would he arrange to meet this person in the chapel?'

'We don't know he was planning to meet him there. The fact that he ended up dead in the chapel proves nothing.'

'But why did he take his sword with him?' Cindy demanded.

'Perhaps for his own protection?'

'Then how did it find its way into the hands of the killer?'

Paco had been growing more and more irritated, and wasn't quite sure why. Perhaps it was because Cindy's unexpected change of mood had unsettled him. Perhaps it was because the task ahead was so daunting – if not downright bloody impossible. Perhaps it was because he was mourning the death of a childhood friend, while, at the same time, trying to be a totally professional police officer.

Whatever it was, he knew it would only take one small spark to make the whole powder keg explode.

It was Felipe who provided the spark. 'It's nice to have Cindy asking the awkward questions instead of me,' he chuckled. 'It feels as if a great weight has been lifted from my shoulders.'

'You'd be far better off if a great weight was lifted off your belly,' Paco snapped.

And instantly, he started to feel guilty. 'I'm sorry, Felipe, old friend,' he said. 'I didn't mean that.'

'It's all right,' Felipe assured him. 'I'm happy to have a big belly, because in the months to come, when the rest of you are starving, I'll still have my reserves of fat to draw on.'

Chapter Twelve

Saturday 13 May 1937

Paco was sifting through the witness statements that Felipe had brought with him. Cindy was reading a book. And in one corner of her pen, Eleanor Roosevelt was scratching her way through the fresh gravel Paco had supplied her with. On the face of it, then, it seemed to be an ordinary domestic scene – perhaps even a *boring* domestic scene.

But it wasn't. The atmosphere in the room – generated by Cindy – was glacial, and had been since they'd got back from the Cabo de Trafalgar.

Paco put down the reports. 'Felipe was right,' he said. 'These things are about as useful to the investigation as a violin would be to a polar bear.'

Cindy didn't laugh. She didn't even groan.

'Do you want to talk about what's bothering you?' Paco asked.

'All right,' Cindy agreed. 'I don't like being made a fool of, and I don't like being ganged up on.'

'What are you talking about?' he asked.

'Down in the bar, Felipe made that joke about the football teams, then pretended it hadn't been a joke at all, just to make me look foolish.'

'Felipe's your friend. He would never try to make you seem foolish,' Paco said, soothingly.

'I don't see how you can say that, when you saw the whole thing with your own eyes, and heard it with your own ears.'

'It's just a misunderstanding, that's all,' Paco said. 'Felipe doesn't make jokes. That's just the way his mind works. He's as down to earth as a badger – and is just as fond of rabbit.'

It was another attempt at levity, but the moment the words were out of his mouth, he could see that they had fallen flat.

'So if that's true, why did you say you didn't know, when I asked you whether or not he was joking?' Cindy demanded.

Ah, she had him there!

'Maybe *I* was teasing you a little bit,' he admitted.

'Well, I don't like it,' she said. 'There are times when it's all right to tease and times when it isn't. And when I'm feeling uncertain of myself and needing some reassurance is precisely one of those times when it isn't.'

He could have told her that he knew she was right, and he'd probably never have behaved like that if he hadn't been under such stress. He could have added that if she hadn't been under stress herself, she wouldn't have reacted so hyper-sensitively. But the first of these would only have sounded like an excuse, and the second like an accusation. Better – far better – to move on to new territory, rather than attempt to re-fight old battles and hope for a better result this time.

'Let's have a bit of fun this evening,' he suggested.

'A bit of fun,' she repeated, slightly suspiciously. 'What do you want to do?'

'I want to do whatever you want to do,' he said expansively.

'Then I want to go to the movies.'

Well, he'd certainly talked himself into that one, hadn't he?

157

'So what do you think?' she asked hopefully.

'If it's what you'd like to do, then why not?' he said, trying to sound enthusiastic.

'It *is* what I want to do,' Cindy said. 'And it will be good for you, too. You need something to clear your head, so that you can tackle the case tomorrow with a fresh mind.'

That wasn't how he worked. Once he was on a case, he was like a pearl diver, staying immersed in it for as long as he possibly could, and only coming up for air when his body told him there was no choice in the matter.

But he couldn't say any of that now – not in this period of reconciliation.

'I'm sure you're right,' he said, forcing a smile. 'A trip to the cinema will really clear my mind.

It was eight o'clock, and they were walking along the Gran Vía. They were not alone. The street was packed with hundreds of other people, all of whom seemed to be heading for one of the cinemas on or near Callao Square.

In many ways, it was like the old days: whole families were out taking an evening *paseo*; people were sitting at crowded bars and pavement cafés, chatting with friends; there was a buzz of anticipation in the air, engendered by the giant film posters.

And yet, no one would actually have mistaken this for the same time a year earlier, because it was all slightly off-key: the *paseos* were less energetic, as was only to be expected from people subsisting mainly on beans and rice; the conversations at the bar tables were less animated, for once you had discussed the day's events at the bullring, there was very little to talk about except death and deprivation; and even the animation of the filmgoers was muted by the knowledge that though they might be going to see a drama, they were living right inside a much bigger one.

And then there was the lighting. The Gran Vía had always been well illuminated – after all, it was the 'grand way' – but when the air raids began, the bulbs in the streetlights had all been painted blue, in order to make it a little more difficult for the enemy pilots to pick out their targets. Now the lamps only gave off a dullish glow – a little like the light in a photographic darkroom – which was bright enough to let you see someone approaching – and even determine their height and their sex – but was not much good for anything else.

It was brighter inside the cinema, though – ominously – the lights did flicker twice, a reminder that the city's electricity supply was, at best, erratic.

This particular cinema, which was the one Cindy had chosen, was just a hundred metres or so away from the Hotel Florida. She hadn't been to the hotel herself, so probably didn't even associate it with Faustino, but Paco couldn't help thinking that instead of snuggling down in his comfortable bed on the fifth floor that night, the matador was lying on a cold slab in the mortuary.

The painted poster – which occupied all the wall space between the cinema's entrance and the roof – announced that the film was called *Give Me Your Heart* and starred an actress called Kay Francis.

'She's one of the biggest stars in Hollywood,' Cindy told him. 'They'd even heard of her in the boonies, where I grew up.'

Paco smiled to himself. He knew what she meant by boonies now, but he hadn't always.

'It's short for boondocks,' Cindy had explained, and when he'd still looked blank, she'd added, 'It's like saying East Jesus.'

It was at that point she'd realised that she really needed to go right back to basics.

'What do you think America is like, Paco?' she'd asked.

Well, he'd replied, when he thought of the United States, he always thought of tall skyscrapers, standing shoulder to shoulder.

And was that all it was? Millions of tall buildings?

No, of course it wasn't. He'd seen the western films. He knew all about the vast empty prairies.

Were there any towns? she'd asked.

Yes, he'd answered, in the middle of the vast prairie there was always a town or two.

A town or two! He seemed to know as little about America as she'd known about the real Spain when she walked down the gangplank and off the boat, she'd said. There were thousands of small towns in the country – maybe hundreds of thousands. She came from one herself, called Jonesville.

'It had one school, one doctor, one drug store and two hardware stores that sold just about everything,' she'd told him. 'There was a movie house, but it was closed during harvest time and in the blizzard season. The railroad didn't run through town, but if the wind was blowing in the right direction, you could sometimes hear its whistle in the distance. There were folk in Jonesville who'd never left Jonesville – and couldn't see why anybody would ever want to. And that, Señor Ruiz, is what you call the boonies.'

And yet she had somehow managed to go to college, and from there had journeyed to Spain, he'd marvelled.

They bought their tickets and went inside.

For the first few minutes of the film, Paco managed to give it his whole attention. Kay Francis – the woman they'd heard of even in the boonies – was certainly an attractive woman, he decided, though, to his mind, she was no competition for you-know-who!

The character Francis was playing fell in love with a married man – a member of the English aristocracy. She knew at the time that he was married, but such was her love for him that she didn't let that stand in the way. Then she became pregnant, and asked her lover to run away with her. And she must have imagined she had a winning hand, Paco thought, because she was carrying his baby, and his wife couldn't have children. Unfortunately for her, his wife held the trump card – she was an invalid. He decided to do the honourable thing – a little late, in Paco's opinion, since he had got himself into a position whereby, in order to do the honourable thing, he must also do the dishonourable thing – and leave the pregnant girl in the lurch.

Maybe that was what had happened to Faustino, who was also a sort of aristocrat in his own way, Paco thought.

He imagined the scene.

The blonde girl stands opposite Faustino in his room in the Hotel Florida, and though her pregnancy is not showing yet, she thrusts her belly towards him.

'*This is your child,*' she says, her voice choked with tears. '*You have to marry me, to save him from being born a bastard.*'

And how does Faustino react to this?

Does he treat her with contempt?

'*How do I know the baby is mine?*'

'*It is – I promise you.*'

'*And what does your promise mean? If you will sleep with one man, the chances are that you will sleep with any man who asks you.*'

But would he really say something like that? It was true he had been planning to leave the blonde for his true love in Mexico, but Paco could not see the boy he had once known – and the man he thought that boy had become – simply abandoning her.

So perhaps the conversation had been more like this:

'*I'm sorry, I do not love you, but I will pay for your child's upbringing. I am a rich man, and he will go short of nothing.*'

Financial security would have been enough for some girls. She and her baby could move to a place where they were not known, and she could pretend to be a widow who collected a nice fat cheque from her dead husband's estate every month.

But what if she didn't care about that? What if what she craved was *genuine* respectability? What if she felt betrayed?

Might she – as he'd suggested to Felipe earlier – have gone to a father or a brother to complain?

Or might she have gone to someone else entirely?

Someone outside her family?

Someone who – unlike Faustino – loved her?

Paco had to think back just two days to come up with a possibility.

He was having a drink with Faustino – in a bar not a stone's throw from where he was sitting at that moment – when Luis stormed in. The young banderillero was clearly looking for a fight, and it soon became obvious who he wanted to have that fight *with*.

But before he could really get started, Faustino had cut him off.

'*Do you want to be a matador one day, Luis?*'

'*Well, of course I do. It is all I've dreamed of.*'

'*And can you think of something you might do that could prevent your dream from coming true? Can you think of a word or action which, while it might have nothing to do with your skill in the ring, could destroy your career?*'

So there it was – Faustino was saying, 'Challenge me over the girl, and I will destroy your career.'

And Luis, faced with a choice between love and following his dream, had chosen to follow his dream.

But then later, he had come to regret this ignoble action. And when Diego had been gored and Faustino took the opportunity to leave the ring, he had followed him. He would have been angry with Faustino, but also angry with himself, because he had behaved like a coward – and in a fit of rage, he had killed Faustino, using the other man's own sword.

It was plausible – very plausible – but then again, so were half a dozen other theories he could come up with, if he put his mind to it.

He was surprised when the house lights suddenly came on, and everyone stood up.

It couldn't be end of the film yet, could it?

But it was.

'Did you enjoy that, Paco?' Cindy asked him, as they were leaving the cinema.

He had promised never to lie to her, but he saw no harm in employing a little harmless deception at that particular moment.

'It was interesting,' he said.

'But did you *enjoy* it?' Cindy persisted.

When he'd been given the opportunity to confess that he'd been too immersed in the case to even notice what was happening on the screen, he should have grabbed it with both hands. But, like a fool, he hadn't, and now he was in too deep to back out.

'Yes, I did enjoy it,' he said.

'What particularly did you enjoy?' Cindy asked.

Oh, cruel hard woman!

'I thought it painted an interesting picture of American life,' he said.

'American life,' Cindy mused. 'So it was an *interesting* picture of American life, was it?'

'Yes, it was.'

'Rather than an *uninteresting* picture of American life?'

'I would say so, yes.'

'Yet so much of it was set in England,' Cindy said.

Was it? It was possible it could have been. To be honest, he really had no idea.

He decided to take a gamble on it being true. 'It was an interesting picture of English life, too,' he said. He paused. 'All right, my mind wasn't really on the film at all.'

'Do you have to work at being impossible, or does it just come naturally?' Cindy asked, forgivingly.

'I do seem to have a talent for it,' he admitted.

They were so happy together, he thought. Any illusions they might once have had about each other – any wide-eyed romantic notion about a partner who would be perfect all the time – had now faded completely away.

And it didn't matter a damn!

The people around them seemed happy and carefree too – despite being under siege, despite the daily struggle to scrape together enough food to put on the table – so though the film had failed to work its magic on him, it had obviously touched those around him.

Yes, things could have been much worse, he mused – and that was when he heard the whine of the approaching shell.

Instantly, the atmosphere on the street changed.

In the daytime, these bombardments were greeted with a stoic acceptance of the inevitable, but it was different on the street that night.

Perhaps it was the ghostly lighting which affected all those people out on the Gran Vía.

Perhaps it was the fact that the films they had been watching had given them a false sense of security.

Whatever the reason, panic ran through the crowd with the speed of a bush fire.

Some men shepherded their families into doorways, and once there, picked up the smaller children, as if holding them a metre or so off the ground would save them if a shell scored a direct hit.

Some groups stayed where they were, possibly frozen with fear, or maybe calculating that if the shell had your name on it, it didn't matter what you tried to do to avoid it.

And then there were the runners, zigzagging in and out of the stationary groups in a vain attempt to outpace the high velocity explosive.

The whining was growing louder and more intense. The shell was very, very close now.

Cindy grabbed Paco's arm fiercely. 'I love you,' she said.

He would have told her that he loved her too – he *wanted* to tell her – but he needed at least a couple of seconds to say it, and that was time the shell was not prepared to allow him.

When it exploded on the street, the sound was intense – like the roar of an angry, wounded giant. And then bits of asphalt and pieces of stone – some of them as small as raindrops, some as large as a man's hand – began to rain down on them, and they covered their heads with their arms, in an attempt to protect themselves.

For a moment after the sounds of the explosion died away, there was silence. Then someone began to moan softly, someone else began to cry, and soon half the street was either shouting or screaming.

It wasn't a coincidence that the rebels had decided to launch their barrage now, Paco told himself. They had deliberately timed it for when they knew people would be leaving the cinemas.

Was there nothing they wouldn't do – no depth they wouldn't sink to?

No, there wasn't, because as far as they were concerned, they had God on their side, and that made it perfectly all right to murder civilians whose only crime was their refusal to submit to the will of General Franco.

'We have to get to where the shell landed,' Cindy said urgently. 'We have to see if we can help.'

They barged their way through the milling crowd until they came to the crater in the road. There were six twisted and contorted bodies lying sprawled on the ground. One of them was a girl. She was probably eight or nine, though it was hard to judge her age accurately without knowing how tall she was, and estimating that was made more difficult by the fact that she had no legs.

A number of people were squatting down next to a woman who was lying just beyond the lip of the crater, but they didn't seem to be doing much.

'Let me get to her,' Cindy said, commandingly. 'I'm a nurse.'

And so she was, in a way. Up at the Jarama front, she'd had some basic training in medical matters, which made her a sort of nurse, ready to patch up men who were sort of soldiers.

The people who'd been crowding the injured woman backed away, and Cindy knelt down beside her.

The woman was in her early thirties. She was wearing a flowery dress – a sure sign that she considered this a special occasion – and the left side of the dress, from her waist almost up to her shoulder, was stained a reddish colour.

The blood was not exactly gushing from her wound, Paco calculated, but it was certainly seeping at a worrying rate.

'Anything you try to do for her might only make things worse,' he whispered to Cindy.

'I know,' she agreed.

She bent in closer over the wounded woman.

'I don't think it would do any harm if I cradled her head,' she said to Paco.

'Nor do I, as long as you're careful,' he agreed.

In the distance, there was the sound of another shell exploding.

Cindy gently lifted the woman's head, and slid her own arm carefully underneath it.

'The doctor will be here soon,' she crooned, and really hoped she wasn't lying.

The woman's eyes had been closed, but now she opened them, and looked up.

'Who are you?' she asked.

'I'm Cindy. What's your name?'

'Maricarmen.'

'Does it hurt, Maricarmen?'

'I can't feel a thing. Does that mean I'm going to be all right?'

No, Paco thought, On the contrary, it probably means you're dying.

'Does it?' Maricarmen persisted. 'Does it mean I'll be all right?'

'We'll have to see what the doctor says,' Cindy told her.

'My daughter!' Maricarmen cried. 'Where's my daughter?'

It took all of Cindy's self-control not to turn her head towards the legless body of the girl.

'She's nine,' the woman said. 'She's wearing a brown dress. She was right next to me when the shell landed.'

'They've already taken her to the hospital,' Cindy said.

'Hospital! Oh Jesus!'

'Don't worry, there's nothing much wrong with her – just a tiny piece of shrapnel in her leg. She'll be absolutely fine in the morning.'

'Thank God!' Maricarmen gasped. She took a shallow, jagged

167

breath, then continued, 'You've got blood all over your nice dress. Is that mine?'

'Yes,' Cindy admitted.

'I'm so sorry.'

'It doesn't matter.'

'When you get home, soak it in very cold water – and add a little salt.'

'Don't worry about that now, Maricarmen,' Cindy urged. She paused. 'Maricarmen … can you hear me, Maricarmen?'

Paco squatted down and placed a finger against the woman's neck. There should have been a pulse – but there wasn't.

'She's dead,' he told Cindy.

'She can't be! She was just talking to me!'

Another shell exploded, but this was much further away, like some distant echo of another war.

'She was just talking to me,' Cindy moaned softly.

A new group of men appeared on the scene. They were all wearing the boiler suits that had become almost the uniform of men who were not in the military, but they were also wearing armbands and carrying stretchers.

One of the teams of stretcher-bearers came to a halt next to Cindy. The man on the front of the stretcher was portly – though not in Felipe's class – and the man at the other end was almost skeletal-thin.

'She looks dead,' the fat one said.

'She is,' Cindy agreed.

'Is she a relative of yours?' the fat man asked.

'No,' Cindy told him. 'I haven't got a clue *who* she is – except that her name is Maricarmen.'

'Right,' the fat man said crisply, 'if you'll just let us get at the stiff, we'll handle things from here.'

'Where are you taking her?' asked Cindy, with a sudden note of panic in her voice.

'We're taking her to the mortuary, of course,' the fat man told her.

'Listen, that's her little daughter, lying over there,' Cindy said urgently. 'Could you please make sure that once they're at the mortuary, they're together?'

The fat man snorted. 'Do you seriously think that in a place bursting at the seams with corpses, we've got time to fart around with fiddling little details like that?' he asked.

Any minute now, Cindy's going to ask me to punch him, Paco thought, and though I know I shouldn't, I just might.

It was the thin stretcher-bearer who saved the day.

'We'll do what we can to see they're together,' he said. 'I can't guarantee anything, but if it's at all possible …'

'I want to come with you,' Cindy said firmly. 'I want to make sure that mother and child don't get separated.'

'They can't allow that,' Paco said gently. 'They've got their job to do, and you'll only get in the way.'

'You should listen to your husband, señora,' the fat stretcher-bearer said.

'He's not my husband,' Cindy snapped back at him.

'Well, whoever he is, you should listen to him,' the fat man said.

Paco lifted Cindy to her feet, and steered her away from the crater.

'It's time to go home,' he said.

'I lied to her,' Cindy said, the moment they'd closed their apartment door behind them. 'Her daughter was lying a few feet away from her, with her legs blown off, and I said she was fine. I promised myself I'd always tell the truth, whatever the consequences. And I didn't! What kind of person lies to a dying woman?'

'The kind with the guts to do the right thing, even when it goes against everything she thinks she believes in,' Paco said. 'It would have been cruel to tell her that her daughter was dead.'

'But what do I do now?' Cindy asked, looking round the small apartment for inspiration. 'What do I do now?'

'I want you to just stay where you are,' Paco told her.

'Why? What do you …?'

'Please just do as I say.'

Cindy nodded, and Paco gently removed her bloodstained dress and the bloodstained underwear that lay beneath it. Next, he sponged her down, wrapped her in a blanket, and eased her into the apartment's single armchair. He would have liked to make her a hot drink, but from the way the lights were flickering uncertainly, he knew there was very little power coming through the wires that night, and it would probably take at least half an hour to boil a pan of water.

Instead, he poured her a large brandy.

'Sip it slowly,' he said. 'Let it seep into you.'

He sat on the arm of the chair and wrapped his arms around her. After a few minutes had passed, he could feel her beginning to relax.

'I'm sorry,' she said.

'Sorry about what.'

'Sorry that I insisted on going somewhere we could have been killed.'

'We could just as easily have been killed if we'd stayed in,' he told her. 'If the shell had landed on the roof, and we'd been sitting here, we wouldn't have stood a chance.'

'You're right,' she said, 'but I still feel guilty.'

He got off the arm of the chair, and squatted down in front of her.

'I want you to leave,' he said.

'Leave? What do you mean?'

'I want you to go to Valencia while the road is still open. Once you're there, you can either take a bus or wagon to the French frontier, or maybe board a boat for Marseilles or Genoa.'

'Will you come with me?'

'No.'

'Will you follow me, a little later?'

'No, I can't. I have to stay here.'

'Then I'm staying, too,' Cindy said.

'I worry about you getting hurt,' Paco told her.

'And I'd worry about you getting bloody well *killed* when I'm not here.'

He shrugged. 'It's my country, and my fight,' he said.

'If it's your fight, then it's my fight too,' Cindy told him. She reached across and grabbed his shoulders. 'We could easily have been killed out there on the Gran Vía. If we'd been fifty metres further up the road, it could have been your legs that got blown off, and my dress that got ruined by me spilling my guts all over it.'

'I know. That's why I want you to …'

'And if we had been killed, it would still have been worth it.'

'What do you mean?'

'You *know* what I mean.'

Yes, he did. She meant that what they had had together in a few short months had been more than most people got in a lifetime. She meant that if she had been killed, her dying thought would have been that she'd had more than her fair share of happiness.

'I told that fat man with the stretcher that you weren't my husband,' Cindy said. 'But you are – even if it's not written down anywhere. Besides,' she continued, with a lighter note entering her voice, 'I can't leave, because you're always out having adventures, and someone has to look after Eleanor.'

And in the corner of the room, the hen clucked, as if it had been waiting for its cue.

They made love that night. It felt like an age since the last time they had done it. They began slowly and gently, but they were soon wrapped in a passion which seemed to wipe out the whole world – the whole universe – and leave only them.

And as he lay on his back, looking at the ceiling, Paco thought that Cindy had been right, and that if a shell crashed through the roof at that moment, and killed them both, he would have no complaints.

Chapter Thirteen

Sunday 14 May 1937

Eleanor Roosevelt was an example to them all, Paco thought. Two days earlier, she had been happily clucking away in her mountain retreat. Then, without warning, she had been hen-napped by an overweight ex-policeman, crammed into a sack, and, after being given a bumpy ride on the back of a clapped-out old motorbike, had arrived in the city. Most people he knew would still have been in a state of shock, yet the chicken looked completely at ease, and – from the way she cocked her head to one side when he drew close to her – was very receptive to whatever it was he wished to say.

'Why do I always end up with the cases that are almost impossible to solve, Eleanor?' he asked. 'In the last few months, I've dealt with the murder of an unknown girl in Retiro Park, the killing of a Fascist general's dog behind enemy lines, and the assassination of a member of the International Brigade in Albacete. And that's all since I officially stopped being a policeman. What do you think of that?'

The hen turned away from him, as if to indicate that his monologue had sounded promising at first, but had quickly grown tedious.

'Yes, you're right, Eleanor,' he said, 'if I'd just content myself with scratching at the ground and pecking at corn, I wouldn't have any of these complications. But I can't walk away from this particular case, you see, because Faustino was a boyhood friend of mine.'

'You can't walk away from this case because you're constitutionally incapable of leaving a murder unsolved – whoever the victim is,' said a voice from the bedroom doorway. 'And I'd be very careful if I were you, because there's an old Chinese saying that goes something like, "He who talks to chickens, ends up with a bird brain".'

'You're making that up,' Paco said, turning towards her and grinning.

'You're right – I am making it up,' Cindy admitted. 'It sounded pretty good, though, didn't it?' She walked over to the chicken pen, squatted down, and ran her hand through the straw. When it emerged again, it was holding a brown egg. 'Well done, Eleanor!' she enthused. 'What a clever little hen you are.'

'She who talks to chickens, ends up with a bird brain,' Paco said softly.

'What was that you said?' Cindy demanded.

'I was just saying that I didn't mind if you have the egg.'

'Oh no, you're the one about to set off on some big manly detective work, so you must have it,' Cindy said firmly.

'We'll split it,' Paco insisted. 'We'll cut it right down the middle, across the yolk. Agreed?'

Cindy nodded. 'All right – but only because you've talked me into it, you smooth-tongued bastard,' she said.

They were so happy together, he told himself. He wished it could last forever, but he knew that, with the war raging around them, the odds against a fairy-tale ending were pretty damn high.

* * *

Queues had become so commonplace in Madrid that even when you had to step round them, you didn't really notice them anymore.

Queuing had, in fact, become a way of life for Madrileños, for though a ration card apparently guaranteed you would get a certain amount of food, it was not a magic ticket, and when stocks ran out, you got nothing, however entitled you might be. Thus, shoppers had to plan to arrive early, often long before the shops had opened their doors. Sometimes, the women shoppers – and virtually all shoppers *were* women – would wait in line at one shop, while their older children queued outside another one. It would be the job of their younger children to act as messengers between the queues, so that their mothers would know when it made tactical sense to abandon the line they were in, and head for the place in the more promising queue that their daughters were holding for them.

As Paco left his apartment block and headed for the Grand Vía, he saw just such a queue outside the grocery shop further up the street.

In fact, there were two distinct queues. The longer one was made up of women of assorted ages, many of them accompanied by bored, tiny children, who held hands with their mothers, aunts and grandmothers, but made no pretence of enjoying the experience. A number of the older women had brought with them the low chairs that they customarily sat on outside their own front doors, but the younger ones stood chatting to their neighbours in the line – though after a couple of hours, it seemed to Paco, conversation was starting to dry up.

The second line – which was the one that would be given priority when the shop eventually opened its doors – was a much shorter one, and the women in it were all closer to each other in age, which was hardly surprising, considering they were also all pregnant.

Paco recognised one of the expectant mothers. Her name was Dolores, and she was a neighbour of his. She had what some of the other neighbours called 'a bit of a mouth on her,' which did not make her universally popular, but Paco rather liked a woman who said exactly what she thought, provided, of course, that her tirade was fair-minded.

At the moment, Dolores was squaring up – there was no other way of describing it – to one of the women in the line.

'What's your name, sweetheart?' she asked.

'I'm Alicia,' the other woman replied.

She sounded unnerved, and she was right to be, thought Paco, who had come to a halt so he could watch this little drama play itself out.

'We haven't seen you around here before, Alicia,' Dolores said. 'Where do you live?'

'Why do you want to know?' Alicia asked, suspiciously.

'Just making conversation,' Dolores said, in a deceptively casual way that fooled no one. 'It's not a secret, is it?'

'No, it's not a secret,' Alicia replied, and then added, somewhat reluctantly, 'I live on Zurbano.'

'Zurbano,' Dolores repeated. 'That's in Chamberí. You're shopping a long way from home – for a woman in your condition.'

'I heard this was a reliable place to shop,' Alicia said. She laughed, unconvincingly. 'You know how difficult it is to find somewhere like that.'

'Yes, this shop is reliable, all right,' Dolores agreed. 'But even reliable shops will run out of stuff if they get too many customers from outside the barrio.' She paused. 'Just how pregnant are you?'

'Seven and a half months,' Alicia said.

'Never,' Dolores said scornfully. She grasped her own double chin between her thumb and forefinger. 'Look at this! See all the flab?' She paused to allow for a reply, and when one wasn't forthcoming, she demanded. 'Well, Alicia, do you see it or not?'

'Yes, I see it,' the other woman said, reluctantly.

'This is what having a baby means,' Dolores said, pulling at the double chin to emphasise her point. 'Now look at you. That is never the neck of a woman who's expecting.'

'I just haven't put on weight up there – that's all,' Alicia said. 'Some mothers-to-be just don't.'

But she knew the game was up, and her voice lacked conviction.

One of the other women grabbed her from behind, and pinned her arms to her sides.

'Take a proper look at her, Dolores,' she said.

Dolores reached out, and pressed down on the bulge in Alicia's stomach. Something peeped out from below the bottom of Alicia's jumper, and when Dolores grabbed it and pulled, the pillow came away.

'Well?' Dolores demanded, holding up the evidence.

'I can't afford to be standing in queues all day,' the woman who had ceased to be pregnant said sulkily. 'I've got three little kids at home.'

'We've all got little kids at home,' Dolores said, 'but some of us have swollen legs and morning sickness on top of that. If you're strong enough to bear more than your fair share of the hardship – and you most certainly are – then you should bear it willingly, because it only takes a few people to think of nobody but themselves, and none of us will ever get through this.'

'Well, anyway, I'm here now, and here's where I'm staying,' Alicia said.

'If you don't leave now, you'll regret it,' Dolores warned.

'Why? What will you do?' Alicia demanded. She broke free of the grip that Dolores' friend had had on her, and held her fists out in front of her like an old-time bare-knuckle fighter. 'Well, how about it?' she taunted. 'Does any of you fat, droopy-titted cows fancy taking me on?'

'They'd be very ill-advised to try it, in their condition,' Paco said.

'Yes, they would, wouldn't they?' Alicia said, erroneously identifying him as an ally.

'But, you see, I'm *not* pregnant,' Paco said.

'Are you saying that you'd fight me?' Alicia woman asked incredulously. 'What kind of man are you?'

'I'm a man who likes to see justice done,' Paco said. 'But I won't have to fight you – I'll just put you in an arm lock and frogmarch you away, which really wouldn't be very dignified.' He paused for a second to give that thought time to sink in, then continued, 'You've got the chance to get away – which is more than you deserve – and I suggest you take it.'

The woman shot him a hostile look, then turned and stormed off down the street.

'Well, well, you're a proper little knight in shining armour, aren't you, Don Francisco?' Dolores said.

'Not at all,' Paco said. 'I'm just the man who comes round and cleans up the mess after Dolores the fiery dragon's already done most of the work.' He grinned. 'No offence intended.'

'None taken,' Dolores told him, grinning back.

Matadors stayed in fancy hotels like the Florida. Members of their teams had to settle for something rather more modest, and Luis, the young banderillero, was booked into a *residencia* called the Casa Cordoba, just off the Plaza Mayor. When Paco found him, he was sitting in a bar quite close to his lodgings, moodily sipping at a glass of *sol y sombra*.

The man seemed less than pleased when he glanced up and saw

Paco standing there. And he looked rough – God, he looked rough. His face was more hollowed out than ever, and though the redness of his eyes could have been caused by excessive drinking, it could also have come from crying.

'What do you want, Ruiz?' he demanded. 'Can't you see that I'd rather be alone?'

Uninvited, Paco pulled up a chair, and sat down opposite him.

'I'll leave you alone the moment you've answered a few questions,' he said.

'What kind of questions?'

'What kind of questions do you think?'

'I don't know, and I don't care.'

'The questions I have to ask you all relate to Faustino's death.'

Luis shrugged, as if to say, 'so what?'

'I can't help you,' he muttered.

'If *you* can't help me, then who can? After all, you were the one who found his body.'

'What does that prove? Anybody could have found him. It was just by chance that I was the first one to the chapel, and saw him lying there – dead. And that's all I know.'

'But it wasn't really by chance at all, was it, Luis?' Paco asked. 'There was a good reason you were at the chapel – you had followed Faustino from the *tendido*. The question is, why had you followed him?'

'I followed him because I wanted to talk to him,' Luis said. 'Is that a crime?'

'It depends,' Paco told him. 'What did you want to talk to him about?'

Luis shrugged. 'That's not important now.'

'And suppose I say it is important?'

'What does it matter what you say?' Luis asked with a sneer

179

which somehow managed to be as defensive as it was contemptuous. 'You're not a policeman anymore. If I don't want to talk to you, I don't have to.'

That was true, Paco accepted. His old authority had evaporated with the outbreak of war. All he had left in his armoury now were cunning and shock tactics.

'How do I know that you didn't kill him yourself?' he mused, following the shock tactic route.

Luis gulped, as if it had only just occurred to him that anyone *could* possibly think that.

'I … I … He was my hero – my mentor. Why would I have wanted to kill him?' he stammered.

'I don't know,' Paco admitted. 'What I do know is that you had an argument with him a couple of nights ago.'

'That's a lie!' Luis protested.

Paco sighed. 'Oh, come on, man, I was there. I saw it. Why were you in such a rage with him?'

'I wasn't in a rage at all. You're blowing it all out of proportion.'

'Then what would you call it?'

'It was nothing but a simple misunderstanding.'

'And was this "simple misunderstanding" about the girl?' Paco asked, taking a shot in the dark.

'What girl?'

'The girl with the blonde hair.'

'I don't know any girls with blonde hair.'

'That's strange. That's very strange indeed, because, you see, she was Faustino's mistress.'

Luis laughed. 'She was *what*?'

'She was his mistress. And I strongly suspect that you yourself were in love with her.'

Luis was now almost convulsed with laughter. 'Me!' he gasped. 'In love with her!'

'If you didn't want to talk to Faustino about her, then what *did* you want to talk to him about?' Paco said.

Luis slowly calmed down. 'What *did* I want to talk to him about? As I've told you before, it's none of your business.'

'And why did you suddenly need to talk to him at that moment?' Paco persisted. 'You must surely have had plenty of opportunities before the bullfight even started.'

'No, I didn't,' Luis said, and now he was looking sad again. 'Faustino had been avoiding me.'

'And why was that?'

'I don't know.'

'But of course you bloody know!' Paco said, slamming his palm down on the table.

'You remember what Faustino said to me in that bar the other night, don't you?' Luis asked.

'Yes, I remember – but it wouldn't do any harm to have you repeat it to me now.'

'He warned me that if I said too much, I would destroy my chances of ever becoming a matador.'

'That's true, he did – but he can't threaten to destroy your career anymore, because he's dead.'

Luis shook his head, slowly, from side to side. 'And do you really think that's what he was doing – threatening to destroy my career?'

'It certainly sounded like that from where I was sitting.'

'He would never threaten me. Never! And he was right in what he told me – there are some things it is better never to say.'

So Faustino had warned Luis that if he spoke out about something or other, his career would be ruined. But Luis claimed it was not

Faustino who would ruin his career, but someone else. Yet who else would *want* to ruin his career? Who else would have the *power* to do it?

None of this made any sense, Paco thought.

'I may not have the authority to arrest you myself, but I know people who do have that authority,' he said. 'And once you've been locked up for a while, you'll be willing enough to talk.'

'If I am arrested, I will say nothing more than that I did not kill Faustino, and I don't know who did,' Luis told him.

'That could easily be taken as an admission of guilt,' Paco warned.

'I do not care.'

'In the old days, the judicial procedure was long and drawn out,' Paco said. 'It isn't like that anymore. A trial – if that's what you want to call it – can last less than five minutes, and execution could follow ten minutes after that. You must say something – if only to save yourself.'

Luis swallowed hard. 'I did not kill Faustino, and I do not know who did,' he said.

I believe you, Paco thought. I don't want to, because you're my main suspect, but like it or not, I do.

'If you wish to avoid being arrested, you have to give me at least a little *something* to work with,' he said.

A look of indecision flickered across Luis's face. Then he said, 'I will do something for you if you do something for me.'

'Like what?' Paco asked.

'You are a man with some authority – not enough to arrest me, but much more than I have. I want you to talk to Álvaro Muñoz, Faustino's manager. I want you to tell him he must pay the team what we are owed.'

'Why should he owe you anything?' Paco wondered. 'Surely, it should have been Faustino who paid you.'

Certainly that was the way it normally worked, he thought. It was always the matador who collected the money and paid his team. The manager was not really a manager in the sense that he handled the matador's career – truth to tell, he was little more than a dogsbody, who did whatever jobs the bullfighter either didn't have the time to do himself, or lacked the inclination to do.

But then he remembered the conversation they had had that night in the Callao Square bar.

'I have told my manager to make sure all my money is readily available …'

'You told him what?'

'To make sure that all my money is readily available.'

'Why does your manager need to do that? Couldn't you do it yourself?'

'No, I wouldn't know how to.'

'Surely, all it takes is to look at your various bank accounts …'

'I don't have various bank accounts. I don't have even one bank account. We gypsies don't trust banks.'

And it was certainly Álvaro Muñoz who Faustino had instructed to pay for the security team that Moncho had provided at the bullring – something that Muñoz still hadn't got round to doing.

But this was an entirely different matter altogether.

'I am not sure Álvaro Muñoz will have been given the money that Faustino was supposed to have earned yesterday,' he said. 'The promoters will have had plenty of reason to withhold it, because Faustino was murdered before he had killed even one bull, so why should they have paid his manager for a fight that never happened?'

'Álvaro owes us for more than one fight,' Luis said. 'For some time, he has been paying us half of what we earned, and promising that soon we would have the rest. Well, with Faustino dead, "soon" has become "now".'

'All right, I'll talk to him about it,' Paco promised. 'And what do I get in return?'

'You should go and see the priest.'

'What priest?'

'His name is Don Pedro, and he lives in the barrio San Vicente. Faustino always goes to see him when he is in Madrid.'

'Don't you mean *lived* in the barrio San Vicente, rather than *lives* in it?' Paco asked. 'After the revolt, all the priests who weren't arrested or killed quickly ran away.'

'He did not run away. He is still here,' Luis said, firmly. 'I know this for a fact, because Faustino visited him just two days ago.'

'In his church?'

Luis laughed. 'Of course not. His church was one of the first to be burned down.'

'Then where?'

'I don't know, but you will find him somewhere in the barrio.'

'And will this priest – Don Pedro – know anything which will help me in my investigation?'

'It is likely he will know a great deal – though whether he will tell you or not is quite another matter.'

'Just what is it that this priest knows?'

Luis folded his arms across his chest. 'I have fulfilled my part of the bargain,' he said, 'now you must fulfil yours. Go and talk to Álvaro Muñoz.'

Chapter Fourteen

Sunday 14 May 1937

The Hotel Gran Vía was a little further away from the front line than the Hotel Florida, which meant that it was also a little further away from the enemy artillery in the Casa de Campo. Thus, any potential guest might have concluded that the Hotel Gran Vía was a great deal safer than the Florida. It would be a reasoned, logical conclusion, and probably the one that most intelligent people would have reached. In fact, the only thing that let it down as a theory was that it was completely wrong.

What made it so wrong was that the Hotel Gran Vía stood directly opposite the Telefónica Building, which was the tallest skyscraper in the whole of Europe, and as such provided invaluable assistance to rebel artillerymen wishing to adjust the firing range of their guns. And when they did take the occasional pot shot at the Telefónica – just to make sure they had their calculations right – there was a more than fair chance the shell might go slightly off target, and strike the Hotel Gran Vía.

All of which meant, in practical terms, that when choosing whether to book into either the Hotel Gran Vía or the Hotel Florida, the sensible visitor would instead select a hotel which was unlikely be anything like as classy, but would at least be further away from the front line.

The simple truth was that neither of the hotels was safe, and rather than worry about where he was most likely to be killed, the potential visitor might just as well flip a coin to decide which one he would stay in.

When Paco entered the foyer of the Hotel Gran Vía, the receptionist behind the desk lifted his head from his newspaper, and favoured him with a complete and utter lack of interest.

This receptionist was middle aged, with a drooping moustache and gold-rimmed glasses. His eyes were heavy, and his mouth seemed to be set in a look of perpetual disenchantment. He gave the impression of being the sort of man whose only remaining pleasure in life is kicking the odd stray dog.

It was a common enough story, Paco thought. Men like him started out convinced they would become general manager in ten years. Then, when the ten years had passed and they were still behind the desk, they lowered their sights, and were willing to accept the post of night manager. And when even that didn't materialise, they finally came to understand that everyone they had ever known was part of a hostile conspiracy to keep them down.

'Yes?' the receptionist said to Paco.

'I'm here to see Don Álvaro Muñoz.'

'Is he expecting you?' the receptionist demanded.

'Is he in his room?' Paco countered.

'That depends,' the receptionist said. 'Do you wish to see him on a matter of business?'

'Yes.'

'And what is the nature of that business?'

He wants me to tell him to mind *his* own business, Paco thought, because an argument would add a little excitement to his day, as well as confirming his view of humanity in general.

Well, screw him, because there was simply no time for that kind of melodrama.

'I'm representing the management of the Monumental Bullring in Barcelona,' Paco said.

'You don't sound like a Catalan,' the receptionist replied. 'You don't look like one, either.'

'So what does a Catalan look like?' Paco wondered.

'Shifty,' the receptionist said. 'Untrustworthy.'

The man really was the personification of charm and tolerance, Paco thought.

'I'm not a Catalan,' he said. 'I just work for the bullring.'

'Some people would work for the Devil if he paid enough,' the receptionist said. 'So what do your Catalan masters want?'

'They're holding a fiesta next month, and they'd like Señor Muñoz to work with them on it.'

'How long will this fiesta last?'

'A week.'

'A week!' the receptionist repeated, in disgust. 'These bloody Catalans! Don't they know there's a war going on?' And then, since a heated exchange was looking less and less likely, he lost all interest in the conversation, and said, 'You'll find him on the fourth floor, in suite 417.'

When Paco tapped on the door of Muñoz's suite, a voice from inside called, 'Who are you, and what do you want?'

'I'm Paco Ruiz.'

'Who?'

187

'Faustino's friend. His best friend from his childhood. You remember? We met in the Hotel Florida.'

'You still haven't said what you want.'

'I want to talk.'

'Can't it wait?'

'No.'

Muñoz opened the door. He was in his shirtsleeves, and was puffing on a large cigar.

Paco noted that the cuffs on the shirtsleeves were frayed, and stored up the information for later use.

'Look, I'm very busy,' Muñoz said, 'so whatever it is you need to say, say it quickly.'

'Can I come in?' Paco asked.

And before the other man had had time to reply, Paco had edged him out of the way, and was in the suite.

There were two armchairs in the room, and Paco made a beeline for one of them, and sat down.

'Why don't you sit down, too?' he suggested, as if it were his suite and Muñoz was his guest.

'Now, look here …' the fat man began.

'Or you can stay standing, if you prefer,' Paco said. 'I really don't mind, one way or the other.'

Muñoz plopped down in the other armchair. 'I don't know who you think you are,' he said weakly.

'Me?' Paco replied. 'I'm the man you owe money to.'

'What money?'

'The three hundred pesetas that Faustino promised you'd pay the men who provided the security at the bullfight.'

'Oh, that,' Muñoz said, off-handedly.

'Oh that!' Paco agreed.

'As I recall, we hired them to protect Faustino, and since Faustino is dead, they can't really have been said to have made a very good job of it, can they?' Muñoz asked, puffing on his cigar.

He'd eaten enough shit for one day, Paco thought, as he sprang to his feet. With his left hand, he removed Muñoz's cigar from his mouth, and with his right he grabbed the other man's tie and pulled it as tightly as he could.

'When I hire a man for that kind of work, I'm asking him to risk his life,' he said. 'If the only way to protect his client is to step between the client and the assassin, then I expect him to do it, even if it means taking a bullet himself. And that is just what those men would have done, if the situation had arisen.'

'You're ch … choking me,' Muñoz said.

'Shut up, I haven't finished what I've got to say yet,' Paco barked. 'There are no guarantees in protection work, but those men did what I asked them to, and I'm going to make sure they get paid.'

He released the tie, jammed the cigar unceremoniously back in Muñoz's mouth, and sat down again.

The manager closed his eyes, and took several short breaths. Then he straightened his tie, and looked across at Paco.

'All right, I'll have the money for you by this afternoon,' he said.

'Are you sure about that?'

'You have my word. Isn't that enough for you?'

'It might be – if I didn't know that you still owe Faustino's team several months' wages,' Paco said.

'You must have been talking to one of the ungrateful little shits,' Muñoz growled. 'Was it Luis?'

'As a matter of fact, it was,' Paco confirmed. 'Was he lying to me?'

Muñoz shook his head, and suddenly he seemed much older and completely exhausted.

'No, he wasn't lying,' he admitted wearily. 'I haven't paid them because there's no money to pay them with.'

'How is that possible? Faustino must have been one of the most highly paid matadors in Spain.'

'Not *one* of the most highly paid matadors in Spain, *the* most highly paid matador in Spain,' Muñoz said. 'And if he had fought two more *toros bravos* yesterday, he would have entered the record books, and his fees would have gone through the roof. I told him that. I told him he was a fool to even think of moving to Mexico. But he just wouldn't listen to me.'

'So explain to me just how he managed to end up broke?'

Muñoz made a helpless gesture with his hands. 'He earned a lot, yes, but he also spent a lot. If you are his best friend, as you claim, you will have seen that for yourself.'

Paco remembered the exorbitant price Faustino had paid for prawns in the bar opposite the Hotel Florida.

'*Don't worry about how much it costs, Paco,*' the matador had told him. '*It's just a drop in the ocean to me.*'

Yes, but if you weren't careful, you might find that you had spent so *many* drops that there was no longer an ocean left to dip in.

But all he had was Muñoz's word that Faustino was broke, and he was not entirely sure he could trust the man.

'Faustino told me he'd asked you to withdraw all his money for him to take to Mexico with him,' Paco said. 'If it's true that there was nothing in the pot, why didn't you tell him that?'

Muñoz laughed bitterly, 'I did tell him – I told him again and again – but he would never listen, because he didn't want to hear it. "Come on, we must have some money left somewhere, Álvaro," he'd say, "and I'm sure if you look a little more carefully, you'll find it."'

'And did you look?'

'Yes, I did, but there wasn't any point, because I knew all the money had gone.'

'So, when I heard you arguing with him over the fact that you hadn't arranged any advance advertising for the bullfight, why didn't you say it was because there was no money to pay for it, instead of pretending that you hadn't done it because you didn't think it was necessary?'

'Because Enrique Gómez, his mentor – his adopted father – was there in the room, and I didn't want to humiliate Faustino in front of him.' Muñoz sighed. 'So, I humiliated *myself*, in order to spare his pride. It was not the first time I had done that. We all loved Faustino, and we all tried to protect him in our own ways – but like the men you hired, we were not always successful.'

It was plausible, Paco thought, and yet, in the bar, Faustino had seemed so sure he had plenty of money.

'Where were you when Faustino was killed?' he asked.

'Am I a suspect?' Muñoz demanded.

'Everyone who was at Las Ventas around the time Faustino was murdered is a suspect,' Paco told him flatly. 'And you, of course, had the necessary skill to inflict the killing thrust.'

'What do you mean?'

'It was a clean thrust. It didn't even chip the bone. And you were a matador – you would have had the skill.'

'Didn't you hear what Enrique said about me?' Muñoz demanded – and now he sounded both angry and ashamed. 'I only fought in small towns – towns that were so poor that even the priest and the mayor didn't have any money. I did not use a sword, because they couldn't afford to have me kill the bull.'

'I still want to know where you were,' Paco said.

'I was in the corral.'

'And what were you doing there?'

'I was carefully inspecting the horns of the *toros bravos* that Faustino was due to fight.'

'I thought they were always inspected the morning before the fight, by a member of the matador's team.'

'They are, but a lot can happen between the inspection and the bullfight. Some bulls will charge the side of their corrals out of sheer anger and frustration, and that can result in the tips of their horns splintering.'

'Does that mean the bull is no longer in any condition to fight?'

'No, it will have absolutely no effect on him at all. The bull won't even know it's happened, and he will be just as brave and as fierce as he was before he injured himself.'

'So, what's the problem?'

'A splintered horn is far more dangerous from the matador's point of view. If the bull succeeds in goring him, the wound will be much worse than the wound made by a normal horn. Very few matadors survive being wounded by a splintered horn. That is why I would never allow one of my fighters to meet a bull like that.'

'Do all managers make this kind of check on the bulls just before the fight?' Paco asked.

Muñoz shook his head. 'I have never known any other manager to do it, but it is the way *I* do it, because that is the sort of manager I am.'

'How many other clients do you have?' Paco asked.

'I have had many in my time,' Muñoz said vaguely.

'That's not what I asked,' Paco said. 'Tell me how many clients you have now.'

Muñoz shrugged. 'There was only Faustino,' he admitted. 'Believe me, looking after him was a full-time job.'

'So he was your only source of income?'

'Yes.'

'And he was broke?'

'Yes.'

'Which means you are broke?'

'It does.'

Paco looked around him. 'You are broke, and yet you are staying at this fancy hotel. How can you afford it?'

'I can't,' Muñoz confessed, 'but fortunately, the hotel management does not realise that yet, and so it extends me credit.'

'But the day of reckoning is bound to come eventually,' Paco pointed out. 'It always does.'

'True, but until then, I have very little choice but to carry on as I am,' Muñoz said.

'Very little choice?' Paco repeated. 'You make yourself sound like a prisoner.'

'In a way, I am,' Álvaro Muñoz said, 'a prisoner to my situation. Listen, I need a new client – or possibly two new clients – who are already successful bullfighters. But will any matador worth his salt put his confidence in a man living in a cheap *hostal*? Of course he won't! He will want a man who is an established success – a man who stays in an expensive hotel like this one. He will look at me, and he will think, "I am already doing very well, but with this man behind me, I would be doing even better."'

As long as he doesn't notice your frayed shirt cuffs, Paco thought.

But aloud, he said, 'So that's how it works, is it?'

'Of course that's how it works,' Muñoz replied, with enthusiasm. His cigar had gone out, and he paused to light it again. 'Once I have signed up the new clients and have money in my pocket, I will settle my account here, and pay Faustino's team the money that is owed to them. And, of course, I will make sure you get your money – you will be first to be paid.'

'You're dreaming,' Paco said. 'The war is getting worse by the day. There will be no more major bullfights until it is over – and who knows how long that will be?'

'Perhaps you're right,' Muñoz said. 'And if you *are* right, then I might as well drown myself in the Manzanares. But before I do that,' he looked around him, 'I think I'll indulge myself in a little more of this luxury.' He smiled, sadly. 'I really am sorry, Señor Ruiz. If I had your three hundred pesetas, I'd gladly give them to you, but the fact is, I'd be pushed to raise three pesetas right now.'

Chapter Fifteen

Sunday 14 May 1937

Half a dozen workers – and the same number of donkeys – were standing around a shell crater in Callao Square. The men were filling the hole with rubble which they had harvested from bombed-out buildings elsewhere. The donkeys had uncomplainingly carried the rubble to the site, and now stood there stoically, waiting for their burdens to be lessened.

You didn't see many donkeys around any longer, Fat Felipe thought, but in his childhood they had been a common sight, and it had been motor vehicles which were rare – so rare, in fact, that when one appeared, it would be followed down the street by a bunch of screaming, excited children.

His mother had been a washerwoman in those days, on the banks of the River Manzanares. It had been a hard life she'd led, vigorously swirling bed sheets in the water, scrubbing them on the flat stones beside the river, and pegging them out to dry. In the summer, the sun had beaten down mercilessly on her as she worked. In the winter, the river had been as cold as ice, and her hands, when she had finished her day's labour, were almost red-raw. But she – and everyone else around her – had tolerated the conditions because they had no choice, and anyway, that was just the way life was.

'We thought we'd put all that behind us,' Felipe sighed.

And so they had – but the war had brought it all back. Today it was donkeys and ration cards, and who knew what it might be tomorrow.

He wasn't there to reminisce, Felipe reminded himself, looking up at the Hotel Florida – he had a job to do.

He walked into the hotel lobby, and straight up to the reception desk.

The receptionist, a small, dapper man in his late thirties, was writing in a ledger. He looked up at Felipe with some disdain, and said, 'Yes?'

'I am Inspector Cortez of the Observation Corps, and I need to see the room that the murdered bullfighter occupied,' Felipe told him.

He spoke with all the authority he could muster, but from the look of semi-contempt on the receptionist's face, it was clearly not enough. Well, he would just have to try something else.

'I really don't think …' the man began, his eyes already turning back to his ledger.

'Good!' Felipe interrupted him. 'Thinking would be a waste of effort. Just get me the manager.'

'I can't …'

'If you don't do as I ask, I'll sit on you,' Felipe said.

Now, finally, the receptionist looked up again. 'What do you mean?' he asked – and he seemed just a little worried.

Felipe rubbed his big hands across his ample belly. 'I'll sit on you,' he repeated. 'I'll knock you down, and then I'll sit on you. I wouldn't be surprised if I broke a few of your bones in the process.'

'Just wait here, please,' the receptionist said, disappearing through the door behind him, into an office.

He was soon replaced by a serious-looking middle-aged man in a frock coat. 'You have been threatening one of my staff,' he said, accusingly.

'I'm sorry about that,' Felipe said. 'I didn't like it, but he wasn't being very helpful, and I had to do something, didn't I?'

'Did you?' the manager asked sceptically.

'Yes. You see, I'm investigating *El Gitano's* murder, and I need to search his room.'

The manager smiled sardonically. 'Ah yes, you told my clerk you were an inspector in the Observation Corps, didn't you?'

'That's right.'

'I don't believe that any such organisation exists.'

When your bluff has clearly failed, there's no point in sticking with it, Felipe thought.

'You're right, there is no such organisation,' he admitted. 'But I really am trying to track down the murderer, and would very much appreciate your help.'

'I can't have my very important and distinguished guests disturbed by the likes of you,' the manager said.

'I would have thought they'd be more disturbed by the shells which keep hitting the building than they'd be by one quiet, very discreet, investigator,' Felipe pointed out, reasonably enough.

The manager looked him up and down, his expression suggesting that the first words which came to mind when examining Felipe were not 'quiet' and 'discreet', then sighed and said, 'Listen, I've tried my best to reason with you, and that clearly hasn't worked. Very well, then, I'll give you one minute to leave the building, and after that, I'll get the porters to throw you out.'

'I wouldn't do that, if I were you,' Felipe said.

'Oh, you wouldn't!' the manager replied, scornfully. 'And why not?'

'Firstly, because I'm a big man, and they'll probably rupture themselves trying to carry me.'

That was true, but it wasn't enough to deter the manager. It was time to bring his back-up bluff into play.

'You said "firstly." Does that mean there's a "secondly"?' the manager asked, with another smirk.

'Oh yes, there's a secondly,' Felipe replied. 'Secondly – and much more importantly – I happen to know some very powerful people.'

The manager chuckled. 'Do you really? I run one of the best hotels in Madrid,' he said. 'I know cabinet members and senators. Ernest Hemingway, John Dos Passos and Errol Flynn have stayed here. They call me by my first name. Do *you* know them?'

'I've seen a couple of Errol Flynn's films, but I've never seen any starring this Dos Passos feller,' Felipe admitted. 'Naturally, I know all about Hemingway ...'

'You do not strike me as a book ...'

'I thought he was bloody brilliant in *Mutiny on the Bounty*.'

'Hemingway and Dos Passos are not matinee idols – they are famous and much-admired writers,' the manager said superciliously. 'So if you don't know them, who *are* these important people you *do* know?'

'Well,' Felipe said, 'I know Antonio Pérez.'

'Ah, yes, Antonio Pérez,' the manager said. 'Well, I'm most impressed! You really do know some important people, and I'm almost humbled to be in your presence.'

'I thought you might be,' Felipe said.

The manager might have left it there, but he was having so much fun that he decided to carry on.

'Antonio Pérez,' he repeated. 'Isn't he better known as the Conde de Cagada, Grandee of Spain?'

'No,' Felipe said, deadpan. 'He's better known as the Displacement Resettlement Officer. He's married to my cousin, Inmaculada.'

'I don't even know what a Displacement Resettlement Officer is,' the manager admitted.

'There's no shame in that, because the post's only just been created to deal with changing circumstances,' Felipe said kindly.

'Changing circumstances?' the manager said. 'What exactly do you mean by that?'

'Well, you see, there are thousands of people flooding into Madrid all the time, in order to escape the fighting,' Felipe explained. 'The official term for them is "displaced persons", and it's the job of the Displacement Resettlement Officer to find them accommodation. There are all sorts. Some are highly educated folk – doctors, lawyers and the like – and they'd feel perfectly at ease in a place like this.'

'Get to the point,' the manager snapped.

'But a lot more of them are peasants, who don't know what it's like to live more than a couple of metres from a pile of animal shit,' Felipe continued. 'If they were lodged here, they'd be completely lost at first. But it wouldn't take them more than a few days to get used to it and feel at home – and make it look and smell like home, too. And it would only take a quiet word from me in the DRO's ear ...'

'I wouldn't allow people like that in the hotel,' the manager said.

'You'd have no choice,' Felipe told him. 'He gets his orders directly Don Manuel Azaña.'

'He gets his orders directly from the president of the republic!' the manager gasped. 'Is that true?'

'Yes,' Felipe replied.

He spoke with some conviction, because he was reasonably sure that if such a man as the Displacement Resettlement Officer had actually existed, he would, in all likelihood, have got his orders directly from the president.

'You only want to see the room that *El Gitano* was using – is that right?' the manager asked.

'That's right.'

'And if I let you see it …?'

'If you let me see it, I promise to steer well clear of the DRO next time I go round to my cousin's house for coffee,' Felipe said.

The manager hit the bell on the desk with the flat of his hand, and the clerk reappeared.

'Take this … this gentleman … to the room he wishes to inspect,' the manager said to the clerk.

He turned, and walked back towards the office.

'I've just one more thing to say to you before you disappear,' Felipe called after him. 'Actually, now I come to think about it, there are two things.'

The manager turned around. 'Yes,' he said coldly.

'I may be a fat ignoramus, but even I know it was Charles Laughton who was in *The Mutiny on the Bounty*. And as for Hemingway – well, he wrote *A Farewell to Arms*, but I haven't read it, because reading wears out the eyes.'

Then manager scowled, then stepped into the office and slammed the door loudly behind him.

The clerk looked at Felipe with an expression that hovered uneasily between admiration and disdain.

'Follow me,' he said.

'What floor is the room on?' Felipe asked.

'It's on the fifth.'

'Then we'd better take the lift.'

'The lift isn't working, I'm afraid,' the clerk said, and since disdain had rapidly vanquished admiration in his attitude, he said it with a certain degree of malicious glee.

Felipe sighed. 'The things I have to do in order to ensure that justice triumphs,' he said.

It was on the second floor that the smell halted Felipe in his tracks. It wafted alluringly along the corridor, and seemed to be homing in on his nose.

Bacon!

In Madrid!

That was impossible. There was no bacon to be had in the city, and for a moment he lost faith in his power of smell.

But no, whatever his logic and intellect told him, his olfactory senses still detected bacon – nice fatty bacon.

There was no doubt about it.

It had probably been brought in from a world where bacon was taken for granted, by one of the foreign correspondents or businessmen who made the Florida their base, he decided. Whoever it was would have a spirit stove in his room, and would be cooking the bacon in its own fat.

It was too painful to think about.

He had almost got his own hands on bacon the week before. A peasant in one of the villages had shown him a side of the stuff that made his mouth water just to look at it. He had offered everything he could to get his hands on it – money, metres of dark cloth, litres of caustic soda, a huge block of salt – the peasant had turned them all down.

So what *did* he want, Felipe had asked.

A bicycle, the peasant had told him.

But with the money he was being offered, he could buy a bicycle himself, Felipe had argued.

The peasant had replied that no one in that village – or even the next village – had a bicycle to sell.

There were plenty of bicycles in the city, Felipe had pointed out.

He could believe that, the peasant had said, because they had everything in the big city, but though he had seen it light up the sky on dark nights, he had never been there in his entire life – and he was not about to start now.

Felipe thought about going back to the city himself and securing a bicycle, but he knew that by the time he returned to the village, the precious bacon would be gone.

He'd felt a great sense of loss at the time. He was still feeling it now.

'Are we going to stand here forever?' the hotel clerk asked, impatiently. 'I'm supposed to be on duty.'

'Your boss will cover for you,' Felipe told him, 'and we will leave when I'm ready to leave.'

If he couldn't have the bacon himself, he could at least smell it for a little while longer.

The wall at the end of the corridor on the third floor was gone – the result of an artillery shell – and even from the staircase, it was possible to look at the buildings across the street.

'A lot of the journalists come up to the third floor,' the clerk said, walking to the point at which the corridor ended and the plunge down to the street began. 'Can you guess why?'

'Because they're contemplating committing suicide?' asked Felipe, who was feeling his stomach turn to water, even though he was some distance away from the drop.

The clerk, who was obviously sensing Felipe's discomfort – and revelling in it – laughed.

'No, that's not it at all.' He stopped at the very lip of the drop, turned sideways on, and pointed to his left. 'It's because you can see the battle lines from here. Would you like to come and look for yourself?'

You might as well suggest I have a nice lie down on the electric rail in the metro, Felipe thought.

But aloud he said, 'I've no time for such foolishness. I've got an investigation to pursue.'

They reached the fourth floor just in time to see the half-clothed woman emerge from one of the bedrooms. She quickly looked up and down the corridor, then disappeared into the linen cupboard.

A few seconds later, the bedroom door opened again, and a man appeared. He was completely naked, except for a leather flying helmet.

He, too, looked up and down the corridor, then he turned to Felipe and the clerk, and said, '*Kakim putem ona poshia?*'

'What did he say?' Felipe asked the clerk.

'My guess would be, "'Which way did she go?"' the clerk replied.

The naked man spotted the linen cupboard, opened the door, and stepped inside.

'What are you going to do about that?' Felipe asked.

The clerk shrugged. 'Me? Nothing!'

Felipe walked to the linen cupboard and turned the door handle. It was locked from the inside.

He pounded on the door with his fist.

'Are you all right in there?' he asked.

'Go away!' said a female voice from the other side of the door.

'If you're sure you're all right ...' Felipe said.

'I'm fine ... Oooo, where did you learn to do that, Boris?'

Deciding he now had more than enough information, Felipe quickly backed away.

The clerk was smirking. 'Russian pilot,' he said. 'They shag anything that moves, and then drink till dawn. And two hours later, they're up in the air. Still, there's no disputing the fact that since they've been here, there's a lot fewer bombing attacks by the enemy planes.'

Yes, that was true, Felipe thought. The Italian dictator, Mussolini, and the German dictator, Hitler, had been more than willing to help the rebels, but the democracies – Britain, France and the USA – seemed prepared to do nothing to support the legitimate government, so any help they got from the Russian dictator, Stalin, was more than welcome.

By the time they reached the fifth floor, where Faustino had had his room, Felipe felt as if he'd climbed a mountain.

'Has anybody been in the room since yesterday?' he asked.

The clerk shook his head. 'We're short of chamber maids at the moment – two of them were blown up on the way to work – and since the room is paid for until the end of the month, we've left it as it was.'

It was a fine room, Felipe thought – the sort of room that a gypsy boy from Andalucía would never have dreamed he might one day be staying in.

Come to that, it was the sort of room that a washerwoman's son from Madrid would never have dreamed he might one day be staying in – and guess what, he wasn't!

Set in one wall of the room, there was a window that was wider than the whole living room in Felipe's apartment, and when he walked over to it, he got a panoramic view of the street below. He imagined what it would have been like to have looked out of this window a few months earlier, and observed all the busy people scurrying hither and thither, totally oblivious to the fact that they were being watched. It must almost have felt as if you were some kind of classical god, observing the adventures and misdeeds of your earthly subjects. Now, that had all gone, and there was nothing even a little bit godlike in watching six men filling up a hole.

He turned from the window, and examined the rest of the room. The bed was huge, and even a fat man like him could easily have got lost in it. There was also a wardrobe, a dressing table and a small desk.

He examined the wardrobe. It contained several suits with the Ramón Areces label inside them, a number of smart ties, a collection of hand-made shirts and eight pairs of hand-made shoes. All in all, it was just what Felipe might have expected to find there.

The drawers in the dressing table held only what might have been anticipated, too – socks and underwear.

But it was the four silver-framed photographs on the top of the dressing table that really caught his attention.

One of them held a picture of an old man who Felipe recognised as Enrique Gómez, the famous matador and Faustino's adoptive father and mentor.

The other three were of beautiful young women.

These were no doubt Faustino's admirers, Felipe thought, and wondered – without any trace of envy – if the matador had slept with one – or all – of them.

He held one of the photograph frames up to the light. There was something not quite right about the picture, he thought. Everyone posed for photographs, of course, but this pose seemed somehow artificial and not of her own making – not so much posed as *im*posed.

He took the back off the frame, and extracted the picture. It was much thinner than most photographs, and had words printed on the back of it, in a language he thought was probably French.

Not a real photograph at all, then. Rather, it was a picture cut out of a glossy fashion magazine.

Why would Faustino have done that? He wasn't some adolescent girl, in need of a fantasy life, but a fully-grown man – and a famous man, at that.

He took the back off the second frame, and found that it, too, contained a magazine photograph.

So did the third, but here there was a difference, because behind the magazine picture was a real photograph of a man and a woman. The man was the elder of the two, and Felipe guessed he was around twenty-five or twenty-six. The woman – the girl – couldn't have been much more than nineteen or twenty.

The man had his arm protectively placed on the girl's shoulder, and since it was obvious that they were brother and sister, maybe he was serving as her chaperone. They were not dressed like Spaniards, and Felipe thought they were probably either South American or Mexican.

He wondered if this was the Mexican girl that Faustino had fallen in love with. And if she was, why had he chosen to hide her photograph, only looking at it – it could be assumed – when he was alone?

Felipe moved across to the desk. It contained some sheets of thick paper with the hotel's name at the top, a bottle of ink, and a sheet of blotting paper. There was nothing else.

He went next to the bathroom, and gazed with envy on the big enamel bath. When he took a bath at home, it was in a tin bath in front of the fire, and though he had bought the largest bath available, it was still difficult to get even a third of his bulky frame below the waterline.

On the washbasin, there was a bar of soap – which looked expensive, and had the hotel's name stamped into it – a flannel, a scrubbing bush, and a superior-looking cut-throat razor.

He was about to walk away when he noticed a few strands of hair caught in the plughole. He carefully extracted them. They were long, and blonde, but quite dark near the root. They could only belong to the girl who Paco had 'surprised' Faustino with.

He went back into the bedroom, where the clerk was waiting impatiently for him to finish.

'Tell me about the blonde girl,' he said.

For a second, the clerk seemed startled, then a mask of blandness slipped over his face.

'What blonde girl?' he asked.

'Oh, come on, don't play that game with me,' Felipe cajoled. 'You don't miss a thing, and you know exactly who I'm talking about.'

'I make it a rule never to gossip about our clients,' the clerk said.

'Even if the client is dead?'

'Yes.'

'If I was you,' Felipe said, 'I'd make it a rule to avoid being sat on by fat ex-policemen.'

The clerk paled. 'I know very little about her,' he said.

'Then just tell me what you do know.'

'Don Faustino has occupied that room for over a week, and the girl came to see him every day.'

'At what time of day did she come?'

'Usually in the morning.'

'And how long did she stay?'

'For an hour – or perhaps a little more.'

'Does she visit any of the other guests in the hotel?'

'If what you're suggesting is that she's a prostitute, then I think you're wrong.'

'What makes you say that?'

'The hair might mislead you into thinking she's glamorous, but she isn't. She's a thin, timid creature, with pinched features – the sort of girl you could well imagine would end up being a nun. And she wears glasses. I've seen a lot of prostitutes in this hotel, and none of them have ever worn glasses.'

Nor had any of the prostitutes he'd ever met, Felipe told himself. Some had been very short-sighted indeed, but had understood that to put on spectacles would be very bad for business.

'Have you seen her today?'

'No.'

'Do you have any idea where she lives?'

'None at all.'

Felipe sighed. 'All right, that's it. We're done here.'

He headed for the door, but he stopped on the threshold, and took one last look.

There was something missing from the room, he thought – something which you would expect to find in every hotel room, but was strangely absent here.

The only problem was that, for the life of him, he couldn't work out what it was.

Chapter Sixteen

The old building was on the Calle de Fuencarral, a street that ran parallel to Hortaleza, and as he made his way up the stairs which led to Enrique Gómez's apartment, Paco found himself reflecting on how strange it was that a bullfighting legend – a man who he, Ramón and Bernardo, sitting in the Cabo de Trafalgar, had talked about, and argued over, many times – should have been living just a stone's throw away from where they were having their discussions.

When he reached the second landing, he knocked on the door, and could hear the sound of shuffling footsteps inside the apartment. And when Gómez opened that door, he was shocked to see how much the man had aged in less than twenty-four hours.

'I hope I'm not intruding, Don Enrique,' he said.

The old man stared at him with bloodshot eyes, and it was obvious he had no idea who his visitor was.

'I'm Paco Ruiz – Faustino's friend from the old days,' he said.

'Of course, of course,' Gómez said, as realisation dawned. 'Do come inside, Señor Ruiz.'

The apartment was perhaps a little larger than Paco's, but it was

209

packed with so much memorabilia that there was scarcely any room to move.

The walls were covered with bullfighting posters – all of them, of course, featuring Gómez himself – and the swords with which he had he had slain countless bulls hung below them.

A bull's head had been mounted over the fireplace. It would have seemed impressively large wherever it was hanging, but in this smallish room, it seemed gigantic. The bull was staring, glassy-eyed, at a mannequin dressed in a bullfighter's uniform, which stood in one corner.

'I fought him in Malaga, in 1901,' Gómez said, indicating the bull. 'I was only a young man then, still making a name for myself, and I could tell that the people in the audience were asking themselves how it was that a nobody like me should be fighting such a magnificent bull.' He chuckled. 'The answer was, of course, that the bull had been intended for the lead matador – the famous one – but by the time they'd realised the mistake, it was too late, because the bull and I were already in the ring. It could have been my undoing, because I had never before fought a bull with such spirit. But I rose to the challenge. I was magnificent, and the crowd went wild. And I never had to fight a second-string bull again.'

'It was a very lucky break, then,' Paco said.

'Maybe,' Gómez said. 'Or maybe one of the officials could see my potential greatness, and decided to give me a chance to prove myself.'

A true *aficionado* of bullfighting was like a religious zealot, Paco thought. He would do anything – at whatever cost to himself – for the good of the sport. So maybe some official *had* recognised Don Enrique's undoubted greatness, and risked his own job to ensure that this rising messiah was given his due.

'Perhaps I'm being fanciful,' Gómez said. 'Perhaps it was just an honest mistake that led to me getting that bull, but deliberate or chance – whichever it was – it changed my attitude to life.'

'In what way?' Paco asked.

'From that day onwards, I always tried to give a chance to everyone I met,' Gómez said. 'It might just be a little thing – like giving an unemployed man the money for new clothes, so he stood a better chance of getting a job, or it could be something bigger – like taking a gypsy boy under my wing and adopting him as my own son – but it is all a part of the lesson I learned that afternoon.' Gómez paused for a moment. 'You must have a glass of brandy with me.'

It would have been a mistake to refuse, so Paco said, 'Thank you, Don Enrique.'

The old man disappeared into his small kitchen, and when he returned, he was carrying two large brandies. He didn't spill either of them, but that was nothing short of a miracle, given how much his hands were shaking.

He handed Paco one of the glasses. The glass itself was crystal, and must have been expensive when new, but time had not been kind to it, and there was a tiny chip missing from the rim, which could well cut the lip of the unwary.

'Try it,' Gómez urged. 'Try the brandy.'

Aware that the old man's eyes were watching him, Paco took a sip from the safe side of the glass. There was nothing wrong with the brandy, he decided, but it wasn't particularly special, either.

'What do you think?' Gómez asked.

'It's a good one,' Paco said.

The old man was delighted. 'It is a very old, very exclusive brandy,' he said. 'One of my admirers in Jerez sends it to me.'

'I'm certainly enjoying it,' Paco said, a little awkwardly.

It mattered to Gómez to still feel important, he thought.

When you were with him, your emotions were forever swinging back and forth between admiration and pity – admiration for what he had achieved, and pity that he seemed unable to let it go.

'I bought this place when I first adopted Faustino,' the old man said. 'Before then, I would always stay in hotels, but I thought he needed somewhere he could call home.'

'I'm sure you were right,' Paco agreed.

'Not that we were home very often,' the old man continued. 'There were so many places, all over the country, that demanded to see me. Ah, the cities we went to, the rings I appeared in – Cordoba, Seville, Valencia, Barcelona, Badajoz – and the crowds who went wild. We lived like kings – staying in the best hotels, dining at the homes of mayors, landowners and military governors. We even went to Colombia once. They admired me there, too.'

How different their lives – his and Faustino's – had been since the day Enrique Gómez had spotted the young gypsy fighting the bull-on-wheels, Paco thought. He had stayed in the village, while Faustino had travelled the world. He had lived on a diet which consisted mainly of beans, supplemented with a few other vegetables and the occasional scrap of meat, while Faustino dined off suckling pig and lobster. He had attended the church school, where the Jesuit brothers would beat him if he took too long to learn the lesson, while Faustino …

While Faustino what?

'With all this travelling, did Faustino have a private tutor?' he asked.

'I saw to it that he got all the education he needed,' the old man said. 'I got him *everything* he needed. He ate well. He dressed well. And I could not have wished for a more loving and grateful son. He appreciated everything I did for him …' he laughed, 'Everything, that is, except for the girl.'

'The girl?' Paco repeated.

'The whore,' the old man clarified. 'For his sixteenth birthday, I bought him a whore.'

For many Spanish men, going to a prostitute for the first time was a rite of passage, Paco thought.

In his wild youth, when he was first in Madrid, he himself had visited the brothels on Calle Echegaray, accompanied by his friend, José Manuel, who had later become a Catholic priest, then a headmaster, and was now … well, in the bloody confusion of the war, who knew where the hell he was now?

Back then, the young Paco had considered the brothels to be normal – as natural as the sun setting or the river flowing. Now, whenever he thought about it, he felt the guilt rising from his stomach and poisoning his mouth, and though he tried to tell himself, in mitigation, that he had treated the girls with more consideration than most of their clients, it made no difference.

'She wasn't just some painted tart, you know,' Gómez said. 'She was a nice-looking girl – not beautiful by any means, but very pleasant. She could have been someone's sister.'

'She *was* someone's sister,' Paco said softly to himself.

'I wanted to surprise him, so I slipped her into his room while he was eating dinner. I said good night to him at his door, then went along the corridor to my own room. I imagined I wouldn't see him again until late next morning – or maybe even the next afternoon.'

'But it didn't turn out like that?'

'No, it didn't. I heard some shouting, then a door opening and slamming closed, and when I went out into the corridor, the girl was standing there shivering, dressed only in the expensive silky nightgown I had bought for her.'

* * *

'What have you done to anger him?' Enrique demands.

'Nothing,' the girl sobs.

'You must have done something wrong. Did you refuse to let him have his way with you in the manner he wanted to?'

'No, I ...'

'Did you try to rob him?'

'No, I promise.'

'Then what happened?'

'He ... he saw me lying there, and he went crazy. He pulled me off the bed, dragged me to the door, and pushed me out of the room.'

'And that was all that happened?'

'Yes.'

'You didn't say anything to upset him?'

'I might have said, "What's the matter? Why are you throwing me out?"'

Enrique sighs. 'All right, you can go.'

'But all my clothes are inside.'

'I will go and get them.'

Enrique knocks gently on the door, then enters. Faustino is sitting on the bed, with his head in his hands. He looks up, and when he sees Enrique standing there, his eyes blaze with rage.

'I have just come for the girl's clothes,' Enrique says soothingly.

'Did you send that whore in here?' Faustino demands. 'Was it you, father?'

'Yes, it was me,' Enrique replies. 'It is your sixteenth birthday, and it is time you became a man.'

'I lost my virginity a long time ago,' Faustino screams. 'And if I want sex, I don't need you to pay for it, because I will find it for myself.'

'It was the first and last time that he ever shouted at me,' Enrique said, as the tears streamed down his face. 'I miss him so much.'

'We both do,' Paco said.

And it was true – he did miss his old friend

'When the war is over, and they put up the statue of me in front of the bullring in Ronda, I will insist they put a statue of him next to mine. If they refuse, I will not allow them to put up one of me.'

'After the war, the winning side may not wish to erect any statues of matadors,' Paco cautioned.

Enrique laughed again. It was a dry, harsh laugh, the sort of sound any man might make if he coughed in a cavern.

'As a man, I want the Republicans to win,' he said, 'but as an artist, it is a matter of total indifference to me which side eventually triumphs, because both sides have a great respect for the arts – especially those arts which embody the true spirit of Spain.'

Faustino had said much the same thing when the dangers of going behind enemy lines had been pointed out to him, Paco remembered.

'*I am admired as much on that side as I am on this,*' the dead matador had said, '*and they would never think of shooting me.*'

'How did you feel about him going to Mexico?' Paco asked.

'I thought it was a good idea,' Enrique said. 'The two of us are both well-liked and well-respected over there.'

'Do I take that to mean that you'd have been going with him?'

'But of course. He would not think of leaving me behind. He had already found me a small villa close to the one in which he would be living.'

'Where were you when Faustino was killed?' Paco asked.

'Why do you ask that?' Enrique wondered.

'Because it is possible that you might have heard or seen something which would help me to catch the killer.'

'Sadly, I was in the president's box,' Gómez said. 'I would have preferred to be somewhere else, but the president did me the honour

215

of inviting me to share his box, and I did him the honour of accepting the invitation.'

Ah well, another promising lead crumbles into dust, Paco thought.

'Did you know that when he was in Madrid, Faustino would often visit a priest?' Paco asked.

'Of course I knew,' Gómez said. 'I knew everything about him.'

'So you knew he was broke?'

'The priest?'

'No, Faustino.'

'Broke?' Gómez said incredulously. 'He wasn't broke! Who told you that story?'

'I can't remember who it was now,' Paco lied. 'Maybe it was just a rumour I heard.'

'You shouldn't listen to rumours,' Enrique said sternly. 'Especially rumours about famous men.'

Paco bowed his head. 'You're right,' he agreed. 'A man like Faustino was too smart to allow himself to go broke. I bet he checked over the accounts every week – if not even more often than that.'

Enrique said nothing.

'I'm right, aren't I?' Paco prodded. 'He did go over the accounts every week, didn't he?'

'You know what boys are like,' Enrique said evasively. 'They can't be bothered to fill their heads with boring details.'

Paco smiled at the way Enrique had chosen to describe a thirty-seven year old man, but then, he supposed, however long he'd lived, Faustino would have been a boy in Enrique's eyes.

'So the responsibility of checking the books fell on your broad shoulders,' he said.

Enrique was silent for a moment, and then he said, 'You were asking about the priest.'

Which was quite an obvious and rather clumsy way of attempting to change the subject, Paco thought, but since he did want to know more about the priest, he decided to let Enrique get away with it.

'Yes, that was what I wanted,' he agreed. 'What can you tell me about him, Don Enrique?'

'His name is Don Pedro.'

'And his parish is the barrio of San Vicente?'

'Yes.'

'Why did Faustino go to him?' Paco wondered.

'Because Faustino, like many gypsies, was very religious,' Enrique said. 'I would have thought you already knew that.'

'I wasn't asking why Faustino went to see a priest, I was asking why he went to see *that* priest,' Paco explained. 'Why did he bother to go all the way to the barrio of San Vicente? Why not see a local priest?'

'Don Pedro was a local priest once,' Enrique said. 'He worked at the church of Cristo Salvador, which is just down the road from here.'

Cristo Salvador was quite a rich parish in a good neighbourhood, and you would expect any priest who served there to be a golden boy who would eventually be moved on to bigger and better things. So what was the reason for Don Pedro being transferred to a rough barrio like San Vicente?

'Why did he leave Cristo Salvador?' he asked.

Enrique shrugged. 'There was a scandal of some kind.'

'What kind?'

'I don't remember,' Enrique said.

And Paco couldn't quite decide whether he was lying or not.

He finished his drink, and put the glass down.

'I have to go,' he said.

The news seemed to depress Enrique.

217

'So soon?' he asked, plaintively, grabbing hold of Paco's sleeve, as if this was enough to restrain him.

'The more time that passes, the more chance Faustino's killer has of getting away with it,' Paco said.

'You're right, of course,' Enrique agreed, releasing his grip. 'But …'

He left this last word hanging in the air, like a tattered flag.

'But what?' Paco asked.

'But perhaps you will be able to find the time to visit me again, so that we can talk about Faustino some more.'

'I'll do my best,' Paco promised, as he headed for the door.

Chapter Seventeen

Sunday 14 May 1937

Felipe had once seen an American film in which one of the characters said, 'When all you are left with is lemons, then you make lemonade.'

It had seemed to him at the time to be a pretty stupid thing to say, because if you only had lemons what else were you *expected* to make?

Tortilla?

Paella?

But now, when he applied this to his current situation, it was beginning to make sense.

'When all you have to trace a woman with is a dyed blonde hair, then go to a ladies' hairdresser,' he said to himself.

As soon as the first Fascist shells had started falling on the city – months ago now – he'd naturally expected all the hairdressers to close. Some had, but most of them – along with the majority of shoe shops – had stayed open. So it seemed that however hungry they were – and whatever their chance of being blown up – women still wanted to feel special, and what better way to feel special than by having their hair done or buying new shoes?

And now, paradoxically, they had even more opportunities for shopping and hair care than they'd had before Madrid came under siege.

There was a simple explanation for this paradox. Before Franco's rebellion, both the church and custom had dictated that places like hairdressers' close on Sundays. That had all changed. To open on a Sunday was seen as an act of patriotism, and a way of cocking a snook at all those fat pampered priests who once thought they could control the way ordinary people lived their lives.

Felipe had no idea how many hairdressers were still operating in Madrid, but he acknowledged that he had set himself a daunting task. Still, just as before you made your lemonade, you had to assume there was a market for it, so, when you began your search for the elusive blonde, you had to assume that you would find her.

It was logical to begin his investigation with the hairdressing salon closest to the Hotel Florida, and that was what he did.

It was a strange and alien world he suddenly found himself thrust into. The salon had thick carpets and gilt-bordered mirrors, and there was even a statue in the corner of a semi-nude woman who, tragically, seemed to have lost both her arms.

He wished that he and Paco had investigated a murder in a hair-dresser's before the war – murder by thinning scissors, perhaps, or maybe the case of the poisoned shampoo? But since they hadn't, he was left with no choice but to make it up as he went along.

There were two young women busily washing the hair of two middle-aged customers whose heads were bent over basins, and a third middle-aged woman, in a severe suit, who was observing the whole process with a critical eye.

The watching woman noticed the fat man standing awkwardly in the doorway. As she made her way towards him, there was something in her gait which told Felipe that she liked nothing more than putting the riff-raff in its place.

'Can I help you?' the woman asked, with a broken-glass edge to her voice which was designed to shred any feeling of self-worth he might have brought in with him.

'I'm looking for a young woman,' Felipe said. 'I don't know her name, but I do know that she dyes her hair blonde.'

And he held out the sample of hair for her to see.

The woman – who he was already starting to think of as the dragon-lady – seemed to swell up with outrage.

'Just where do you think you are?' she demanded.

'A hairdressing salon?' Felipe asked tentatively.

'A hairdressing salon,' the woman agreed – and managed to sound unpleasant even in agreement. 'A *respectable* hairdressing salon – one that would never allow the disgusting creature who gave you that hair through its doors.'

The girls looked up from their basins, and giggled.

'This is nothing to do with you, Teresa, nor with you, Belén,' the woman said harshly. 'Get back to your work.'

The girls bowed their heads in submission, then did as instructed.

The old bitch thought the girl with the dyed hair was a whore, Felipe thought. Still, he should have been expecting that, because it was just what he'd assumed when he'd first seen the hair. It was, in fact, a reasonable assumption for anyone to make, because decent Spanish girls simply didn't dye their hair – their mothers would be scandalised, and their fathers wouldn't stand for it.

'She's not a prostitute,' he said. 'She wears glasses.'

The woman nodded, as if to acknowledge that, based on this new information, it was unlikely the owner of the hair was a fallen woman. But if the girl was no longer the object of her contempt, she needed some other target, and she reverted to what had probably been her original plan.

'What business does a man like you have asking about any woman who is not a member of his family?' she asked.

'I'm conducting an investigation …' Felipe began.

'Are you claiming you're a policeman? Because, apart from the *guardias de asalto*, I thought there weren't any policeman anymore.'

'All right, I'm not a cop any longer,' Felipe said weakly, 'but I used to be, before everything went wrong.'

'I don't believe you were ever a policeman,' the dragon-lady said. 'You look too fat to have ever been an officer of the law, and even if I did know a girl like the one you're looking for, I wouldn't tell you about it.'

'But you *don't* know one, do you?'

'Well, no, but …'

'Thank you for your time,' Felipe said, heading for the door.

'I would report you – if there was anybody to report you to,' the dragon-lady called after him.

The floor of the second salon was tiled, rather than carpeted, the mirrors lacked a gilt surround, and the chairs were not padded. In other words, it was a definite step down from the last one, Felipe thought gratefully, and armed with the story he had carefully worked out beforehand, he was feeling altogether more confident.

The owner was an improvement, too. She was quite smartly dressed, but lacked the green scales and fiery breath of the woman in the previous encounter.

'I wonder if you can help me,' Felipe began. 'I have a cousin in Jaén, called Conchita. Her young daughter has run away from home, and my cousin has asked me to find her.'

'Do you have a photograph of her?' the owner asked.

Felipe shook his head. 'Unfortunately not.'

The salon owner frowned. 'That's strange.'

Yes, it is, Felipe told himself.

Very, very strange.

You should have thought of that before you told your story, shouldn't you, you great fat fool? he chastened himself.

'No photographs at all?' the salon owner said.

'There obviously *were* some photographs of the girl,' Felipe replied, improvising wildly, 'but she took them with her when she ran away.'

'She probably did that to stop people like you from showing her picture around places like this,' the owner said.

'Yes, that's exactly why she must have done it,' Felipe said, grateful for her help.

'And what makes you think she came to Madrid?' the woman asked.

'Ah, my other cousin, Alberto, works as a coalman, and he caught sight of her on the street, but when he called after her, she hurried away.'

'I see,' the owner said, and her face indicated that she shared his concern that an innocent young girl from the provinces should have gone missing in the big city. 'But what I don't understand is why you should come looking for her in a hairdressing salon.'

'The girl is a typical Andalusian beauty – brown eyes and lovely black hair,' Felipe said, 'but when Alberto saw her, her hair was blonde, so she must have had it dyed, mustn't she?'

'Yes, she must,' the woman agreed. 'But I'm afraid she didn't have it done here.'

'How can you be sure?'

'Because we don't do hair dyeing.'

As he stepped out into the street, Felipe was feeling distinctly more optimistic. True, the salon owner hadn't been able to help him find the girl, but her unintentionally creative contribution to his cover story had made it much stronger.

So maybe next time he would be more successful.

Chapter Eighteen

Sunday 14 May 1937

The barrio of San Vicente was among the poorest in Madrid. It was one of those places that dirt-poor peasants, fresh in from the countryside, naturally gravitated towards, an area of so little importance to the authorities that gypsies could set up their encampments on waste land – of which there was an abundance – confident that no one would think it was worthwhile moving them on.

The area lacked the wide tree-lined avenues and pleasant parks that could be found in other parts of the city, and had none of the glamorous shopping arcades and swish restaurants which many Madrileños simply took for granted. Instead, it was full of decaying buildings, tightly packed together and tottering unsteadily over filthy neglected streets.

Some of the buildings had given up the struggle to remain upright, choosing instead to collapse into heaps of perished plaster and crumbling bricks.

Or perhaps they hadn't fallen over at all. Perhaps they had been reduced to their current state by enemy shelling.

It was hard to tell.

There was no public transport available. The tramline came to a final stop long before it reached the barrio. The metro, it was true, did pass under the edges of San Vicente, but no one had thought to install a station to give the locals access to it. As for omnibuses, the company's drivers had long since made it plain that they were not prepared to operate in such a dangerous area. There were not even any taxis – the people who lived there could not afford them, and why would anyone who *could* afford them ever think of visiting San Vicente?

What the barrio did have plenty of was whores, but then, there was nowhere on earth where there weren't whores. They stood on every street corner, but they were not the exotic courtesans of the Salamanca barrio, nor even the bovine country girls who sold their bodies on the Calle Montera. No, these whores were old and fat – and probably riddled with disease. They all called out to Paco, offering him sex for the price of a couple of glasses of wine. When he turned them down, he smiled apologetically, trying his best to suggest with that smile that the rejection had nothing to do with them personally, but was merely a reflection of how little time he had to spare in the busy life he was leading. But hiding behind those smiles of his there was deep pity – and a real anger that society should allow any woman to fall so far.

He had reached a bar which was, in reality, little more than the front room of a slum dwelling, and decided it was as good a place as any to start his search.

There were several men in the bar, slumped lethargically in chairs which looked as if they might come apart at any moment. None of the men were wearing uniforms, but that was not surprising, Paco thought, because why should a man fight – and probably die – in order to save a society in which he had no real stake?

All the customers looked at him suspiciously when he entered the room, and he sensed their eyes following him as he made his way to the counter.

'What can I do for you?' the barman growled.

'I'd like a glass of wine, and some information,' Paco said.

'I'll give you the drink if you've got the money to pay for it,' the barman told him. 'As far as the information goes, it will depend on what you want to know.'

Paco paid for his drink, and took a sip. The wine tasted almost like vinegar.

'So what's so important to you that you'd lower yourself to come to a place like this?' the barman wanted to know.

'I'm trying to get in touch with someone,' Paco said.

'Who?'

Once he'd actually said the name, things could turn ugly, Paco thought, but if he wanted to find his man, there was very little choice in the matter.

'I'm looking for a priest called Father Pedro,' he said.

Behind him, he heard the sound of chairs scraping, as the other customers rose to their feet.

'There are no priests left in Madrid,' the barman said. 'We've driven out the ones we didn't kill.'

Paco sensed that all the other customers had formed a semi-circle behind him, but his instinct told him that it would be a fatal mistake to turn round and check.

But were any of them armed?

That was a stupid question! Were any of them armed? They were *all* armed. In a barrio like this one, even the mice carried switchblades.

He realised he was in a cold sweat. What happened in the next few minutes, he told himself, would determine whether he walked out of the bar under his own steam, or was carried out – lifeless – and dumped on some convenient derelict site.

'My information is that Don Pedro is still here,' he said.

'Are you carrying a weapon?' the barman asked.

Two possible answers sprang to mind.

The first was that he had a bomb, and if anyone laid a hand on him, it would detonate, killing them all.

The second was the truth.

'No, I'm not armed,' he said, opting for the latter.

Back in his apartment, he had calculated that while it might be dangerous to leave his pistol at home, it would be even more dangerous to bring it with him.

He hoped he'd got that right.

'Are you a priest hunter?' asked an unfriendly voice behind him.

'If you found him, would you kill him – or maybe hand him over to somebody else who'd do the job?' asked a second, even less amiable.

'I don't want to harm him,' Paco said. 'I think he might be able to help me solve a murder.'

'A murder, is it?' the barman asked, sceptically. 'And what murder might that be?'

'The murder of *El Gitano*,' Paco told him.

The barman's face clouded over. 'He used to come in here whenever he was in Madrid,' he said. 'If we ever had any trouble with the local gypsies, he would find a way to fix it so they were happy and we were happy. He was not just a great matador – he was a great man.'

'But who are you to go investigating his murder?' asked one of the men standing behind Paco.

'I am a detective.'

'There are no detectives, any more.'

'You're right, of course,' Paco agreed, 'there are no detectives any more. But there used to be – and when there were, I was one.'

'How do we know that?' the barman wondered. 'Anybody can stroll in here and claim to be a detective, but that doesn't mean …' He paused. 'Hang on, I know you, don't I? Haven't I seen your picture in the papers?'

Paco sighed – partly with relief, partly in exasperation.

'You were the one who found the headless body in the left luggage at Atocha station, weren't you?' the barman asked.

'Yes,' Paco admitted, 'that was me.'

The other customers were no longer behind him, but standing where he could see them from the corners of his eyes, to both his left and his right.

'Nobody knew who the hell the stiff was at first – well, he didn't have a bleeding head, did he? – but you worked out it had to be the Count of Casla,' the barman said.

'Better known as Count Can't-Keep-My-Pants-On,' one of the others shouted – and the rest of the men laughed.

'It turned out that the count had slept with the wife of one of the grooms – well, more like raped her, if you ask me – and that the groom had threatened to kill him,' the barman said. 'So what did the count do? Fight him like a man? Not that cowardly bastard. He wouldn't soil his aristocratic hands. He got some of his underlings to beat the shit out of the groom, then threw him off the finca. I've got that right, haven't I?'

'You've got it right,' Paco agreed.

'All the bosses in that bloody police force of yours – the captains and colonels or whatever you call them – wanted it all done and dusted by suppertime, didn't they? Arrest the groom, try him, and have him garrotted. What could be easier?'

Yes, there certainly had been pressure from the police hierarchy, Paco thought, but that wasn't the half of it.

He had travelled up to Villa de Casla – the small town in Leon that was all-but owned by the count, because the evidence he'd managed to collect suggested it was on his own estate that the count and his head had become no more than casual acquaintances. And once he was there – Jesus, the pressure had been intense.

The chief of police, in whose gaol the groom was being held, claimed he had heard the man confess in his sleep, and when Paco asked if there were any other witnesses, he had asked how many the policeman from Madrid would like.

The mayor had shown Paco a charming house on the edge of Villa de Casla, and when Paco had asked what it had to do with the crime, the mayor had replied it didn't have anything to do with it. Then why were they there? Paco had wondered. Ah, the mayor had replied, he just thought the policeman from Madrid might like to see a place that it was in his gift to bestow on anyone who he considered to be a particular friend of the town.

The provincial governor had invited him to dinner – and sent his Rolls Royce to pick him up. Paco should not think of him as a provincial parsnip-head, he explained, as they worked their way through the sumptuous banquet. He had studied in Madrid, and made many influential friends there. In fact, though he hated to boast, he had the power – even at a distance – to make or break the careers of many men in the capital.

'But you wouldn't arrest him, would you?' the barman asked, 'because you were on the side of the common man.'

Actually, he was on the side of justice, Paco thought, and in another case, where all the evidence had seemed to point to a rich businessman, he had proved that the guilty party was, in fact, his manservant.

But perhaps it was better not to mention that.

One of the men caught in his peripheral vision stepped forward, so that Paco only had to turn slightly in order to see him head-on. He was a big man with a broken nose and scars on both cheeks, and in his right hand he held a wicked-looking knife with a serrated edge.

'It was the countess what done it, wasn't it?' he said. 'Her and her secret lover.' Then he noticed that Paco was staring at his knife, and grew positively embarrassed. 'Sorry about that,' he mumbled, sliding the knife back into its hidden sheath, somewhere in his threadbare jacket. 'I forgot I was still holding it.'

'That's quite all right,' Paco told him – because that was the kind of thing it was a good idea to say, when somebody ceased to threaten you with fifteen centimetres of finest Toledo steel.

'I'd love to have seen that stuck-up bitch's face when she realised she wasn't going to get away with it,' the man said. 'It must have been a real picture.'

'It was,' Paco agreed.

And that was no lie. The woman's family had been titled for hundreds of years. She knew the way the world was supposed to turn. There were the lower orders, who humbled themselves before their betters, and their betters, who sometimes condescended to notice them. The aristocrats were always right, and the peasants were always wrong, even when they weren't. And now this grubby little inspector from Madrid – this man who spoke with an Andalusian accent, and was little better than a peasant himself – was trying to arrest her! Well, she wouldn't have it.

Nor did she. While she was in her boudoir, supervising the maid who was packing her trunk for the journey back to Madrid, she took a pistol with a pearl handle out of a secret drawer, and blew her own brains out.

'The lover didn't get to kill himself, though, did he?' the man with the scars asked. 'They garrotted that bastard.'

'Yes, they did,' Paco said.

'And did you watch it?'

'No.'

As arresting officer, he'd been entitled to watch the execution. Indeed, it had even raised a few eyebrows when he'd said he wouldn't be going.

He was not sure how he felt about capital punishment in general, but he was certain he was against the garrotte, because it seemed to him that whatever he'd done, a man had the right to die with some dignity, and there was no dignity in being strapped in a chair and choked to death.

'Let's talk about Don Pedro, shall we?' Scarface suggested.

'All right,' Paco agreed.

'Some of the men in this bar hate the Church …' Scarface began.

'*Some* of us hate it? I'd say it's more like *all* of us,' one of the other men called out.

'And if the archbishop of Toledo walked in here now, they would slit his throat without even thinking about it,' Scarface continued. 'But there's not a man here who hates Don Pedro, because he's one of us, and has only ever tried to help his less fortunate brethren.'

'I understand that,' Paco said.

Scarface was silent for a moment, then he said, 'Can you promise me that you mean Don Pedro no harm?'

'Yes, I can promise you that.'

232

'Then have another wine – I'll pay for it this time – and while you're drinking, one of the boys will find him.'

Wonderful, another glass of vinegar, Paco thought – but at least this time it was free.

Chapter Nineteen

Sunday 14 May 1937

It was the fifth hairdressing salon that Fat Felipe had visited, and though he really didn't want to let his old boss down, his feet were starting to warn him that if he went on doing this for much longer, there would be serious consequences.

Just two more, he promised himself – I'll do two more, and then I'll call it a day.

This salon was larger than any of the ones he'd called at previously. Here, there were four girls fussing over the hair of four women, and there were another two clients waiting.

There was one thing about the place that struck him as strange – the apparent absence of anyone in charge. The proprietors of two of the other salons had been fire-breathing dragons, while the owners at the other two could have been somebody's kindly auntie – but scary or reassuring, they had all been there, supervising the work of the salon, and unless this large and obviously successful business belonged to one of the young girls, that was clearly not the case here.

He walked up to the girl working closest to the door, and said, 'I'm looking for the boss.'

'He's looking for the boss, Josefina,' she said to the girl on her left, and there was a hint of mischief in her voice.

'Is he indeed, Isabel?' replied Josefina, smirking. 'Then you'd better tell him where she is, hadn't you?'

'You'll find her in her office, over there,' Isabel said, pointing to a door in the far wall.

'Would you do me a favour?' Felipe asked.

'Depends what it is,' Isabel replied.

'Could you please go into the office, and tell your boss that I'd like to talk to her?'

Isabel chuckled. It was a deep, earthy chuckle – the kind of chuckle with which a married woman announces to her selected target that she's ready to begin an affair.

'I'd like to help you, but I daren't,' she said, though Felipe found it hard to imagine there was anything she wouldn't dare to do.

'Doña Elena doesn't like us leaving our clients under any circumstances,' Josefina explained, 'but she won't mind if you just knock on the door and introduce yourself.'

Something wasn't feeling quite right about this whole conversation, Felipe thought, but he had no idea what it was.

'You're sure she won't object being interrupted?' he asked.

'Oh, Doña Elena she won't object at all,' Isabel told him. 'If I know her, it will be quite the reverse, in fact.'

Not without some misgivings, Felipe knocked on the office door.

'Come in,' said a voice.

He opened the door, and stepped inside. It was an office, but only inasmuch as it had a desk in it. The soft velvety furnishings, the paintings of voluptuous women which adorned most of the wall space, and the overpowering smell of a sweet, sticky perfume, all combined to make the place seem much more like a boudoir than a place of business.

Sitting behind the desk was a large woman. She was wearing a tight red dress, which struggled to contain her body in much the same way as a sausage skin might strain if it had been overstuffed with meat. Her head was in proportion to the rest of her body – which made it about the size of a young giant pumpkin – and her face was painted with reckless abandon. And to top it all – literally – she had dyed her hair a blazing red.

'Come in,' she said. 'Close the door behind you, and take a seat.'

Felipe did as he'd been told. 'I wonder if you can help me,' he said began, drawing some degree of reassurance from his now-familiar script. 'I have a cousin who lives in Jaén, and her daughter …'

'You're a big man, aren't you?' the woman interrupted him, as she stood up and walked around the desk. 'I like big men. A healthy appetite for food indicates a healthy appetite for some other things, don't you think?' she concluded, as she took up a position in front of the door.

Felipe twisted round so he could see her properly.

'I'm looking for a girl who dyes her hair blonde,' he blurted out, having decided to abandon the subtle approach in favour of getting this over with as quickly as possible – and then making his escape.

'Oh, you like blonde-dyed hair, do you?' the big woman asked coquettishly. 'I could dye my hair blonde if you'd like me to …' she leered at him, '…and not just the hair on my head, if you know what I mean.'

Felipe cleared his throat, and rose shakily to his feet.

'I … I have to go,' he croaked.

'But you've only just arrived,' the woman protested.

As he turned, Felipe felt sweat forming on his brow. He couldn't get out of the door with her standing there, he told himself, and if she refused to move, he would simply have to lift her out of the way. He was confident he could do it, but the very thought of touching her made his skin crawl.

'I absolutely refuse to let you leave this room until you've had a drink with me,' the woman said. 'You'll find a bottle of ponche and two glasses in the desk drawer.'

'I don't think …' he said.

'I'm serious,' she teased. 'You're not leaving until you've had a drink with me.'

It was then that he noticed the framed photograph on the desk. The man in the photograph was wearing a matador's costume, and he had signed it, *El Gitano*.

'Where did you get this?' he asked.

'Now don't try changing the subject, just when we were getting friendly,' the woman said.

Felipe felt a sudden – and surprising – surge of anger. He slammed his large hand down on the desk, which shuddered, but did not break.

'Don't try giving me the run around, señora,' he said harshly. 'I asked you a straight question, and I expect you to give me a straight answer. And I want you to do it now!'

'I … I …' the woman said, completely knocked off balance by this sudden and unexpected show of masterfulness.

'Come on – spit it out!' Felipe said.

'It belongs to a client,' the woman said. 'She brought it in to show me, and I admired it so much that she said I could borrow it for a while.'

It could all be just a coincidence, Felipe thought, but he had conducted enough investigations to know that coincidences were far less common than most people thought.

'Was this client a young woman with dyed blonde hair?' he demanded.

'Yes,' the woman admitted.

'What's her name, and where does she live?'

'Her name is Nieves.'

Nieves! That was the name of the woman who had signed the note to Cindy, telling her that Faustino had got her a ticket for the *corrida*, and would leave it at the ticket office with the other two.

'Give me her address,' he snapped.

'I don't know her address, but I know she lives in the barrio, because I've seen her in the shops.'

'What else can you tell me about her?'

'I think she's some kind of teacher.'

'Anything else?'

'Nothing, except that she seems to be a nice girl.'

'Does she have a family of any kind? A husband, perhaps?'

'I really don't know. Honestly, I don't.'

Felipe walked over to the woman and pointed his index finger directly in her face.

'I'll be looking for this girl, but I don't want her to *know* that I'm looking for her,' he said. 'Do you understand?'

The woman bit her lower lip. 'You frighten me,' she said.

'Do you understand?' Felipe barked.

'Yes, I understand.'

'Then step aside, and let me out.'

The woman stood meekly one side, and as he was opening the door, she said, 'You will come back, won't you?'

'I thought I frightened you,' Felipe growled.

'You do – that's why I want you to come back.'

So that was the secret of success with women – or, at least, with a certain kind of woman – Felipe mused, as he left the salon. If he'd known that a few years earlier, his life might have taken a completely different course.

Except that it wouldn't have, he thought with an internal chuckle, and for two very good reasons. The first was that his wife – who was a third his size – would have killed him if he'd so much as looked at another woman. And the second was that, given the choice between an extra-marital affair and a plate of kidneys in sherry, he'd go for the kidneys any day of the week.

Chapter Twenty

Sunday 14 May 1937

The priest was an old man with white hair, and his face was marked with as many lines as a contour map of the mountains. There was nothing about the way he was dressed to distinguish him from any of the other men in the bar, but he carried with him an aura that could only belong to someone at peace with his god. As he crossed the bar to Paco's table, the ex-detective noted that all the other customers were treating him with a respect which bordered on awe.

The moment he sat down, the barman placed a large glass of brandy in front of him.

'That's the last drop of the good stuff we have left on the shelf, Kiki,' he said. 'Enjoy it.'

'Kiki!' Paco repeated, amused.

'That is my *nom de guerre*,' the priest said, 'though it is ironic that someone whose life has been devoted to peace should need one, is it not?' He took a small sip of his brandy, then continued, 'Are you a believer, Señor Ruiz?'

Paco had no wish to lie, but even if he had felt the urge to, he could tell it would be pointless, because he was sure this man would see right through him.

'No, I'm not a believer,' he said, 'but it is not one of those protestant creeds which dominate half of Europe that I have abandoned – I am an atheist from the True Faith.'

The priest smiled, wanly.

'That is the sort of joke that men make to take away the pain which their tragic loss of faith brings them,' he said. 'Let us pray you will eventually find your way back. But we are not here to discuss your immortal soul, are we?'

'No, we're not,' Paco agreed. 'Tell me, Father, where are you living, now the presbytery has been burned down?'

The priest smiled again, and there was more genuine humour behind it this time.

'I know what you are doing,' he said.

'Do you? And what is it?'

'You are asking me a simple question – the answer to which is of no interest to you – before asking one of the questions that really does matter. It is called "softening me up".'

Paco smiled back. 'You're quite right about the purpose of the question, of course, but, as it happens, I really am interested in the answer.'

'There are many kind people who offer me shelter in this barrio, but I do not stay with any of them for long, because it is too dangerous for them. And sadly, though my work is far from done, I am afraid I will have to leave the area soon.'

'Because you're in danger of being killed?' Paco wondered.

The priest shook his head. 'That is not it. There *is* always the danger I'll be killed, of course, but my life is not important. What worries me is that others may be killed trying to protect me – and I cannot allow that to happen.'

'Why were you demoted from your old parish, and sent to serve here?' Paco asked.

'A priest can do God's work everywhere and anywhere, and in that sense, it is impossible for him to be demoted.'

'But you do know what I mean, don't you?'

'Yes, I know what you mean. I was moved because the bishop considered me too liberal. He thought that in this parish, which is less educated and hence – he blandly assumed – less tolerant, practising such liberality would be made more difficult.'

'In other words, he didn't want to get his own hands dirty silencing you, so he palmed the job of shutting you up onto the people of the barrio San Vicente.'

The priest smiled again. 'That is so,' he agreed, 'though I am sure the bishop would not see it quite like that.'

'So what particular liberal views were they that the bishop found so objectionable?' Paco asked.

'We have talked more than enough about me,' the priest said firmly. 'Ask me the questions that you came here to ask.'

'You have heard that Faustino was murdered, yesterday?'

'Yes, it was a great loss. He was a sinner – as all of us are – but he was also a good man, trying hard to do the right thing.'

Paco wondered if the priest knew that not only had Faustino had a mistress right there in Madrid, but also that he'd been about to abandon her.

'I want to track down his murderer,' he said, 'and I was wondering if you knew anything that might help.'

'I know none of the people that Faustino knew,' the priest said. 'We moved in entirely different worlds.'

'But he must have told you things.'

'He told me a great deal, but mostly under the seal of the confessional.'

'And does that matter, now that he's dead?'

The priest nodded. 'Now that he's dead, it matters more than ever. His secrets are the only thing he left behind that I can protect.'

'The other night, when I visited him in his hotel room, there was a woman there. Do you know anything about her?'

'If it was the woman I think it probably was, then I have never met her, but I know she was called Nieves, because he once showed me a letter from her.'

Nieves! The woman who had written to Cindy!

'What kind of a letter?'

'I'm not sure I know what you mean,' the priest said.

Oh yes, you do, you crafty old priest, Paco thought.

'Was it a romantic letter, in which she declared her love for him? Was it perhaps a reproachful letter, in which she claimed he had been unfair to her?'

'No, it was nothing like that. It was a purely practical letter, in which she was arranging a meeting. It's true, the letter contained a brief description of her, but that was only so that Faustino would recognise her when he saw her.'

'So they'd never met before this.'

'That is correct.'

'Where did they meet?'

'I believe it was at a pavement café in the Puerta del Sol.'

'And how soon after that did she become his mistress?' asked Paco, trying not to sound as if he was springing a trap.

'And, as I suspected would happen, we are already running into difficulties,' the priest said.

'What do you mean?'

'If I say that he told me about her in confession, and so I can't talk about her to you, you will assume that she *was* his mistress, because if she wasn't, I would surely tell you.'

'And isn't that true?'

'No. It is not the content of his words in the confessional which is important, it is the fact that he has uttered them at all. So he may have told me something as harmless as the fact that she was a friend of his sister's – if he had one – and I still couldn't tell you that.'

'In other words, she may have been his mistress or she may not have been, but whatever she was, you can't tell me.'

'Exactly.'

'And yet, you could tell me the girl's name, and that she had written him a letter setting up a meeting.'

'Yes, because that happened *outside* the confessional.'

'So if he didn't show the letter to you in your role as his confessor, why *did* he show it to you?'

'I can't tell you that,' the priest said.

'Don't you know?'

'Yes, I know – but I can't reveal that information to you without also revealing something that *was* said in the confessional.'

'I'm going to tell you what I think,' Paco said. 'I think that Faustino was having an affair with this Nieves, but then he either told her he was breaking up with her because he had a new love in Mexico, or she found out that for herself. Whichever it was, she went to see Luis, Faustino's banderillero – or perhaps it might have been someone else – and asked him to avenge her honour, and either because he loved her too, or because she paid him, he agreed to do it.'

'Even if this was true, how would I know about it, when I have never met either Nieves or Luis?' Don Pedro asked.

'You might not have the complete picture, but Faustino would certainly have told you some of it.'

'You were studying my face as you were speaking, weren't you?' the priest said. 'You were hoping for some slight twitch of my muscles or flash of my eyes to tell you that you were on the right lines.'

'Yes,' Paco admitted, suddenly feeling like a guilty child.

'And did you find what you were looking for?'

'No.'

'I shall say this, and I will say no more,' the priest told him. 'I do not know who killed Faustino or why they killed him, but what I think can say, without betraying my sacred vows, is that you have everything – and I do mean *everything* – completely wrong.'

Chapter Twenty-One

Sunday 14 May 1937

Paco had drunk three glasses of wine in the bar in San Vicente – two while he was waiting for Don Pedro to arrive, one while he had been talking to the priest. It had been a far from pleasurable experience, but he had recognised that to turn the wine down would have been discourteous, and – given the volatile nature of the other customers – probably dangerous as well.

Now, he was back in his own barrio. It was not a rich one, by any means, but at least it did not have the stink of poverty and desperation that permeated San Vicente – at least it was somewhere a man could get a *decent* drink.

There were a couple of dozen bars he could have chosen, but his inbuilt, homing pigeon instinct led him straight to the Cabo de Trafalgar, where he knew he'd find a very excellent white wine from Rueda.

'I was hoping you'd turn up, because I've got a letter for you from a Señor Álvaro Muñoz.' Eduardo, the new barman said, as he walked through the door.

Now why would Muñoz want to send him a letter, given that the last time they met, Faustino's manager couldn't wait to push him out of the door?

'The letter was ...' the barman began.

'First serve me a glass of white wine, and *then* give me the letter,' Paco interrupted.

The barman grinned. 'Pleasure before business,' he said. 'You're a man after my own heart.'

Eduardo poured the wine, and Paco took a sip. It had a magical effect, and already, the vinegar he'd been forced to ingest with the priest was becoming a distant memory.

'All right,' he said, 'let's see the letter.'

Eduardo produced an envelope with something of a flourish. Even at first glance Paco could tell it was quality paper, and when he took it off the barman, he saw the crest of the Hotel Gran Vía.

'A bellboy brought it round,' Eduardo explained. 'He said Muñoz had told him you'd give him two pesetas for his trouble. I paid him myself – out of my own pocket.'

'And now you'd like the money back?'

'Yes, but there's absolutely no hurry. Any time in the next two minutes will do.'

Paco grinned, found a couple of pesetas in his pocket, and laid them on the bar.

It was just typical of Muñoz to expect other people to meet his expenses, he thought.

He opened the envelope and glanced at the single sheet of paper.

Señor Muñoz has been hurt very badly and is in the Hotel Palace hospital, he read. *He would like to see you urgently.*

There were times – after a particularly bloody skirmish on the front line, for example, or when a bomb or shell had fallen on a crowd of people – when the Hotel Palace hospital was in complete chaos. On these occasions, the entrance steps became slippery with blood, and the lobby was jam-packed with stretchers on which the wounded moaned and groaned while they waited their turn for attention. Further into the building, under the rotunda's huge glass cupola, teams of doctors worked frantically at saving lives, and sometimes, they even succeeded.

Thankfully this was not one of those days, and the hospital looked as normal as any hospital which was in reality a hotel – and which had been hastily converted using whatever materials were available – could be expected to look.

Álvaro Muñoz had been put in a ward which had once been one of the grand suites. One of his legs and both of his arms were in plaster, his chest was strapped up because of broken ribs, and his face looked as if it had been fed into a meat grinder. He was, to put it in medical terms, a complete bloody mess.

'Who did this?' Paco said, because it seemed the only thing *to* ask in the circumstances.

'Who do you *think* did it?' Muñoz asked.

'From the thoroughness of the beating, my guess would be a loan shark,' Paco said.

'Yes, that's who it was,' Muñoz agreed. 'At first … at first, the interest was fifty percent a month, then it was fifty percent a week, then it was fifty percent a day. I … I haven't given them any money for over a week, because I had no money left to give them – and so they … they did this to me.'

'The other thing I would guess is that the reason you went to a loan shark in the first place was because you've got a gambling problem,' Paco said.

'It's … it's not a problem,' Muñoz gasped.

'Isn't it?'

'No, it's a lot worse than any problem – it's a sickness.'

It was suddenly all starting to make sense, Paco thought.

'Did Faustino really spend all the money he'd made?' he asked.

'No, of course he didn't. The reason there was none left was because he entrusted it to me, his … his faithful manager, and I gambled it all away.'

'The letter you sent said you wanted to see me urgently,' Paco reminded him.

'Yes, I … One of my lungs is punctured. The doctor thinks I might die.'

And as if to demonstrate the truth of the remark, he coughed, and droplets of blood appeared on his sheet.

'I'm sorry …' Paco began.

'I didn't ask you to come here because I want your sympathy,' Muñoz croaked. 'There's something I must get off my conscience while I'm still alive.'

He was about to confess to Faustino's murder! Paco thought. And it was now obvious *why* he had killed him. He had spent all *El Gitano*'s money, and murder was the only way to escape exposure. He'd had the opportunity – he'd found Faustino alone in the chapel – and he had the skill, because he'd been a matador himself, and must have had *some* experience with a sword, whatever he might claim.

'Go ahead,' Paco said. 'I'm listening.'

'I … I want to help you to find Faustino's murderer, and the only way I *can* do that is by telling you where you *shouldn't* be looking,' Muñoz said.

Prepared as he'd been for a confession, this *non-confession* knocked Paco completely off-balance.

'So you're saying that you didn't kill him yourself?' he asked.

Álvaro Muñoz looked about as shocked as his pulped features would allow him to.

'Kill him?' he repeated, aghast. 'Good Christ, no! I loved the man.'

'Do you swear to that?'

'I do. I swear to it with what may be my dying breath.'

He believed Muñoz, Paco told himself, because even a man who had lost his faith – as he had himself – would not tell a lie knowing that the shadow of death was hovering overhead, and was ready to sweep down and claim him at any moment.

'So where is it that I *shouldn't* be looking for the killer?' he asked.

'You should … shouldn't be wasting your time trying to track down the man who wrote all those threatening letters, because … because that was me.'

'What did you hope to achieve by that?'

'Faustino was planning to go to Mexico within weeks of that last bullfight in Ventas.'

'I know.'

'So he would have wanted all his money by then – and I couldn't give it to him. But if the fight was … if the fight was …'

'Cancelled?'

'Yes, cancelled, or he didn't take part in it, then I would be safe for a while, because I knew he would never have left Spain before he had the opportunity to kill two more bulls.'

'And who was to say, with this war going on, how long it would be before another bullfight could be arranged?' Paco said.

'Exactly.'

'So if you could have frightened him off, you would have been buying yourself more time.'

'Yes.'

'But he would still have wanted the money eventually.'

'I know, but by then, my luck might have changed, and I would … would win back all the money I lost.'

'Did you really think that might happen?'

If Muñoz could have shaken his head, he would probably have done so. As it was, he had to content himself with rolling his eyes.

'A gambler always thinks it might happen – and knows it never will,' he said. 'I am a very bad man. I deserve all this.'

'Nobody deserves this,' Paco told him. 'What's the name of this loan shark of yours?'

'He is called … called Jorge Casado now, but I don't know if that's his real name.'

'It probably isn't,' Paco said. 'Do you know where he bases his operation?'

'Yes, I know.'

'Then give me his address.'

'Why … why would you want that?'

'Because I think I might pay him a visit.'

'Are you insane?' Muñoz asked. 'Casado is an evil bastard, and all his men are vicious brutes. If you … if you go anywhere near them, you'll get what I got – or maybe even worse.

It was a possibility, Paco admitted to himself – a *real* possibility – and he didn't relish the prospect at all. But there were some things that could not be avoided, whatever the personal cost, and this was one of them. He had given Moncho his word that he would pay him and his team for their work at the bullring, but he couldn't pay them, because Muñoz couldn't pay him. And since the reason Muñoz couldn't pay him was because he had given all his cash to the moneylender, then it fell to the moneylender to honour the debt.

'I've got enough on my conscience as it is. Don't let me die with you on it, too,' Muñoz pleaded.

'I'm sorry,' Paco said softly, 'but it's something that I have to do.'

Chapter Twenty-Two

Woodend waited until they'd had a few drinks in the Cabo de Peñas before he floated the idea he had been mulling over for some time.

'Do you know what I've been thinking?' he asked, trying his hardest to sound casual. 'I've been thinking that after two days of breathing in this city filth, what we need is a bit of good, fresh mountain air in our lungs.'

He hadn't been thinking that at all. What *had* been preying on his mind was the thought that the fourteenth would be the fortieth anniversary of Faustino's murder – a murder that Paco felt responsible for – and the further his friend could be kept away from the Las Ventas bullring that day, the better.

Paco looked pensive, but said nothing.

That was not a good sign, Woodend thought. He looked around the room for some fresh inspiration, and saw that the English couple were there again, playing cards.

'What are you playing?' he asked.

The man looked up. 'German whist,' he said, and then, feeling further explanation was probably necessary, he added, 'it's like ordinary whist, but it only needs two people to play it.'

'And who's winning?'

'Why does everybody always want to know who's winning?' the man asked, in mock exasperation.

Woodend grinned. 'It's that bad, eh?'

'She's taking me to the cleaners,' the man replied ruefully, returning his grin.

'Listen, my friend and me are thinking of taking a trip to the countryside,' Woodend said. 'Could you recommend anywhere?'

'The area around Miraflores is beautiful,' the man said.

'We camp there most weekends,' the woman added. 'We find it recharges our batteries.'

'It recharges their batteries,' Woodend said to Paco. 'Don't you think our batteries could do with a recharge?'

'Yes,' Paco agreed.

Woodend suppressed a sigh of relief. 'So we'll go to this Miraflores place, shall we?'

'No, not there,' Paco replied. 'I have somewhere else in mind.'

'Might I be so bold as to ask where?'

Paco smiled enigmatically. 'I remember you telling me about those excursions you had in Lancashire, where you'd be taken to a famous beauty spot, but until you got there, only the bus driver knew where you were going. What was it that you called them?'

'Mystery tours.'

'That's right. Well, our excursion tomorrow will be a mystery tour for you.'

Saturday 14 May 1977

It was only when they were three-quarters of an hour into their mystery tour, and passing through Galapagar – once the centre of royal

254

hunting expeditions – that Woodend saw the huge cross looming up in the distance, and he realised he had made a mistake the previous day by not pinning Paco down on the question of their destination.

He'd seen pictures of the cross in books, and, as a renegade Methodist, it had disturbed him then, but looking at it in real life was far worse.

'That's the cross in the Valley of the Fallen,' he gasped.

'Yes,' Paco agreed.

'And we're heading straight for it.'

'Yes.'

'You're surely not intending to stop there, are you?'

'I am.'

'Why didn't you tell me you were planning to come here?'

'Because you would have tried to talk me out of it,' Paco said, 'and perhaps you might have succeeded,'

'Is there any point in me trying to talk you out of it now?' Woodend wondered.

'No, now that I have it in my sights, my mind is made up,' Paco said firmly.

Woodend noticed that his friend was clutching the steering wheel so tightly that his knuckles had turned white.

'Don't do this thing, Paco,' he pleaded. 'Let's go back to Madrid, and get rolling drunk.'

'I have to face my demons,' Paco told him, in a voice which was suddenly both cracked and frightened. 'For forty years, I have kept them locked up, but it has always been a great effort, and the older I get, the greater that effort becomes. If I don't do something to vanquish them now, they'll take over my life completely.' He turned his head, and Woodend could see there were tears in his eyes. 'I need to do this, Charlie,' he said. 'I have to do it for Cindy.'

Woodend sighed. 'Aye, I suppose you do,' he admitted. 'I just wish I was still allowed to smoke, because – by Christ – I could use a Capstan Full Strength right now.'

As they drew closer to the great cross, Paco's face took on a neutral expression, and when he spoke again, it was in the flat, emotionless voice of a tour guide repeating his script for the five hundredth time.

'The cross is the largest in the world. It is one hundred and fifty metres – or five hundred feet – high. Two buses could pass one another on its arms.'

'Although both drivers would probably be shitting themselves,' Woodend said, in an attempt to lighten the mood.

'The cross can be seen from a distance of thirty-two kilometres – twenty miles,' Paco continued, as if he'd never spoken. 'Beneath the small mountain on which the cross rests is the basilica. It is actually larger than St Peter's Basilica in the Vatican, though in order not to diminish the resting place of Peter himself, part of it was deliberately left unconsecrated, making it officially smaller than it is in actuality. It was blasted and hacked out of the granite mountainside, and the whole thing took eighteen years to complete.'

'You were one of those who did the hacking, weren't you?' Woodend said.

'Yes.'

'What was it – some kind of chain gang?'

'Oh no,' Paco said, 'I volunteered.'

'You volunteered! Why? Wasn't it nasty, dangerous work?'

'Yes, it was very nasty – and very dangerous, too. Many of the comrades I worked side-by-side with eventually died of lung disease, because of all the granite dust they inhaled. And as for me – well, you've seen how I limp when a cold wind blows in from the sea.'

'So, I'm still confused as to why you'd volunteer.'

'They offered us a deal – two days off our prison sentences for every day we worked in the valley. I was serving a long sentence, and so I jumped at the chance of cutting it in half.'

'Just how long was it?' Woodend asked.

'Thirty years.' Paco said.

'That's disgusting.'

'I considered myself lucky to get it.'

'Lucky! How the hell can that be lucky?'

'Do you remember I told you about a man called Moncho?' Paco asked.

'He was the one who'd lost half his left leg fighting in the mountains, wasn't he? The one you hired to guard Faustino at the bullring?'

'Yes, that's him. Well, when the Fascists began rounding up men who'd fought on our side, his wife took away his wooden leg, and hid it at a neighbour's house. She did not think they would execute a cripple. She just couldn't imagine that the Fascists would be so lacking in honour as to carry any man to the site of execution, and then turn their guns on him.'

'So what did she think they would do?'

'She thought they would leave him alone.'

'And did they?'

'No, they took him away. And only then, did it occur to her that they didn't have to carry him to the site of execution at all. You see, they were only using firing squads because they had so many people to kill in a hurry. Under normal, more leisurely circumstances, they would have used the garrotte, and there was no reason why they couldn't kill Moncho that way.'

'Jesus!' Woodend said.

257

'A month later, his wife – his widow, by then – received an official letter to say that her husband had been found guilty of crimes against the state, and duly executed.'

'Poor bloody woman,' Woodend said. 'Imagine having to live with the knowledge that, in attempting to save your husband from the firing squad, you'd condemned him to an even more unpleasant death.'

'She didn't have to live with the fact for long, because Cindy was able to tell what really happened.'

'How would Cindy know that?'

'My wife loves to help others,' Paco said. 'It's a compulsion.'

'You're telling me,' Woodend replied. 'I don't think there's a single good cause in Calpe and district that she's not involved in.'

'And once I'd been arrested, she felt the need to be involved in good works more than ever.'

Woodend nodded. 'Yes, I can understand that.'

'The problem was that, in the early years of the dictatorship, anyone who had been involved with the Republican cause – even marginally – was not allowed to work for official charities. So she looked for unofficial ways to be useful, and one of these was to help the whores on Calle Echegaray.'

'What did she do for them?'

'She did all kinds of things. She taught them about personal hygiene, which at least cut down their chances of catching the clap by a little. She wrote letters to their families for them – many of them were illiterate. And she listened – because sometimes, all the girls wanted was someone to talk to.'

Woodend nodded again, but said nothing.

'At any rate, sometimes the prostitutes talked to her about their clients,' Paco continued, 'and there was this one girl who'd been with a young soldier who'd told her about a big man with the lower half of one leg missing, who they'd executed by firing squad that morning.'

'So they had shot him after all!' Woodend exclaimed.

'Yes, but the point of this story is not that he died by firing squad, but *how* he died by firing squad.'

That didn't make much sense, but it certainly sounded intriguing.

'Go on,' Woodend said.

'Moncho asked for some crutches, so he could walk to his execution with some dignity, and they agreed. I'd like to think they did it through humanitarian feelings, but the truth is more likely to have been that the idea of carrying a big man like him wasn't very appealing, and would have been even less appealing – not to say bloody dangerous – if he chose not to cooperate. So they got him the crutches, and when he asked if he could have them the night before the execution, so he could practice walking with them, they agreed to that, too.'

I can see their reasoning, Woodend thought. The last thing they would have wanted would be to have him falling over on the way to his execution.

'The following morning, he was taken from his cell, and hobbled up to the wall he was to be shot against,' Paco said. 'Then, at the last minute, he called out to the lieutenant in charge of the firing squad that he had some important information about a plot against Franco. The lieutenant had probably heard this kind of thing countless times before – desperate men trying to buy their freedom with useless information – but Moncho just didn't look like that kind of man, so the lieutenant must have decided he had nothing to lose by listening to him.'

'Which was a mistake,' Woodend guessed.

'Which was a mistake,' Paco agreed. 'The lieutenant walked across to the wall, because if there really was a plot afoot, he didn't want Moncho bawling it out for all the world and his brother to hear.'

'That makes sense,' Woodend said. 'If there was a conspiracy, you'd want to avoid word getting out that you'd uncovered it, because that would give the conspirators a chance to run for the hills.'

'Exactly,' Paco agreed. 'Now you remember that Moncho asked if he could have the crutches the night before the execution.'

'Yes.'

'He said it was so he could practice walking, but what I think he wanted to practice was keeping his balance with one crutch, while using the other as a weapon. But whether that was the reason or not, it was what actually happened – the moment the lieutenant got close enough, Moncho grabbed his right crutch in the middle, and swung it like a hammer. It caught the lieutenant a blow on the side of his head. He went down, but before he'd even hit the ground, the execution squad had panicked and opened fire, not only killing Moncho, but killing him, too. I think that was exactly what Moncho had been hoping for. As he would have seen it, his final action in life had been to rid the world of one more Fascist.'

'It was a good way to go,' Woodend said soberly.

'Yes, it was, but you see, in his place, I would not have had that option,' Paco said. 'My hands would have been tied behind my back, and if I had struggled, I would only have robbed myself of what little dignity I had left. I was willing to die in battle, Charlie, but I had no wish to be shot like a dog – and *that* was why I considered thirty years' imprisonment a good deal.'

'What I don't understand is why they *didn't* shoot you,' Woodend said. 'I mean, from what you've told me, it seemed to be a set policy to shoot all Republican officers.'

'It was.'

'And did they know you'd been an officer?'

'Oh yes.'

'So why didn't they shoot you?'

'I will tell you about it some other time.'

'Why not now?'

'Because it is a distressing story – and the Valley of the Fallen will provide us with enough distress for one day.'

They had reached their destination, and stood on the paved esplanade looking across at two white granite colonnades which described perfect quarter circles and came to rest each side of the entrance to the basilica.

At first, Woodend had no idea why just looking at the colonnades was enough to make him shiver. And then it came to him.

It is Berlin, in 1945. Much of the city has been destroyed either by bombing or by the advancing Soviet Army. Hitler is dead. Goebbels is dead. The population is starving, and in rags. They scavenge through the wreckage, looking for something they can eat or something they can sell. And some even sell their own daughters – or anyway, rent them out for a night – because the price of a hymen is at least one pack of cigarettes, and even a single cigarette is valuable currency.

Woodend is behind the wheel of a jeep, and has been driving his boss, Major Cathcart around the city. Now, on Mauerstrasse, their progress is halted by a column of tanks, moving from one war-torn part of the city to another war-torn part of the city.

The hold-up does not bother Woodend, because it will give him time to think. He does not know what those thoughts will involve yet – sometimes they are about the woman waiting for him back home, who he never really believed he would ever see again; sometimes they review the horrors he has witnessed in the previous few weeks – but he will manage to deal with whatever his brain decides to throw in his direction, because that is the kind of man this war has made him.

'Gone to sleep, Sergeant Woodend?' asks a voice to his left.

Woodend sighs. Cathcart, he has already learned, is not a man to welcome silent contemplation. Cathcart needs the sound of his own voice – and other voices responding to it – to reassure him that he exists.

'No, I'm not asleep, sir,' he says.

'Then tell me what you think of that building over there.'

He is pointing to one of the few large buildings in the city that has survived intact. It is made of white stone – probably limestone – and has been built on a more grandiose scale than is necessary for purely functional use. It is austere and geometrically precise, but the same could be said about many other buildings Woodend can think of. What makes this one different is its aura. It has no soul, and though he has nothing to base his feelings on, Woodend knows it was designed and built by men totally devoid of human compassion.

'Well?' Cathcart says. 'What do you think?'

'Why do you want to know what I think, sir?' Woodend asks, because his reactions are private, and he will only reveal them if he absolutely has to. 'After all, I'm no expert – I'm just a common or garden NCO.'

Cathcart laughs. 'I've always thought you have a great deal of solid common sense, sergeant – sometimes even more than some of my fellow officers. So what is your opinion?'

'It's evil,' Woodend said, bluntly.

Cathcart nodded. 'Now that is interesting, because, you see, until Berlin fell, this was the Ministry of Public Enlightenment and Propaganda.'

That was what the colonnades reminded him of, Woodend thought – the Propaganda Ministry in Berlin – because they, too felt as they had been designed by men without compassion, and they, too, emanated evil.

He took a deep breath and told himself that he was not there to re-live his own horrors, but to do his best to mitigate his friend's.

He turned to Paco, who was staring intently at the entrance to the basilica.

'Are you all right?' he asked.

'Franco said this monument was built in the spirit of reconciliation,' Paco replied. 'It was no such thing. If he had truly believed in reconciliation, he would have paid disability pensions to every soldier badly mutilated in the war, not just those on his side.'

'But there are Republicans buried here, aren't there?' Woodend asked.

'Yes, there are some, but that was nothing more than a gesture to the outside world,' Paco said.

'What do you mean – the outside world?'

'Franco wanted to join the United Nations, have the economic blockades lifted, and sign a deal with the Americans to lease air bases here. To achieve that, he had to pretend to be at least half-way civilised, but underneath he never changed – he was a barbarian who hated all Republicans until the day he died.'

'You've shown you have the courage by coming here,' Woodend said. 'Shall we go now?'

Paco shook his head. 'No, it isn't enough to just come here. I have to go into the basilica.'

'Are you sure?' Woodend asked worriedly.

'Yes.'

'Would you allow me to come with you?'

'I need you to stay here,' Paco said. 'I need to know you will be waiting for me when I come out again. Do you think you can do that?'

'Are you sure that's what you want?'

'Yes.'

'Then I can do it,' Woodend said, accepting that he had no choice in the matter. 'Good luck.'

He watched his old friend walk towards the basilica. It was a warm, dry day, but the Spaniard's limp had never seemed quite so pronounced before.

Woodend looked across the esplanade. It was relatively early in the season, but the valley was already having its fair share of visitors. There were American tourists in Bermuda shorts, with heavy cameras hanging around their necks. There were German tourists in leather shorts and sensible walking boots, and French tourists in sexy shorts and berets.

Several parties of nuns were in evidence, enjoying this day away from restrictions and rules. Some pointed at the cross, and talked animatedly. Others sat on a bench, drinking wine from plastic cups and nibbling at boiled eggs. And a few were just wandering around, surreptitiously examining the Levi jeans and Lacoste polo shirts which the wearers were unconsciously modelling for them.

Everybody was having a nice day out, he thought – with the obvious exception of his poor bloody mate.

It was half an hour before Paco emerged again. He seemed smaller than Woodend remembered him, and he was dragging his leg behind him as if it were quite useless.

'I have been trying to locate the exact spot where I received my injury,' he said. 'I thought I would have no difficulty at all, but it turned out to be impossible. Perhaps my memory has faded over time, or perhaps the tunnel to hell I was working on has changed too much for me to recognise, but whatever the case,' he shrugged, 'I could not find it.'

'What exactly happened to you in there?' Woodend asked.

'Oh, a granite boulder fell on me. It would never have happened if the man in charge had taken the proper precautions, but why should he, when he had a whole concentration camp of political prisoners from which to draw his labour force?'

'They at least took you to hospital, didn't they?'

'Yes, they did. It wasn't much of a hospital, but the doctors and nurses did what they could for me, when they had the time. But then the day came when the administrator announced they would need my bed for someone else, and I would have to leave.'

'They were setting you free,' Woodend said.

'They were throwing me onto the scrap heap,' Paco said bitterly. 'Cindy came to the hospital and took me home. I was still too weak to walk, and she carried me up the ninety-two steps to our apartment.'

'By herself?' Woodend said, shocked.

'By herself,' Paco agreed.

'But why didn't she just ask the neighbours to help?'

Paco laughed. 'Things had changed while I'd been in prison. The Fascists' grip had tightened on the city, and squeezed the spirit out of the people. Cindy did not ask for help because there would have been no point. No one would have dared to give help to a criminal. They would be afraid they might be arrested themselves.'

'But you'd been released!' Woodend protested. 'You were starting with a clean sheet.'

'I was still a criminal,' Paco said. 'I would remain a criminal in the eyes of the authorities until the day Franco died. But that doesn't matter anyway. Even helping an ex-criminal could be an arrestable offence if the authorities decided it was.' He laughed again. 'The Fascist mind is both illogical and arbitrary, and that

265

is the source of its power, Charlie. Most people are so worried that they might be arrested for something they *haven't* done that they never get around to doing anything that might be a threat to the state.'

'God, you can be quite depressing sometimes,' Woodend said.

'I suppose I can,' Paco agreed. 'You remember earlier that you proposed we went back to Madrid and got rolling drunk?'

'Yes?'

'It's starting to look like a very good idea.'

'Hallelujah!' Woodend said.

Chapter Twenty-Three

Except where the concrete rendering had fallen away to reveal crumbling red brick, the single storied building was the colour of dried mud. Once – perhaps not so long ago – it had been firmly in the countryside, and its owner had probably kept pigs and chickens, while his wife had woven cloth or painted pottery. But then the city had grown, swallowing up the villages and hamlets which surrounded it with all the voraciousness of a hungry barracuda, and now the old farmhouse stood sandwiched between two much larger modern buildings.

As was characteristic of most Spanish houses, there were thick bars on the windows, and the shades were pulled down, so it was impossible to see inside. What was most *uncharacteristic* about the place was the door. It was made of hardwood, and had three locks on it. As an experiment, Paco stuck his little finger into the keyhole of the largest lock, and was not entirely surprised when it disappeared right up to the knuckle.

He took a step backwards, and examined the door from further away. If the keyhole was as deep as that, then the door was not one piece of wood but two, with a steel plate between them. Charge that with a battering ram, and you'd just bounce off – which was not at all a comforting thought for a man who intended to be on the other side of that door in the near future.

He tugged on the bell pull, and heard the bell ringing inside.

He waited.

There was the sound of bolts being drawn, and then the door opened. The man framed in the doorway was tall and broad, with cold eyes and a broken nose – the kind of man who, back in the days when Paco was a policeman, would have had him reaching for either his handcuffs or his pistol.

'What do you want?' the man demanded.

'I want to see Jorge Casado,' Paco told him.

'Why?'

'I represent one of Señor Casado's clients,' Paco said. 'I am here to pay off his debts.'

'And which client might that be?' the thug demanded.

'I am only authorised to speak about my client's business matters to Señor Casado in person,' Paco said, primly.

'What I don't understand is this,' the thug said, suspiciously. 'Normally, we have to chase up the people who owe Mr Casado money, and remind them of their obligation. Yet here we have a client who is in such a hurry to pay off his debts that he sends somebody like you around to do it for him. Now why is that?'

'Does the name Álvaro Muñoz mean anything to you, by any chance?' Paco asked.

The thug grinned. 'Ah, yes, I see the way your client's mind is working now – he doesn't want to end up in the next bed to blubbering Álvaro.'

'Exactly,' Paco agreed.

The thug nodded. 'You stay here, and I'll see if Señor Casado is prepared to see you.'

He closed the door, and slid all the bolts firmly back into place.

The building was like a fortress, Paco thought, as he stood out there in the street. There was no sign over the door that said, *Abandon Hope, All Ye Who Enter Here* – but there might as well have been.

He should walk away now, while he still had the chance, he thought. But how could he do that when Moncho's lads were still owed their money, and people like Álvaro Muñoz kept getting the shit kicked out of them?

The thug returned two minutes later.

'Hold your hands above your head,' he said.

It wasn't a suggestion, and Paco did as he'd been instructed.

The thug ran his hands expertly up and down Paco's body. He was silent until he found the knife in its sheath fastened to Paco's ankle, and he grunted with satisfaction.

He straightened up. 'What's this?' he asked, holding out the weapon.

'What does it look like?' Paco asked.

'Do you always carry a knife?'

'Don't you?'

The thug grunted again. He was happy to have found the knife. He did not guess that Paco had put it there precisely so it *would* be found, since, in this thug's world, nobody walked around without some kind of weapon, and not to have had one would have been to invite suspicion.

'Can I have my knife back?' Paco asked.

'Not now, no,' the thug said. 'You'll get it back when you leave – or maybe I should say *if* you leave,' he added with a sneer.

It still wasn't too late to walk away from all this, Paco's gut told him. Walking away could really not be simpler. All he had to do was put his right foot in front of his left, then his left in front of his right, and keep repeating the process until he was well clear of this decaying house with its reinforced door.

'Are you coming inside or not?' the thug asked impatiently.

'I'm coming in,' Paco said.

Then he stepped through the door into a narrow corridor.

'It's the room at the end,' the thug said.

And as Paco made his way down the dimly lit corridor, he heard the other man drawing the bolts, turning the keys, and sealing him inside.

May was one of the best months of the year in Madrid. The snow on the mountains had long since melted – so the winds which blew into the city no longer had a chilling edge to them – and the ground had not yet stored up the reservoir of heat that made the summer so intolerable.

This particular day in May seemed especially wonderful. The trees were in full leaf, and still had their springtime sheen, the birds chirped cheerfully, and the machine-gun fire and artillery boom seemed so far away that it could easily be dismissed as someone else's business.

Fat Felipe was sitting on a bench in a small park in the centre of the barrio. He was testing out his new theory. If he were to keep walking around the neighbourhood, and the suspect was doing the same, this theory argued, they would both be covering the same ground, but might never come into contact. If, on the other hand, he was to stay in the park, the chances were that would see her, since the park was *so* central, and most of the residents would cross it at least once a day as they went about their business.

It was a good theory, and if it turned out to be incorrect, well, at least he'd be giving his aching feet a break.

It was around half-past ten that he spotted her. She was walking across the park like a Hollywood starlet – head held haughtily high, hips swinging defiantly and invitingly – but it was plain to Felipe that she had neither the temperament nor the hips to pull it off.

She sat down on the bench opposite, and opened a magazine, which immediately absorbed her. From where he was sitting, Felipe could see that the magazine was a glossy one, and had that slightly worn look of something that had been read again and again.

He stood up, lumbered across to her bench, and sat down again. Almost hypnotised by the contents of her magazine, she didn't even give him a glance.

'You seem to be really enjoying that,' he said loudly.

Now she did look up – startled. Then, seeing the speaker was a jolly fat man, she visibly relaxed.

'Yes, I am enjoying it,' she said.

The receptionist at the Hotel Florida had described her as a very plain girl. He'd certainly been right about that, and her attempt to make herself more attractive by dyeing her hair blonde had somehow only served to underline that plainness.

'What is it?' Felipe asked. 'A film magazine?'

'That's right,' she said, holding the magazine up for him to see.

The front cover was dominated by a picture of a blonde woman, but none of the writing which surrounded the photograph made any sense to Felipe, so presumably it was in a foreign language.

'She's a very pretty lady,' he said.

'Isn't she,' the girl gushed. 'Her name is Sonja Henie. She's a Norwegian champion figure skater, and one of the biggest names in the movies. So you see, you don't have to be an American to be a star in Hollywood.'

She surely couldn't think …

But she did!

She actually thought that if a beautiful Norwegian figure skater could become famous in America, then she could, too.

It was heart-breaking. It really was.

'I nearly went to America myself,' the girl said. 'There was this rich man who had promised he would pay for my ticket.'

'So what happened?'

A tear ran down the girl's cheek.

'He died,' she said.

It was almost impossible to believe this girl had been Faustino's mistress, but what other possible explanation could there be?

Maybe he got a perverse pleasure out of taking someone so obviously unattractive to bed.

'Don't go soft on her,' he heard a voice – which he recognised as Paco's – say in his head. 'You're an investigator – investigate!'

'Why would Faustino Vargas pay for your ticket to America?' he asked sharply.

The girl jumped. 'Faustino Vargas? Who said anything about ...?'

'Your name is Nieves, and every morning, you went up to Faustino's room in the Hotel Florida. Perhaps you imagined he was in love with you, and perhaps you didn't. At any rate, you learned that he was going to abandon you and move to Mexico.' She looked so devastated that, despite his resolve, he found himself softening. 'It was a terrible betrayal, and I can understand why you asked someone to kill him, but you must see now that it was wrong.'

'You ... you think I was his mistress, don't you?' the girl asked, and the astonished expression on her face looked real enough.

'Well, weren't you?' asked Felipe, starting to feel less sure of himself.

'No, I certainly wasn't.'

'Then what exactly *were* you?'

'I was his bloody teacher!' the girl bawled.

The room at the end of the corridor was square. As it was adjacent to the back alley, it was more than likely that there was a window in the wall facing that alley, but since all the walls were lined with large steel cabinets, there was no way to know for sure. This lack of a window meant that the sole source of illumination was a single overhead light bulb, and that the air was thick with cigarette smoke and sweat.

The furnishings consisted solely of a desk, one upright chair behind it, and two upright chairs in front of it.

There were two men in the room.

The one sitting behind the desk – Jorge Casado, presumably – was in his late thirties. He was of medium height and medium build. He had black hair, dark, unforgiving eyes, and a pock-marked skin.

The other man was tall and broad, and could almost have been the slightly uglier twin – if such a thing were possible – of the thug who had let Paco into the building. He was standing in the corner, near the door, and while his boss had shown some curiosity about Paco's arrival, this man's face was a blank.

'Take a seat,' Casado said.

Paco sat, and as he did, he heard the door open, and the other thug enter the room.

All three of them were now in the same place.

That was good.

That was what he had been hoping for.

But even when things were going exactly according to plan, three against one still didn't feel very comfortable.

'I've seen you before,' Casado said. 'You used to be a cop.'

'I've seen you before, too,' Paco told him. 'But the last time I saw you, you weren't called Jorge Casado, and your main business was running a string of prostitutes.'

Casado smiled. Two of his teeth were capped with gold.

'Ah yes, the good old days,' he said. 'I have fond memories of those girls of mine.'

'And I expect they have fond memories of you, too,' Paco replied. 'Especially the ones whose faces you slashed with a razor.'

'I only did that to the ones who stepped out of line,' Casado said. He sounded slightly petulant, as if he thought Paco was being unfair to him. 'I had to do it, once in a while, just to show the others they'd better be careful from then on. And when all's said and done, how many of the girls did I actually slash? It was something like three or four, wasn't it?'

'It was six,' Paco said.

'What a good memory you have,' Casado said admiringly. 'So it was six. Considering the size of my stable, that's not a lot, you know. Besides, I only did it to the ones who were well past their best, and who I'd probably have thrown out soon, anyway.' He laughed. 'I let some of the pretty ones get away with murder.'

'And didn't it bother you just a little bit?' Paco wondered.

'Didn't what bother me just a little bit?'

'Slashing the girls.'

'Not at all,' Casado replied, making an expansive gesture with his hands. 'It was just normal business practice in my line of work.' He sighed. 'I do miss those days. Still, times change, and we have to change with them, don't we? Most of my whores' customers are now on the other side of the battle lines, and the soldiers on this side think the girls should be patriotic, and screw them for free.'

'So now you're into loan sharking,' Paco said.

'Amongst other things,' Casado said airily. 'And what about you? You've gone from being hot-shot cop … an inspector, if I remember rightly …'

'Yes, I was an inspector.'

'Gone from being an inspector to acting as messenger boy for a man who's such a loser that he has to borrow money from somebody like me. It's a bit of a comedown, isn't it?'

'Like you said, we must all move with the times, and do what we can,' Paco said. 'Was it you who beat up Álvaro Muñoz so badly?'

'Why do you want to know?' Casado asked, with an edge of suspicion creeping into his voice.

'Oh, it's nothing more than professional curiosity,' Paco said.

'No, it wasn't me,' Casado told him, relaxing. 'I don't do that sort of work these days. I got Sergio and Carlos to do it instead.'

'Which one is which?' Paco asked.

'Professional curiosity again?'

'That's right.'

'The one who let you in is Carlos, which means the other one must be Sergio, doesn't it?'

'And beating Muñoz up was just an extension of your normal business practice?'

'Correct. I'm a great believer in making an example of people who let me down. And it works, doesn't it, because here you are with money from one of my other clients.'

How long had he been stalling now, Paco wondered.

Had it been five minutes?

Or could it even have been six?

Moncho had said he would only need four minutes at most. Well, the one-legged man had already been proved wrong, Paco

275

thought – and he was painfully aware that he couldn't hold Casado off for much longer.

'Speaking of money,' the loan shark said, 'where is it?'

'Well, it's like this, Jorge,' Paco said. 'I've got some men working for me – nice guys, I'm sure you'd like them – and Álvaro Muñoz owes them three hundred pesetas. The problem is, Muñoz hasn't got any money – and the reason for that is that you took it all off him. So what's the result? I can't give my boys the money that they've earned.'

'My heart bleeds for you,' Casado said.

'So how do my men get what they're owed?' Paco wondered. 'Well, I suppose *you'll* have to pay them.'

The room fell silent, and suddenly felt much colder. The seconds ticked by, and as they did, Casado's expression changed from complacent amusement to black rage.

'I don't like jokes – especially jokes that are at my expense,' he said. 'They make me angry. I'm angry now. Can you see that?'

Oh, God, yes, Paco thought. What are you doing, Moncho? What – in God's name – are you bloody doing?

But aloud, he said, 'It's no joke. I'm giving you a chance to do the right thing. Take it while it's there – because you won't get another one.'

'Do you remember what I said about making an example of Álvaro Muñoz?' Casado asked. 'Well, it obviously wasn't enough for some people, so we need a second one – and you're the lucky winner.' He turned to his men. 'I don't particularly want you to kill him, Carlos, but if he does die, you can be certain I won't lose any sleep over it.'

Two pairs of hands grabbed Paco's arms, lifted him out of the chair, swung him across the room, and smashed him into one of the metal cabinets. The collision drove the air from his body, and started his wound throbbing. His head was pounding, his vision was hazy, and when the two thugs let go of his arms, it took him all his effort not to fall over.

Carlos, who had around a twelve-centimetre height advantage over Paco, leant forward, and grinned. He didn't have gold-capped teeth, like his boss. His teeth were rotting – and his breath stank.

'How would you like it if I carved you up using your own knife?' he asked.

'I don't think I'd like it all,' Paco admitted.

Carlos produced the knife, and held it up in front of Paco's face.

'I'm feeling in a generous mood today, so I'm going to give you a choice,' he said.

'A choice?' Paco repeated. 'What do you mean?'

And he was thinking as he spoke, 'Are you trying to pick the lock with a hair grip, Moncho? Because I'd just like you to know that if that *is* what you're doing, then I'm a bloody dead man.'

'What do I mean?' Carlos repeated. 'I mean that I'm giving you the choice of where I start. We could begin with your face, if you like. Or maybe we should find out just how difficult it would be to slice off your *cojones*.'

He couldn't wait any longer, Paco decided. Whatever it cost him later, he was going to have to act now.

It was a three-stage manoeuvre. In stage one, Paco kneed Carlos in the testicles. In stage two, he pushed the doubled-up Carlos out of the way, so that he could get at Sergio. And in stage three, he kicked Sergio – who was only just starting to react – on the knee-cap.

'Well, well, well, I do like to see a man of spirit,' Casado said, from behind his desk. 'But you must realise this is going to make things even worse for you than it was going to be anyway.'

Carlos and Sergio had both collapsed by the door, so there was no way of getting round them.

Not that it would have mattered even if there had been.

Say the door had been open – which it wasn't – and he'd been able to clear the sprawling bodies of the thugs with one giant leap – which he couldn't – what good would that have done him? He'd have been in the corridor – certainly – but there was only one way out of the corridor and into the outside world, and that was through the reinforced door with the three locks.

The two thugs were climbing to their feet. What he'd just done to them would have knocked any ordinary man out of the game for half an hour, but these were hard cases, and in another ten seconds, they'd be ready to attack.

One of them would come at him from the left, the other would come from the right. They would be on their guard now, so if he managed to get in even one punch, he could count himself lucky.

Well, shit!

The sudden roar thundered down the corridor, like an out-of-control express train, and the walls shook as its vibrations hit them.

Sergio and Carlos froze, then looked at their boss for instruction.

Casado himself was staring at the door with horror.

'What the hell was that?' he gasped.

Paco breathed a sigh of relief. 'I'd guess it was the noise of somebody blowing your front door off,' he suggested.

'I'll deal with this bastard, you see what's happening out there,' Casado told his thugs.

Carlos opened the door, and the stink of the explosion flooded into the room. The corridor was a dense cloud of smoke and dust, and the second the two thugs stepped out of the room, they were swallowed up by it.

Casado was just reaching into his desk drawer when Paco slammed the drawer closed, trapping his hand inside.

Casado screamed with pain, and Paco smashed his fist into the other man's face, then pushed him off his chair. By the time the loan shark had struggled back to his feet, Paco had opened the drawer and extracted the pistol.

Casado looked around, as if deciding what to do next.

'Sit down again,' Paco said, aiming the pistol squarely at his head.

Casado sat. He seemed unsure of how to use his uninjured left hand – whether to soothe his damaged right wrist with it, or probe exactly what damage had been done to his nose. He finally settled on his nose.

In the corridor, a full-scale battle seemed to be raging – men cursing, the heavy thud of bodies hitting walls, the grunts of pain …

Suddenly, there was nothing – a silence so complete it was almost possible to believe that the minute or so of desperate combat had never happened.

There was the ominous thud, thud, thud of a wooden leg, then out of the fog stomped Moncho, followed by three of his men.

'If you're wondering where your bodyguards are,' he said to Casado, 'they looked a bit peaky, so I told them to have a nice lie down.'

'That was one hell of an explosion,' Paco said.

Moncho grinned. 'It was, wasn't it? It's a while since I've blown anything up, you see, and I seem to have got it a bit wrong. I was only intending to get rid of the door, but I appear to have demolished the entire front wall.'

Casado dabbed his nose gingerly with the back of his hand.

'It was three hundred pesetas you wanted, wasn't it?' he asked.

Paco laughed. 'Three hundred pesetas? That was then. You're in the loan shark business, so you must know that if somebody doesn't pay you when you ask them, the price goes up.'

Casado sighed. 'So how much do you want?' he asked, giving in to the inevitable.

'All of it,' Paco said. 'Any money we can find in this place, we're taking away with us.'

'But that's …' Casado began.

'Extortion?' Paco suggested. 'Robbery?'

'Yes.'

Paco shook his head. 'No, it isn't,' he said. 'It's normal business practice.' He looked around the room, at all the steel cabinets. 'What's in them?'

'Nothing,' Casado said.

'Now you know that isn't true,' Paco rebuked him. He nodded to one of Moncho's men. 'Open one up.'

But the cabinet was locked.

'Where's the key?' he asked.

'Don't know,' Casado said sullenly.

'If you make me look for it, I'm likely to get very annoyed,' Paco said, in a voice which sounded deliberately playful, and was all the more menacing because of that.

Casado reached into the drawer and produced a key.

When Paco opened the cupboard, he found himself staring at row upon row of tins of corned beef.

'You can be shot for profiteering,' he said. 'But maybe I'm being unfair – maybe it's all for your personal use.'

'You're a real comedian,' Casado said.

'I try,' Paco told him. He turned to Moncho and said, 'Can you get a couple of big carts to shift this stuff?'

'No problem.'

'So you're going to steal it from me, and then sell it on the black market,' Casado said. 'You pretend to be better than me, but you're not – when there's a chance of making some money, you're just the same as I am.'

'Tell your lads they can take a few tins for themselves, and give the rest to the soup kitchens and hospitals, Moncho,' Paco said, ignoring him. 'The same goes for any cash you find. Take the money you're owed, and give yourselves a bonus for this little adventure. The rest goes to the people who really need it. Got that?'

'Got it,' Moncho agreed.

'In that case, I'll be going – because I've still got a murder to solve,' Paco walked to the door, then stopped, and turned round. 'We always knew that you were the one who was slashing the whores, but they were too frightened to talk, and so we could never prove it,' he said to Casado.

Casado sneered. 'And nothing has changed, because you still can't prove it now,' he said.

'Yes, that's true enough, but you see, something *has* changed.'

'What?'

'Spain, you moron! The judicial system as we knew it has collapsed, and now I don't *have to* prove anything,' Paco said. He turned to Moncho. 'Before you leave, do you think you could you do me one small favour?'

'Sure,' Moncho agreed. 'What is it?'

'I'd very much appreciate it if you'd break both of this arsehole's legs. Do the same for his two mates out in the corridor, as well.'

'Why don't you just kill me, and have done with it, you bastard?' Casado asked.

'Because that would be giving you the easy way out,' Paco told him. 'Up until this very moment, you've been living in a jungle you're partly responsible for creating, and within that jungle, you've been a merciless predator, pouncing on any sign of weakness. Now, you're about to learn what it's like to be on the other side – to tremble when you hear a predator approaching. I'd wish you good luck – but you don't deserve it.'

Chapter Twenty-Four

Monday 15 May 1937

Paco and Felipe were the only two customers in the Cabo de Trafalgar. They could have chosen any of the bar's tables, and the fact that they had selected the one at the far end of the establishment – where they could both have their backs to the wall and also keep an eye on the door – was merely indicative of the troubled times in which they were living.

They were drinking a red wine from Cariñena, and Felipe had just finished explaining how he found Nieves.

'That was good detective work,' Paco said approvingly, 'very good detective work, in fact.'

Felipe simpered like a virgin receiving her first compliment from a gentleman admirer, and said modestly, 'Oh, it was not so hard.'

'So she's a teacher?'

'Yes.'

'And what was she teaching Faustino?'

'To read and write. He was illiterate. Did you know that?'

'No,' Paco said, 'but I bloody well should have done.'

'He told Nieves that when he finally joined his lover in Mexico,

283

it would greatly shame him if he had to admit that he was illiterate.'

'When did these lessons start?'

'A week before he was killed.'

'And he was planning to leave for Mexico in a month, wasn't he?'

'That's right, he was.'

'Five weeks isn't very long at all to teach somebody to read and write.'

'That's what Nieves told Faustino. But he thought that if he put his mind to it, he could manage it easily.'

The problem with so many people was that they were too ignorant to realise just how ignorant they were, Paco thought. If some young boy had told Faustino that he could learn how to be a matador in five weeks, he would have laughed in that boy's face. There is a great deal to learn, he would have said, and even if you have a natural talent, it takes years to develop your skills.

But reading and writing? Unlike bullfighting, there were millions of people who could do it with ease – so how hard could it be?

He should have known about Faustino's weakness, Paco rebuked himself. He should have seen it long ago, because the truth had been right there under his nose from the first time they'd met in the Puerta del Sol.

Faustino had tried to make himself inconspicuous by pretending to read a newspaper, but because he didn't actually know how to read, he'd held the paper far too close to his face.

He'd been spotted by a crowd of his admirers, and they'd asked for his autograph. He'd been happy to sign his name – more than happy, in fact, though he seemed to make rather heavy work of it – but when one woman had asked for a more personal dedication, his mood suddenly changed, and he had become almost belligerent.

And why?

Because he'd learned how to sign his own name – and that was the full extent of his writing skills.

Then there was time in the bar opposite the Hotel Florida, when Faustino had shown him the threatening letters. Paco had asked which one of the letters he should look at first, and Faustino had wanted to know why that would matter.

'*Most men in your situation would want me to start with either the first one they received, or the one that disturbed them the most,*' Paco had explained.

'*They're all the same,*' Faustino had said brusquely.

And so they were to him – because at worst, each and every one of them was just a slip of paper with unintelligible symbols on it, and at best was a series of letters he recognised, but couldn't yet make into words.

Whatever the case, it meant that Faustino had had to give his manager much more power and control than most managers were given, and Álvaro Muñoz had taken advantage of the situation to rob him blind.

'The priest hinted at all this,' Paco told Felipe. 'I think he wanted me to know, but he didn't want to break the seal of confession.'

'I'm not quite sure what you're getting at,' Felipe admitted.

'Don Pedro not only volunteered the information about the letter Nieves had written, he made sure I knew just how mundane the content was. And why did he do that?'

'So you'd ask yourself why Faustino felt it necessary to show it to him?' Felipe suggested.

'Exactly! He wanted me to work it out without him having to betray a sacred oath – and it went right over my head.'

'Don't be too hard on yourself, *jefe*,' Felipe said. 'When I searched Faustino's room in the Hotel Florida, I knew something was missing, but I didn't know what. Maybe if my mind hadn't been overcome by the smell of bacon on the second floor – thickly-cut bacon, I knew that, because thin rashers don't have the same smell at all, and it had just the right amount of fat, so that it blended with the meat …'

'I think you're getting off the point,' Paco interrupted.

'Sorry,' Felipe said. 'But that bacon …' He pulled himself up abruptly. 'What I should have noticed was there was nothing to read in the room – and everybody has *something* to read, even if it's only the sports paper. Also, there was hotel stationery in the desk, but no sign of a pen.'

'Was it Nieves who read him the threatening …' Paco began.

He stopped talking, his attention distracted by a new arrival.

The man was perhaps twenty-five or twenty-six, and wearing a military uniform. He was clearly drunk, but it wasn't the kind of happy drunk where the person under the influence wishes to express his love for all humanity. What this man's stance and swagger revealed was that he was looking for trouble. Paco had seen it before in men who had been on the front line too long.

The young man walked up to the bar, glanced bleary-eyed at the shelves, and said, 'Give me a bottle of that brandy.'

'A glass of brandy?' Eduardo the barman said. 'No problem.'

'Are you stupid – or just deaf?' the young man demanded, belligerently. 'I didn't ask for a glass – I want the bottle.'

'That's fine with me, comrade,' Eduardo said, in a tone that what was both steady and neutral. 'But if you want the whole bottle, I'll have to see the colour of your money first.'

'I'm a soldier …' the young man began.

'I can see that.'

'And I've been out on the front line risking my life for scum like you. So when I say I want a bottle, you give me a bottle.'

286

'You can have a glass on the house, and then I think you'd better leave,' Eduardo said.

The young man reached into his jacket, and produced a pistol. 'I've killed other men with this, you know,' he said, 'and if you're not very careful, I just might kill you.'

Paco's own pistol was already in his hand, and pointing squarely at the young man's head.

There was no telling with the lad might do next. His tortured brain might tell him it would be a good idea to kill the barman, then rush out onto the street, firing at random.

No one would blame him if he took the lad out now, Paco thought. They would say he'd been a clear and present danger, and had brought it on himself. And they would be right.

But he couldn't do it – he simply couldn't take a life when there was a chance of saving it.

He laid his own gun gently on the table.

'I think I can handle him,' he whispered to Felipe.

'And what if you can't?' the fat ex-policeman wondered.

'I *can* handle him,' Paco insisted – and hoped it was true.

He stood up, holding his arms well away from his sides, and gave a gentle cough. The soldier swung round. He aimed his weapon at Paco's chest, but said nothing.

Paco walked slowly across the bar, making sure to keep his arms clear of his body. When he was around two metres from the young man, the latter said, 'That's far enough.'

Paco came to a halt, 'Why don't you put that gun away?' he suggested.

'Who are you?' the young soldier demanded.

'Captain Paco Ruiz. And you?'

'Lieutenant Jaime Alonso.'

'You should never draw your weapon unless you intend to shoot someone, Jaime, and since you clearly don't want to do that, why not put it back in its holster?' Paco suggested.

'You don't know I don't intend to use it,' Jaime said in a voice which was almost a scream. 'Jesus Christ, even *I* don't know if I'll use it or not.'

Paco could feel the sweat forming on his forehead and under arms.

Had he got it wrong? he wondered.

Had he misread his man?

'What front are you on?' he asked.

'The Jarama Valley,' the young soldier told him.

'I've been there myself. It's rough.'

'Bloody rough,' the young soldier agreed. 'But it's not just the front … it's … it's everything.'

Paco nodded. 'We could sit down, and you could tell me about it,' he said soothingly. 'What do you think of that idea?'

'Yes, we could sit down,' Jaime said dully.

'And you could put the gun away?'

'No, I keep hold of the gun.'

'Fair enough,' Paco said, trying to sound as if he meant it.

They sat down at the table, and Paco signalled Eduardo for two brandies.

'So how did it start?' he asked.

'I'm from Granada,' Jaime said. 'I had a *novia* there. We used to see each other in the park at the weekend. We'd listen to the band together. Of course, we always had a chaperone – some female relative of my girl's mother. She had a moustache. Do all chaperones have moustaches?'

'Pretty much,' Paco said, laughing. 'I think it's one of the rules.'

Eduardo arrived with the brandies, and Jaime knocked his back in one.

'I was already in the army when the Fascists overran Granada. I have not been able to get back there since, but a friend managed to get word to me that my beautiful girl's father has married her off to one of Franco's majors. And then there's my parents.'

'What about them?'

'They have a small farm. At first, the Fascists treated them like they treated all the other small farmers …'

'Badly, but bearable,' said Paco.

'Yes, that is exactly it. But then some nasty person – some *cabrón* – told the local captain about me, and now, once a month, he visits my parents and demands money. He calls it a "payment", but it is a bribe – a bribe to allow them to go on living.'

'I'm sorry,' Paco said.

'Nothing seems to be working out,' Jaime said. 'On Saturday, I went to the bulls. *El Gitano* was appearing, and I told myself that if I could see Spain's greatest living matador just once, then I would have at least one happy memory to take into battle with me. And what happened? He was murdered!'

'I know,' Paco sympathised.

It was easy to forget how important Faustino was to people – even those who had never met him or even seen him, Paco thought. This young man had just listed three bad things which had happened to him – he had lost his fiancée; his parents were being persecuted; and he hadn't been able to see *El Gitano*. There was no doubt that that the third ranked much, much lower than the other two, but it still *was* in the top three.

'I've been promising myself that when we've won the war, I will have my revenge on all those people who have wronged me and my family,' Jaime said. 'But what if we don't win the war?' He paused, and looked imploringly at Paco. 'You do think we *will* win, don't you?'

'I think we're set on an inevitable course and that we must disregard the consequences and simply follow it as honourably as we can.'

'You're right,' Jaime said. 'I'm suddenly feeling very tired.'

'Get your head down, and have a good rest,' Paco suggested.

The moment Jaime's head touched the table, he was asleep. Paco waited for perhaps a minute before gently prising the pistol from his hand, taking out the bullets, and slipping them into his own pocket. That done, he returned the gun to Jaime's holster.

'He'll probably be out for several hours,' Paco told Eduardo. 'When he wakes up, give him a black coffee, and tell him I said he should go back to his billet.'

'Will do,' Eduardo promised.

Paco returned to his own table.

'Nice job,' Felipe said admiringly.

'Thank you, but for God's sake don't mention it to Cindy,' Paco said. 'If she knew the risk I've just run, she'd cut my *cojones* off.'

'And looking at it from her point of view, I'd have to say that she'd be quite right to,' Felipe told him.

'If we could get back to business, was Nieves the one who read the threatening letters to Faustino?' Paco asked.

Felipe shook his head. 'When I mentioned them to her, she was shocked. So maybe it was the priest.'

'That's doubtful,' Paco said. 'I don't think Faustino would ever have shown him the letters, just in case Don Pedro told him not to fight.'

'Would it have mattered if he had done?'

'Oh yes, Faustino would have put his art before the wishes of anyone else in the world, but he would never put it before the wishes of God.'

'Then maybe his father read them to him,'

'Not him, either,' Paco said. 'When I asked him if he or Faustino checked over Faustino's account each week, he couldn't wait to change the subject.'

'So he's illiterate and innumerate too?'

'Almost definitely.'

'*I saw to it that he got all the education he needed,*' Enrique had said, when talking about the young Faustino, but that clearly hadn't included literacy.

What had motivated him? Had he really thought that it was unnecessary to learn how to read and write? Or had he feared that an educated Faustino would stop admiring him so much, and might even begin to look down on him?

'So if the priest didn't read the letters to him, and Nieves didn't read the letters to him, and Don Enrique didn't read the letters to him, who *did* read the bloody letters to him?' Felipe asked.

'There's really only one person left, isn't there – the person who, by necessity, must have shared the secret of Faustino's illiteracy?'

'Álvaro Muñoz?' Felipe gasped.

'Yes.'

'But he's the one who wrote the letters in the first place!'

'So who better to read them with conviction?'

Paco imagined Faustino and Muñoz sitting across a table from each other, the manager with one of the letters in his hands. He could picture the look of concern on Muñoz's face – the man was a born showman – and hear the cracked concern in his voice.

'*These letters sound very serious, Faustino. I really think we should cancel the fight.*'

'You're right, he could have done it – and no one would have thought of suspecting him,' Felipe said. 'What a cunning bastard the man really was.'

Yes, he had been cunning, Paco agreed, but he had also been pathetic and desperate. Not that that excused him – a weak man could do just as much harm as an evil one.

'We need to talk more about Nieves,' he said.

'Oh yes,' Felipe replied, guardedly. 'Is there anything in particular that we need to say?'

'Well, we can start by agreeing that the fact that Faustino hired Nieves to teach him to read in no way rules her out as a suspect, can't we?' Paco suggested.

'Can we?' Felipe asked, sounding somewhat bemused.

'Yes. She could easily have fallen in love with him, and imagined that he was falling in love with her. So she tried to persuade him to stay. She said she could be a better wife to him than the girl in Mexico …'

'No,' Felipe said. 'He wasn't her type. She didn't go for macho bullfighters. She wanted someone softer and more romantic, like Clark Gable.'

'She may not have started out attracted to Faustino, but the more time that she spent with him …'

'No!' Felipe said.

'You're not normally so forceful in your opinions,' Paco said, surprised.

'It's not often I'm so convinced I'm right,' Felipe said.

'All right, then,' Paco said, 'convince me too.'

'This girl's whole life is centred on what goes on in Hollywood, and when she told Faustino that she couldn't make him completely literate in five weeks, he told her to try, and promised that whatever the result – success or failure – he'd pay for her trip to Los Angeles.'

'It was that important to her?'

'It was all she wanted in the world. She thought if she went to

Hollywood, she could become a star. So, you see, Faustino's death was a bloody tragedy for her, because he was her meal ticket.'

'It's still not adding up for me,' Paco said.

'Why not?'

'There's no possibility she could have become a star, is there?'

'She'd have had about as much of a chance as a brothel madam has of becoming Pope,' Felipe said.

'And Faustino must have seen that himself.'

'He couldn't have missed it.'

'Then there are two reasons why this story about offering to pay for her ticket has to be a lie. The first is that he would have seen that it would be like pouring money down the drain. And the second was that he'd have known that it would be cruel to send her to Hollywood full of hope, only to have those hopes crushed. He was not a cruel man. He would have spared her that – which means that she's lying.'

Felipe shook his head. 'With respect, *jefe*, I don't think you knew Faustino as well as you thought you did, because there's one important part of his character you've missed out.'

'And what's that, exactly?' Paco asked, surprised at how belligerent Felipe was sounding.

'Ambition,' Felipe said. 'He valued it in himself, and he respected it in others. He told Nieves that she had virtually no chance of succeeding, but if that was what she really wanted, she should try anyway. He also said that if she needed more money when she was in California, he'd send it to her.'

'He didn't have the money,' Paco pointed out.

'But he didn't know that. He thought that Álvaro Muñoz would find it somewhere.'

Yes, he was the perpetual optimist, Paco agreed silently.

'I still don't see why he would single her out for such generosity,' he said, reluctant to give up his position.

'She says that Faustino told her that he could sense just how strong her dream was. He said that he'd had just such a dream once, and that it had been realised because a successful man, who was a complete stranger to him, had helped him. That would be Enrique Gómez, wouldn't it?'

Felipe was right, he thought – it all made sense, and it all hung together.

Faustino was generous.

Faustino did believe in chasing dreams.

So it was more than likely that what she'd said had been true – and that meant she had no reason to want to see him dead, but a very strong one for wanting him to carry on living.

'All right, we rule her out,' he said. 'So where do we go from here? We're agreed that the motive for killing Faustino was personal, rather than anything else, aren't we?'

'Definitely,' Felipe agreed.

'Then we've only one possible suspect left, haven't we?'

'Luis the banderillero?'

'Luis the banderillero.'

'But why should Luis want to kill Faustino?' Felipe asked.

'I'm damned if I …' Paco began.

Then he stopped, and his eyes glazed over, as if he had been suddenly blinded by a very bright flash.

And in a way, that was just what had happened – there *had* been a brilliant bright flash in his brain, caused by the collision of several ideas which, until that moment, had been floating around independently.

The argument that Luis had had with Faustino in the bar, and what Faustino had then said to shut Luis up.

A possible reason why Faustino had felt a desperate need to confess to a priest, and not just any priest, but one whose liberal views had resulted in him leaving his previous parish under a cloud.

The way Faustino had reacted when Enrique hired a whore for his sixteenth birthday.

And the photographs that Felipe had found in Faustino's room, most of them of women, cut out from magazines – but one of a man and a girl, which he had hidden in the back of the frame.

'Are you all right, *jefe*?' Felipe asked, worried.

'We always knew the motive for the murder,' Paco said. 'The problem was that we were looking at it from entirely the wrong angle.'

Chapter Twenty-Five

Monday 15 May 1937

Luis was sitting at a table in the bar opposite his cheap hotel. He had his customary *sol y sombra* in front of him, but he had barely touched it, and he was smoking a cigarette with all the miserly carefulness of a man who does not know when he will be able to afford another one.

He did not see Paco approaching – it was doubtful, given the troubled look on his face, that he was actually *seeing* anything in the real world – and when the other man sat down opposite him, he jumped like a startled rabbit.

'What do you want this time?' he demanded.

'The same as I wanted the last time – to talk to you.' Paco said mildly.

'Have you got my money?' Luis demanded.

'No, but a friend of mine – a man called Moncho – has it, and he'll make sure you get it soon.'

'Well, when I get the money, maybe I'll agree to talk to you and maybe I won't – but I don't want to talk to you now.'

He started to rise to his feet, then he felt Felipe's big hands grab him by the shoulders and slam him back down into his seat.

'You can't do this to me,' he protested.

'But of course I can,' Paco replied calmly. 'Where have you been for the last ten months? Might is right these days, and I have might on my side – there is a pistol in my holster, and my corpulent friend, who is standing just behind you, could break every bone in your body just by bouncing up and down on you.'

'All right, if we have to do this, then let's get it over with as quickly as possible, for Christ's sake,' Luis said.

'Did Faustino ever tell you the story about his sixteenth birthday?' Paco asked.

'No!' Luis said, far too quickly.

'I'm almost certain you're lying to me, but that doesn't matter, because it's a story worth repeating,' Paco said, apparently unconcerned. 'It seems that Enrique Gómez bought Faustino a whore for his birthday, and left her in the boy's room as a surprise. But, as it happened, the surprise was on Enrique, because Faustino threw her out immediately. And then he said something strange. It ran along the lines of, "I don't need any help losing my virginity. I lost it a long time ago." Doesn't that strike *you* as strange, Luis?'

'I don't know,' the banderillero replied.

'Interesting that you, of all people should have no opinion on the matter,' Paco mused. 'All right, then, I'll tell you why it seems odd to me. Until the last few months, it was impossible for a young girl to meet a young man without her father's knowledge and consent – and even if that consent was given, there'd be a chaperone present. But I know what you're thinking. You're thinking, "If he couldn't have sex with a respectable girl, then, maybe he went to a prostitute." Am I right? Is that what's going through your head?'

'I don't want to play your games,' Luis said.

'The problem with that theory, you see, is that a prostitute – even the lowest of the low – wants paying, and where would a boy of fifteen – or maybe even fourteen – get the money from?' Paco clicked his fingers, as if he had just had a revelation. 'Of course, that's it – he must have stolen the money!'

'Faustino would never, ever, steal!' Luis said, suddenly sounding very angry. 'How dare you suggest that?'

'I wasn't really suggesting it at all – I just wanted to see how you'd react,' Paco told him, 'and you're right, of course, Faustino would never steal. So exactly how he lost his virginity remains a mystery. Let's put that to one side for a while, and move on. When my big, heavy friend here searched Faustino's room in the Hotel Florida, he found several photographs of pretty women in picture frames. But that's only what you'd expect, isn't it? A famous matador is bound to attract any number of women. But here's the curious thing – the photographs were cut out of magazines. Why would he do that? Was he trying to create a false impression, do you think? And if so, what could possibly be his motive?'

'I don't know, and I don't care.'

'My colleague did find one real photograph, although it was hidden behind another one. It was of a young man and a young woman. We assumed, naturally enough, that the woman was the girl Faustino was in love with, and the man was her brother. Isn't that right, Felipe?'

'They certainly looked like brother and sister,' said Felipe, who was still poised behind Luis's chair, in case the young man decided to make a sudden dash for freedom.

'Yes, they are almost certainly siblings,' Paco said. 'Have you ever seen that photograph?'

'No,' Luis said, and it was obvious that he was lying.

Paco frowned. 'Really? I was almost certain you would have seen it. Still, no matter, because, as it happens, I have it right here with me. Would you care to take a look at it now?'

And without waiting for a response – without, in other words, waiting for an almost definite refusal – Paco took the photograph out of his pocket, and slid it across the table.

Luis didn't want to look at it, but he just couldn't help himself – and once he *had* looked, he couldn't turn away. He was doing his best to make his face a blank and keep his emotions on an even keel, but the rage bubbling up inside him fought its way to the surface anyway, and when it did, he placed his thumbnail on one of the faces in the photograph, and twisted and twisted it until the face was destroyed.

Paco made no move to stop him, and when Luis had fallen back – clearly exhausted by the whole thing – he said, 'Well, that was most interesting to watch. Moving on again – Don Pedro, Faustino's priest friend, was transferred from his prosperous parish into a poor one, as a punishment for being a very bad boy. Do you know what it was that he'd done wrong?'

'I don't know, and I don't care.'

'I've only just found out myself, by asking around. It seems he was nice to homosexuals. Oh, I don't mean he was one himself – he wasn't and isn't – but that didn't prevent him from treating them decently. He allowed them to attend mass, and he listened to their confessions. His superiors didn't like that at all, so they moved him to a rough parish, presumably in the mistaken belief that his new parishioners wouldn't be as tolerant as his old ones had been, and so he would be forced to suppress his views.'

'Why should a priest like that be of any interest to me?' Luis asked.

'I don't know,' Paco said, 'but he was certainly of interest to Faustino, wasn't he?'

'If you say so,' Luis mumbled.

'That night in the bar opposite the Hotel Florida, you were very angry that Faustino was with me, weren't you? Was that because you thought I might be his new lover?'

'I couldn't see why someone as beautiful as him would ever want someone like you,' Luis said contemptuously, 'but you were in the bar with him, and he was buying you expensive food, and so I thought …'

He fell silent.

'You thought I must be, at the very least, a one-night stand,' Paco said, finishing the sentence off for him. 'Do you remember what Faustino said to you then, Luis?'

'No, I don't.'

'Of course you do,' Paco said easily. 'He asked you if you wanted to be a matador one day, and when you said you did, he said that if that really was the case, you'd better choose your words carefully, because a wrong word at the wrong time could destroy your career. I thought he was threatening you, but he wasn't. What he *was* doing was warning you that you had to hide your true self from the world. That's certainly what he did. That's why he had the photographs of women in his room at the hotel – so the maids would see them, and think he was a real macho man.' He paused for a moment. 'When did Faustino seduce you, Luis?' he asked.

'He did not seduce me!' Luis screamed. 'He did not seduce me!'

'Are you saying you never went to bed with him?'

'No, I am not saying that at all,' Luis told him, a little calmer now. 'When I was a boy, he was my hero. He was the reason that I wanted to become a matador. And when he allowed me to join his team, I thought I was the luckiest boy in the world. He was wonderful with me – he was calm, he was patient, and even though he was having sex with other men, he never laid a hand on me. I still worshipped the matador, but now I found myself falling in love with the man. So he did not seduce me – I seduced him.'

'And then you learned that he was moving to Mexico, to be with his new lover,' Paco said. He picked up the photograph, and held it up for Luis to see. There was only a hole where the man's face had once been. 'This is him, isn't it?'

'Yes,' Luis agreed, defeated.

'And you were so hurt by his desertion of you that you followed him into the chapel in the bullring, and killed him with his own sword.'

'No!'

'No?'

'I followed him because I needed to speak to him, and he had been deliberately avoiding me. I wanted to beg him – on bended knee, if necessary – not to go to Mexico. I wanted to tell him that whatever this new lover did for him, I would do it, too. I wanted to say that whatever this new lover *was*, I could *become*. But when I got to the chapel, he was already dead.'

'Why should I believe you?'

'I do not think I could have killed Faustino,' Luis said, 'but I suppose it is always possible, because he cast me aside and broke my heart. But there is something more important than the heart.'

'And what is that?'

'The soul!' Luis said, and his eyes were blazing with passion. 'Even if I could kill my lover, I could not kill *El Gitano*, one of the greatest artists who ever lived. It would be like slashing an El Greco canvas or trampling on a Stradivarius violin. Killing Faustino would be a loss to those who loved him. Killing *El Gitano* would be a loss to the world.'

And Paco's felt his stomach turn to water, as he realised that though he didn't want to, he couldn't help believing the young banderillero.

In a world in a state of flux, there are still some things which never change, and Paco was not the least surprised to find that there were still

301

ninety-two steps between the street and the tiny apartment in Calle Hortaleza. He had been up and down those steps hundreds of times, but never before had they seemed so formidable – such a challenge.

Cindy was not at home, but there was a note pinned to the door.

There's been a new attack on the front line, and there are heavy casualties, so I've gone down to the hospital to see if I can help. Don't know when I'll be back.

I love you.

Cindy xxx

There was a part of him which was glad she was gone, because he was so proud of what she was doing, but there was another part – a bigger part – that was crushingly disappointed, because on this night, of all nights, he really needed to talk to her.

He heard the sound of the hen scratching in her grit, and squatted down beside the small coop.

'I've run out of suspects, Eleanor,' he said dispiritedly. The hen cocked its head to one side, encouragingly. 'None of the people who could possibly have had a motive for killing Faustino seem to have done it. The stream's run dry, the trail's petered out. I feel as if I've let him down twice – I not only couldn't prevent him being killed, but I can't even find the bastard who did it. So where do we go from here? Why don't you put your mind to it, and see what you can come up with?'

The hen clucked.

'You're right,' he agreed. 'It is still early, but I should go to bed.'

His body felt heavy, and taking off his clothes seemed like a supreme effort. He was so exhausted he thought he would fall asleep immediately.

But he didn't. He lay in his bed and gazed into the blackness, reading his failure on a ceiling he couldn't even see.

He was still awake when Cindy arrived home – smelling of antiseptic and vomit – at three o'clock the next morning.

Chapter Twenty-Six

Sunday 15 May 1977

The previous day, in the Valley of the Fallen, had been emotion-ally draining. The evening which followed it – spent touring the bars around Hortaleza – had been positively bacchanalian, and, as a result, both Paco and Woodend woke up the next morning with prize-winning hangovers.

Left to his own devices, Woodend would have spent the morning as immobile as it was possible to be, while, at the same time, drinking endless cups of black coffee.

Paco, however, was having none of that.

'It's our last day in Madrid,' he said, speaking softly, in order not to offend his aching brain cells. 'If I do not show you Retiro Park before we leave, I'll be in big trouble with Cindy.'

'We could always pretend we'd been to the park,' Woodend suggested.

'So if Cindy asks, you'll say we visited the Retiro, will you?' Paco asked.

'All right then, we'll go to the bloody park,' Woodend groaned.

* * *

By the time they reached the Retiro, they were both feeling a little less delicate, and though they were in no state to run a marathon, they were reasonably confident they could survive a gentle wander through the park.

They visited the Crystal Palace, and strolled along the pleasant tree-lined avenues.

'Yesterday, you said that when the time was right, you would explain to me how you avoided the firing squad, despite being an officer,' Woodend said as they ambled. 'Is the time right now?'

Paco sighed. 'I suppose it is as good as it ever will be,' he said. 'There were three officers on each military tribunal, though God alone knows why they needed three, because the verdict was almost inevitable. If you were a Republican officer, you were guilty, and if you were guilty, you were executed. A well-trained monkey could have run that court.'

'But they didn't execute you,' Woodend said.

'No, I happened to know one of the officers on my board – a man called Major Ramirez …'

'You were on the same cocktail circuit, were you?' Woodend interrupted.

Paco grinned. 'Hardly. I got to know him back in the days when I was a policeman. His eight-year-old son was kidnapped on the way home from school, and the case was assigned to me.'

'And you rescued him, I take it."

'That certainly would have been a nice ending to the story, wouldn't it?' Paco said. 'Unfortunately, there are few happy endings in real life. By the time the family realised the boy was missing, he was already dead. I assume he'd seen the kidnappers' faces, or they'd decided a dead boy would be less trouble than a live one, but whatever their reasoning was, they killed him shortly after the snatch.'

'Did they ever offer any explanation?'

'They didn't have the opportunity. I tracked them down to a shack on the edge of Madrid. I told them to come out with their hands up, but instead they came out shooting. I killed one of them, Felipe killed the other. Major Ramirez was devastated at losing his son, but seemed to draw some small comfort from the fact that we had avenged him.' Paco stopped to light a cigarette. 'I was found guilty and sentenced to death at my trial, but an hour later, I was informed my sentence had been commuted to thirty years' hard labour. That would have been Major Ramirez's doing.'

'If he'd really been grateful, he might have done a little better than thirty years,' Woodend said.

'Don't underestimate what a big step that was for him,' Paco said. 'By holding out against execution, he could be said to have been flying in the face of the Generalissimo's direct orders. It could have ruined him. It *may have* ruined him, for all I know.'

'How did you feel when you were given the news?' Woodend asked.

'I told you in the Valley of the Fallen that I considered myself lucky to get a thirty year sentence, and, in a way, that was true,' Paco told him. 'Yet at the same time, I felt guilty about being given special treatment. It seemed an insult to my fellow officers that I should live and they should die. It was all very confusing, but fortunately conditions were so hard, and simply surviving was so difficult, that I didn't have much time to dwell on it.'

'Do you still feel guilty?' Woodend asked gently.

'About not being shot? No. I was given no choice in the matter. Besides, while a man who runs from death is undoubtedly a coward, a man who embraces it is nothing less than a fool.'

'That's rather good,' Woodend told him. 'Who is it a quote from?'

'From nobody,' Paco said, sounding slightly puzzled. 'I said it. About thirty seconds ago. You heard me.'

'Well, I am impressed,' Woodend said. 'I'm not thick, by any means, but I doubt if I could have come up with something as succinctly elegant as that.'

For a moment, Paco looked embarrassed, then he grinned. 'I'm a Spaniard,' he said. 'We're born that way. Spanish babies even crap with succinct elegance.'

'Now that I would like to see,' Woodend said.

Their wanderings had led them to the artificial lake, and they noted that there were a fair number of rowing boats on the water. Some of the boats had been hired by families, and the fathers rowed while the mothers constrained the small children. Others contained young couples, and in these the men pulled hard on the oars to demonstrate their prowess and the women lounged luxuriously backwards, to show that they *could be* lady-like, when the situation called for it.

'Shall we take a boat out?' Paco asked.

'Would Cindy expect us to?' Woodend asked.

'Not particularly.'

'Then we bloody won't.'

'Thank God for that,' Paco said, almost to himself.

There was a great deal of activity around the lake, as there always was on a Sunday. People of all ages were wandering around with a relaxed aimlessness. Some were smoking cigarettes; some were eating ice creams. And all of them were making happy, animated, excited noises quite alien to the rhythms of dourness and understatement which dominated Woodend's native Lancashire.

Some sort of entertainment was available every few metres. There was a puppet show, which, though vaguely related to the British Punch and Judy puppets, could never be mistaken for them. There were stilt walkers, and there were jugglers. And there was a magician.

Paco and Woodend joined the wide circle surrounding the magician.

'For my next trick I will require a jacket of some kind,' the magician said. He scanned the crowd. 'You sir,' he continued, pointing, 'would you like to lend me your jacket?'

The man he had singled out was dressed in his Sunday best, and the jacket he was wearing was a black and white check, which was not to Woodend's taste at all, but looked quite expensive.

The man hesitated. He didn't want to surrender his best jacket to the magician for some unspecified trick, his expression said, but he didn't want to be seen like a bad sport in front of all these people either. Eventually, and not without some signs of trepidation, he took off the jacket, and handed it to the magician.

The magician walked to the other side of the circle, taking the precious jacket as far out of the man's reach as was possible.

'And you, sir,' he said to a man who was smoking, 'could I borrow your cigarette for a moment?'

The man grinned as he handed the cigarette over. And why wouldn't he? For though he was starting to get a rough idea of what the magician was about to do, the jacket wasn't his, was it?

The magician returned to the centre of the circle. He was holding the jacket in his left hand and had positioned it – and himself – in such a way that while everyone could see the outside of it, no one could see the lining.

In his right hand, he was holding the burning cigarette. Now he placed it under the coat, so that it had completely disappeared from sight.

'Don't worry, sir,' he called out to the owner of the jacket, 'your pride and joy is perfectly safe with me.'

But even as he was speaking, the cigarette emerged through what, it was becoming apparent, could only be a hole in the jacket. The first indication had come when just the glowing tip of the cigarette had appeared in the middle of one of the jacket's white checks, but then the rest of it began to slowly rise, like a cobra being charmed by an Indian fakir's flute.

People glanced at the jacket's owner, who was standing there mortified.

The magician himself had been looking the other way, but now, when he finally turned towards the jacket, an expression of real horror came to his face. He extracted the cigarette, threw it to the ground, and stamped on it with some vehemence. Next, he folded the jacket so the burn hole was concealed, and quickly handed it back to its owner.

'I'm terribly sorry, sir, that trick doesn't usually go wrong,' he said, 'but once you've had it invisibly mended, you'll hardly notice the burn.'

Having said his piece, he wisely beat a retreat.

The owner of the jacket held it up to assess the extent of the damage, then, obviously puzzled by what he found, turned it over.

'There's no hole in it!' he said.

'Indeed there isn't,' the magician agreed.

The crowd applauded, and the magician bowed.

'For my next trick,' he said, 'I will make half my audience immediately disappear.'

And then he produced a hat, and held it out in front of the people nearest to him for their contributions.

He had been right about some of the audience disappearing, but Woodend stayed, and when the hat reached him, he dropped a handful of change in it.

'A curse on you bloody foreigners,' Paco said, in mock-anger.

'What do you mean?'

'You always over-tip for everything, which makes things very difficult for the locals. And now you've squandered all your money, I suppose you're expecting me to buy you a beer.'

'That's right,' Woodend agreed, grinning.

They sat at a café facing the artificial lake. The beer was Mahou Five Star, their heads had cleared, and the weather was perfect.

'The important thing when you're watching a magic trick is to be looking in the right direction,' Woodend mused.

'And what was the right direction in the trick we just saw?' Paco asked.

'I don't know,' Woodend admitted. 'If I had known, that's the direction I would have been looking in, and I'd have seen how the trick was done.'

'This conversation isn't about magic at all, is it?' Paco asked.

'It is, in a way,' Woodend answered. 'It seems to me that what a good detective learns to do is to look in the places which are not obvious – the places most people wouldn't even think of looking – because that's how he'll discover how the trick was done. Do you see what I mean?'

'I'm not quite sure,' Paco admitted. 'Are we talking about Faustino's murder here?'

'Yes, we are,' Woodend replied. He paused. 'Let me put things slightly differently. Sherlock Holmes once said, "When you have eliminated the impossible, whatever remains, however improbable, must be the truth".'

'So now you're Sherlock Holmes, and I'm your Dr Watson,' Paco said, amused.

Woodend shook his head. 'No, nothing as grand as that. When we came to Madrid you were Don Quixote and I was Sancho Panza, but now, after a few days here, you're the old Paco – Inspector Ruiz – and I'm standing in for Fat Felipe.'

Paco smiled. 'Go on.'

'The last thing you told me about the case was that you'd talked to Luis, and ruled him out as the killer, which meant you were left without a single suspect.' Woodend took a slug of his beer, and wished he had a cigarette to go with it. 'You did tell me you caught the killer in the end, didn't you?'

'Yes.'

'So this is what I think you did,' Woodend said. 'You worked out what direction you hadn't looked in – or to put it in Holmes' words, you considered which improbabilities you were left with.'

'You're right of course,' Paco agreed. 'I conferred with my colleague, Eleanor Roosevelt – the world's greatest hen detective – while I was giving her some corn the next morning, and she agreed with me that there was only one road left to take.'

'So what did you do?'

'I went to see Colonel Sanz, the area commander, who I had not seen since the bullfight. He said he was far too busy to engage in a long conversation with me, and I said I'd only keep him a second, because I only had one question, and that question could be answered with a single word.' Paco smiled again. 'Do you know what that question was, Charlie?'

'Maybe not the exact question, but I think I can have a pretty good stab at guessing the general content,' Woodend said.

Chapter Twenty-Seven

Monday 15 May 1937

Enrique Gómez was effusive in the welcome he extended to Paco.

'I see so few people these days,' he said, almost by way of an apology for his enthusiasm. 'Will you have a glass of brandy with me?'

'Yes,' Paco said, 'I think I will. I think we'll both need one.'

Gómez poured the drinks – his hands seemed less shaky than they had the last time Paco had visited him – and they both sat down.

'Did I ever tell you about the *toro bravo* I fought in Cordoba, back in 1911?' the old matador asked, and without waiting for an answer, he continued, 'They call that part of the country the cauldron of Spain. Did you know that?'

'Yes,' Paco said, 'but that's not …'

'It was certainly a cauldron that summer, but the *señoritos* of Seville still came to see me. Imagine it – these men who thought they were so important that they expected everyone else to go to them, travelled over one hundred and forty kilometres in that heat to see *me*! And in those days, a hundred and forty kilometres really *was* a hundred and forty kilometres. But it was worth their journey, because when I faced that bull …'

'It's over, Don Enrique,' Paco said quietly.

'What do you mean?'

'You told me that you watched the bullfight from the president's box, didn't you?'

'Yes. As I think I explained, it was, in a way, a great honour to be invited, but it was certainly no more than I was ...'

'I talked to Colonel Sanz, less than hour ago,' Paco interrupted him. 'He confirms that you were in the box, but also says that you left as soon as Faustino had walked out of the ring.'

'Yes, I remember now. I wanted some fresh air.'

'He also says that when you returned, fifteen minutes later, you looked very distressed.'

'Of course I was distressed. I had just seen a fellow matador gored in the ring.'

Paco shook his head sadly from side to side. 'It's time to come clean, Don Enrique,' he said.

Gómez nodded, acknowledging the truth of the remark. 'Yes, it's time to come clean,' he agreed. 'What do you want to know?'

'All of it,' Paco said.

'All of it. Of course,' Gómez said heavily. 'I begged Faustino not to enter the ring again in Spain, but he said that he had to do it. Very well then, if he had to do it, he had to, and I reconciled myself to it, because he was my adopted son, and I loved him dearly. Of course, I knew it would pain me to see him kill the bulls – especially the second one – but I thought I could manage that pain. And then I made my big mistake.'

'What mistake?'

'I accepted the invitation to sit in the president's box.'

'Why was that a mistake?'

'Because the president and Colonel Sanz wouldn't stop talking about what great things Faustino was about to achieve. "I'm told that when *El Gitano* has fought these two *toros bravos* today, he will have killed more bulls than any matador this century," Sanz said. "That's right, he will have,' the president agreed. "Do you think he is the greatest matador of all time?" the colonel asked. "That's certainly what a lot of people who know about bullfighting are saying – and I'm inclined to think they're right," the president answered.'

Gómez threw his glass against the wall. It smashed, and for a few moments, he and Paco watched as several small brown streams of brandy trickled down the wall on their journey to the ground.

'Those two men – Sanz and the president – were talking as if they didn't even realise I was there,' Gómez said. 'Or perhaps they did realise it, but it didn't *matter* that I was there – because *I* didn't matter!'

'They can't have thought that,' Paco said soothingly. 'The president would never have invited you into his box, if that had been his attitude.'

'The president probably invited me as a favour to Faustino,' Enrique said. 'I counted for very little – and I would count for even less when he had killed those two bulls. I wondered if there was something I could do, even at this stage. Then Diego was gored, and Faustino left the ring. It seemed like a sign I couldn't ignore.'

Faustino is in the chapel. Diego's death has unnerved him. He has watched the fight himself, with the eyes of a professional, and he knows that the reasons Diego was gored were because he failed to read the bull right and because he had decided that the best way to please the crowd was to act more like a showman than an artist. So yes, as much as any man's death is his own fault, Diego is responsible for his own demise.

He knows this, but he doesn't quite believe it, because deep inside him there is a small voice which whispers that this a message from God which is aimed directly at him – a warning that he should not disobey

314

the commandments by defying his father, that if Enrique does not want him to fight, then he shouldn't.

Yet he knows he must *fight. He has gone against all the conventions and left the ring in the middle of the* corrida *so that he can pray to the Blessed Virgin to intercede with God, and ask that he be allowed to do what he knows he has to do.*

On his knees, he holds out his sword in front of him.

'Bless this sword,' he implores. 'Make it the instrument of my victory and thy triumph.'

He realises he is not alone, and turning around, he sees Enrique Gómez in the doorway.

He stands up, and places the sword reverently on a side table.

'Why are you here, Father?' he asks.

'You will fight three bulls today, not just the two, won't you?' the old man asks.

'Yes, as you know better than anyone, that is the custom when one of the other matadors is unable to kill his own bulls.'

'That makes matters even worse than they were,' Gómez moans. 'Instead of you having killed one more bull than me, you will have killed two more.'

'Father, you were a great matador,' Faustino says. 'You live in the hearts of all the people who saw you fight.'

'And when they are all dead? What will my legacy be then?'

'You will have the statue ...'

'No, it will be you – the matador who has killed more bulls than any other – who will have the statue. Please, my son, I beseech you, do not fight today. Go to Mexico, and find true happiness there.'

Faustino sighs. 'Father, I love you,' he says. 'I would do almost anything for you. I would even die for you if you wanted me to. But my whole life, since the day you adopted me, has been leading up to this moment, and

I cannot give it up and be denied my triumph. Can you honestly say that if you were in my place, you would act any differently?'

Gómez doesn't want to think about that last question – can't bring himself to think about it – so instead he picks up Faustino's sword.

'So you'd die for me, would you?' he demands.

'Yes, Father.'

'You'd just stand there, and let me kill you?'

'Yes, father.'

And Gómez plunges the sword into Faustino's heart.

'He didn't really believe I was going to kill him,' Gómez said, 'but if he had, I don't think he would have behaved any differently. Faustino was a good, dutiful son. It was only *El Gitano* who would have defied me.'

'And yet it was you, his father, who robbed him of his life,' Paco said.

'No!' Gómez said. 'The eyes which saw him there in the chapel were the eyes of a father, and they were full of love. The hands which held the sword which killed him were the hands of the matador, Enrique Gómez.'

'But they're both you,' Paco said.

'Yes,' Gómez admitted, 'they're both me.'

'Are you sorry you killed him?' Paco asked.

An expression of pure anguish and misery filled Gómez's face. 'But of course I'm sorry.'

'Then why did you run away? Why didn't you stay, and face the consequences of your action?'

'Why didn't I stay?' Enrique Gómez repeated, as if not quite able to believe that anybody could be so stupid. 'I killed Faustino to protect my statue. If I had admitted to killing him, they would never have erected the statue, and he would have died in vain.'

He walked over to the cabinet, picked up a glass, and poured himself another brandy.

'I will never see that statue myself,' he continued, 'because by the time they put it up, I will already have drunk myself to death.'

'Why don't you go and see a priest – perhaps even Don Pedro?' Paco said, though he was surprised to hear his atheist self make such a suggestion. 'He may be able to grant you absolution and bring you a little peace.'

'I have no use for priests,' Gómez told him. 'Besides, I do not want to lose my guilt. I want to carry it around until the end of my days, like a heavy weight. It is what a man does.' He took another slug of brandy. 'Have you seen the wound that killed Faustino?'

'Yes.'

'Did it chip any of the ribs?'

'No, it didn't.'

Gómez nodded. 'I thought so. You can always tell when it is a clean thrust. I am an old man, and I never thought I would achieve greatness again, but that …' and a look of mad pride came into his eyes. 'That was the finest thrust of my entire career.'

Chapter Twenty-Eight

Monday 16 May 1977

They had entered Madrid by the southern route – passing through Albacete and skirting around the ancient city of Toledo – but on the return journey, they took the northern, more scenic route, with a side trip to Cuenca.

Paco didn't say much as they negotiated the twists and turns, and seeing the sheer drops that lay just beyond the edges of the roads, Woodend was grateful that his friend seemed to be paying so much attention to his driving.

The previous evening, they had made a final tour of the tapas bars near their hotel, and while they ate and drank, they had talked about food, the town of Calpe, their wives, and the time each of them had spent working in their respective police forces.

What they had *not* talked about was the reasons for the visit to Madrid. Woodend would have been quite willing to talk about it, but since Paco seemed reluctant to raise the subject, he'd been happy to let it lie.

You need time for your brain to process these things, he thought, as he looked out of the car window at yet another steep drop, but sometime or another in the near future, it will *have* to be discussed.

They reached Cuenca at lunchtime. Woodend was impressed – as well he might have been. The town stood on an outcrop of rock between two deeply cut river gorges. It had been fortified since the early Middle Ages, and at times had belonged to the Moors, and at other times to the Christians. Now, it was mostly invaded by tourists, who came to see its famous hanging houses, which were built right up to the edge of the cliff, and had balconies which seemed to hover over the gorge.

'I know a lovely little restaurant in the old town …' Paco began. He smiled, awkwardly. 'I *did* know a lovely little restaurant in the old town – forty years ago. I expect it closed down a long time ago.'

But it hadn't. It was still there, with its low ceiling beams from which hung strings of garlic and legs of mountain ham.

The waiter – whose parents must still have been children the last time Paco visited the establishment – smiled and said, 'What can I get you, *caballeros*?'

'Do you still have *zarajos* and *morteruelo*?' Paco asked, more in hope than expectation.

'Of course, they are the specialities of the house. Which would you like?'

'Both,' Paco said, beaming. 'And make it double rations.'

The waiter looked dubious. 'I think you'll find our single portions are more than generous,' he said diplomatically. 'And you must remember that both dishes are rather rich.'

'I may look like an old man,' Paco said. 'In fact, I may – much to my own surprise and astonishment – actually *be* old man – but today I have the appetite of a crocodile that has been fasting for Lent. So bring us double rations, and you'll not see any of it go to waste.'

319

The *morteruelo* was served in a clay pot with chunks of freshly baked bread. The waiter described the red wine which came with the dish as 'robust', and that was exactly what it was.

'Felipe would have loved this,' Paco said wistfully. Then he stopped eating, and looked Woodend squarely in the eye. 'Thank you.'

'For what?'

'For accompanying me on my quest. For being both my squire and my friend.'

'Think nothing of it,' Woodend replied, and then – hoping he wasn't sounding too anxious, he added, 'Has it worked? Did you succeed in vanquishing your demons?'

'I didn't vanquish them, no, and I was foolish to think I ever could,' Paco said. 'But at least I have faced them, and that's a start. And the next time we clash, I will have my new allies behind me.' He shook his head. 'No, I'm wrong to call them that. They're not new at all. They've always been there – but I didn't know it.'

'You've lost me,' Woodend admitted.

'I'm not surprised. What else could you expect when I'm talking complete rubbish?' Paco asked, looking very embarrassed.

'I'm not going to let you get away with that,' Woodend said. 'Tell me what you meant.'

'I am too old to be fanciful,' Paco said.

'If you're not too old to order double rations of *morteruelo*, you're not too old to be fanciful,' Woodend said firmly.

Paco sighed. 'All right,' he said. 'When we were in Calpe and I thought of Madrid, I remembered the friends I'd lost, and the people I didn't even know who lay bleeding in the streets. I remembered the sheer hell of working on the Valley of the Fallen, and the agony of learning to walk again.'

'And now?' Woodend asked gently.

'And now when I think about it, I will remember Eleanor the feathered detective, and Fat Felipe's obsession with bacon. I'll think about making love to Cindy when we were both so tired we could hardly even walk, and of the crowds on the streets, laughing and joking, even though they knew death might only be minutes away. Those memories are my army now.'

'And they'll flatten the demons every time,' Woodend promised.

The waiter arrived, with a large plate weighed down by *zarajos*. Woodend suspected they were something vaguely intestinal, but they smelled delicious, so what the hell.

'Is there anything more you'd like to say on the subject of our little excursion?' he asked.

'No,' Paco said. 'In fact, I'd prefer to talk about something else entirely. Why don't you suggest a topic?'

'Well, you never did get around to telling me what happened to Enrique Gómez in the end,' Woodend said.

'No, I don't suppose I ever did,' Paco agreed.

He was teasing, of course. While he was speaking, he did a pretty fair job of keeping his face straight, but once he had stopped, a slight crinkling at the corners of his mouth gave him away.

With a theatrical sigh, Woodend joined in the game. 'If there's one thing I really enjoy, it's having the piss taken out of me by a stupid old fart who has had the bloody nerve to drag me halfway across Spain,' he said.

'That is a most inaccurate statement to make,' Paco retorted.

'Indeed?' Woodend asked. 'And is there any part of it you find particularly inaccurate?

'Yes, there is – I have dragged you nothing *like* halfway across Spain.' He took a sip of the excellent wine. 'If you want to hear the rest of the story, you only have to ask, you know.'

Woodend put his hands together in supplication. 'Please, Uncle Paco, tell me the rest,' he said.

'Enrique said he needed to go into his bedroom, and promised he wouldn't be long,' Paco said.

'You weren't afraid he might try to escape?'

'We were three floors up. Besides, when a man opens his soul to you one minute, he is not going to run away the next.'

'That's true,' Woodend agreed.

'When he came out again, he was wearing his full matador's costume. The effect it had on him was amazing. He had gone into his bedroom as an old man, and emerged thirty years younger. The costume seemed to fit him perfectly. It was almost as if it was not a costume at all, but a time machine.'

'Lucky old him,' said Woodend, patting the pot belly he had earned, but still resented.

'He asked me if I would escort him to the front line, and I said yes.'

'I see,' Woodend said.

'And what does that mean, Charlie?'

'As a result of considerable effort on your part, and on the part of Fat Felipe, you'd just succeeded in tracking down a murderer. I would have thought your next step would have been to arrest him, and hand him over to the appropriate authorities.'

'I had no power to arrest him,' Paco said. 'And what were the appropriate authorities? The judicial system had all-but collapsed, as had the prison system. If I'd handed him over to the military, they would have either told him to go away or shot him on the spot. So I took him down to the front line, as he requested.'

'And what happened once you were there?'

'Some of the men in the trench were old enough to have seen him fight, and those that were not had heard their fathers and uncles talk about it, so his arrival created something of a stir. After all, he was a hero to these men, and they flocked around him.'

'So he'd just gone down there for a spot of adulation, had he?' Woodend asked.

'Yes, in a way – but perhaps not in the way you might imagine,' Paco said enigmatically.

'Explain,' Woodend demanded.

'He asked for a ladder, and when they brought one to him, he laid it against the side of the trench that bordered no-man's land, and climbed up it. Then he stood on the lip of the trench, and looked across at the enemy lines, which could not have been more than a hundred metres away.'

'And no one shot at him?'

'Not then. Remember, he was wearing his matador's costume, which must really have puzzled and intrigued the enemy.' Paco paused. 'Did I mention that he had his sword with him?'

'No, you didn't mention that you'd allowed a murderer to retain his lethal weapon,' Woodend said.

'Well, I had. He had his sword with him, and he raised it above his head and began walking towards the enemy lines. Someone shouted, "Viva Enrique! Long live the king of matadors!" and then all the men in our trenches were shouting it "Viva Enrique! Long live the king of matadors!" When he was about halfway across no-man's land, the men in the enemy trench began shouting it, too. "Viva Enrique! Long live the king of matadors!" Then there was a new sound – a man, probably an officer, shouting through a megaphone. "Drop your sword, and put your hands in the air."

'Enrique froze. The men in our trench looked at each other ques-tioningly, with real distress in their eyes. Was this how it ended? they were thinking. Were there no real heroes left anymore? And then Gómez began to walk towards the enemy lines again, his sword held high above his head. There was fresh chanting. "Viva Enrique! Long live the king of matadors!" "Viva Enrique! Long live the king of matadors!" "Drop your sword, and put your hands in the air," the man with the megaphone said. "This is your final warning." But he didn't drop his sword, and the last thing Enrique Gómez heard before the machine gun bullets almost cut him in two was, "Viva Enrique! Long live the king of matadors!" I don't think he had ever been so happy in his entire life.'

'Can I ask you a couple of questions?' Woodend said.

'Of course,' Paco agreed.

'Then here's the first one: didn't Enrique realise that in behaving as he had, there was absolutely no chance that Franco would allow a statue of him to be erected once the war was over?'

'We can never know for certain what was in his mind, but I think he did appreciate that,' Paco said. 'I think that was the point of the whole thing – by deliberately ruining his own chances of immortality, he was paying his debt to Faustino in the only way he could. What was your other question?'

'You remember you said there was a great deal of chanting – "Viva Enrique! Long live the king of matadors!"'

'Yes?'

'Who started it?'

Paco grinned sheepishly.

'That may have been me,' he admitted.

Notes and Comments

Chapter One

Seat 600

The Seat 600 was first popular family car in Spain, and helped to kick-start what became known as Spain's economic miracle. It was based on the Italian Fiat 600, and had a 633cc engine (hence the name). Between 1937 and 1973, Seat produced nearly 800,000 of this model (Paco's was one of the earlier ones!) and it became as iconic in Spain as the Mini was in England.

Fascists

Most history books talk about the Spanish Civil War in terms of a conflict between the Republicans and the Nationalists, but throughout this book I refer to Franco's side as either the rebels or the Fascists. There are four reasons for this. The first is that the action in the book takes place exclusively on the Republican side, and that is how they referred to their enemies. The second is that Franco's people were rebels – the Republican government was democratically elected, and they sought to overthrow it. The third is that by any measure, they were Fascists, and many of their actions closely mirrored those of Hitler and Mussolini. And lastly, I find the term 'nationalist' misleading, since it implies that the only Nationalists were on Franco's side, and whilst there were many internationalists and regionalists (not to mention anarchists!) on the Republican side, there were also many Republicans who considered themselves to be fighting for Spain.

Executions

Cindy's comments on the number of executions may seem a little exaggerated, and indeed, exaggeration is quite common in the case of eyewitnesses, but, if anything, she is understating this case. A.V.Philips, a British journalist reporting from Madrid at the time, estimated that there had been 100,000 executions in Spain by the end of 1939. An Italian diplomat, who was also an eyewitness, claimed that there were between 200 and 250 executions a day in Madrid alone. Rodríguez Vega has written that two million people had been in prisons or concentration camps by the end of 1942. Those lucky enough to dodge a bullet were given prison sentences of up to thirty years. And, as a final act of vengeance, disabled men who'd fought on the rebel side were granted a war pension, while those who fought on the Republican side (as honourably, or perhaps even more so, than the rebels), got nothing.

Chapter Two

Gran Vía

To forestall any emails pointing out to me that that in 1977 Gran Vía was called José Antonio: José Antonio Primo de Rivera was the leader of the fascist Falange, and was executed in Valencia on 20 November 1937, on the same day and in the same month that Franco's death was announced in 1965. (There is a school of thought which suggests that this was no coincidence, and that, aware of the symbolism, Franco's successors either ordered the thirty-seven doctors attending him to keep him alive until that date, or hushed up the fact that he died earlier. But I digress!)

Franco considered José Antonio an effete intellectual, which made him pretty close to being the scum of the earth, but once he was conveniently dead, he became useful, and by raising him to near-sainthood, Franco managed to attach José Antonio's followers to his own cause. Thus Gran Vía – the Fifth Avenue or Oxford Street of Madrid – was renamed in his honour. To the Madrileños, however, it remained what it had always been, the Gran Vía.

Casa de Campo

The Casa de Campo (literally 'country house') was created in the early sixteenth century as the royal hunting grounds. In 1931, after the monarchy was overthrown, it was opened to the public. It is roughly five times the size of Central Park in New York.

There is darker side to the Casa's history. Shortly after the Fascist revolt, the Republican government all-but disintegrated, and a period of anarchy ensured. It was during this period that the Casa de Campo served as the killing fields, the place where a number of Republican vigilante groups and ad-hoc militias executed men who they had decided were enemies of the state. There is no doubt that many of those killed lost their lives simply because someone in the militia disliked them or because (and this was far too common) they owed them money.

To be fair, however, once the government had more-or-less re-established control, the killings virtually ended. This was in marked contrast to the Fascist side. Here, once Franco had a firm grip on his forces, terror was used as a form of control and intimidation.

Murder in Albacete
This investigation takes place in the third Paco Ruiz novel, *The Fifth Column.*.

Chapter Five

Ramón Areces, the tailor who made Faustino the Matador's suits, went on to found El Corte Ingles – the English Cut – which is currently the largest chain of department stores in Europe, and the third largest in the world.

Barrio de Salamanca
The barrio de Salamanca, located just off Goya Street in one of the most affluent parts of Madrid, is traditionally known for its right-wing sympathies, and support for Franco showed no sign of abating with his death. When I lived there in the early 1980s, there were still a large number of stalls on the street selling Franco souvenirs – key rings, lapel badges, etc – and anyone seen reading the liberal El País newspaper while drinking a beer in the Cervecería Cruz Blanca ran a fair chance of being beaten up.

Duros
The duro was five pesetas, so a hundred pesetas was twenty duros. Quoting prices in duros was common practice when buying and selling everything, from a kilo of apples (one or two duros) to a flat

in the centre of the city (which could be several million duros).

Chapter Six

Real Madrid and the Mediterranean League

Real Madrid: The official records of the Franco regime show Adolfo Meléndez as president of the club at the time when Antonio Ortega was, in fact, in charge. Unfortunately, Ortega was not around to dispute this, since Franco had had him shot in 1939. The title Real Madrid was restored by the Generalissimo.

The Mediterranean League: Since Real Madrid was not allowed to compete, and Atlético Bilbao (the leading club at the time) could not compete since most of its players were either soldiers on the Republican side or had fled to France, Barcelona won the competition without much effort.

The Free Spain Cup

This was meant to be competed for by the four teams at the top of the Mediterranean League, but since Barcelona had decided to go on a tour of Mexico and the USA (from which only four players returned), Levante, Valencia CF's local rival, was allowed to enter. Levante won, and at the end of the dictatorship, sought to have the cup recognised as official (there would have been no chance while Franco was still alive). Unfortunately, the Royal Spanish Football Federation refused to recognise either the Mediterranean League or the Free Spain Cup. The Federation still refuses. This annoys Barcelona, but since they have won more trophies than you could shake a stick at, they can probably live with it. It is, however, particularly galling to Levante, since the Free Spain Cup is the only trophy they have ever won.

Chapter Eight

The Massacre in Granada

This massacre is particularly interesting to me since it explodes two popular myths – (1) that the Jews and Christians were always and everywhere oppressed by the Moors, and (2) that all Moors were mates, and that Moorish Spain was always one big happy kingdom.

Here's what actually happened – on 30 December 1066 (less than a week after William the Conqueror had been crowned King of England) a Muslim mob stormed the royal palace and crucified Joseph bin Naghirela, a Jew and vizier (chief counsellor) to the king. The mob may simply have resented the fact that a Jew held so much power in an Islamic kingdom (a power which he ostentatiously displayed), though at least one source claims they were incensed when it was revealed that Joseph intended to betray the city to the King of Almería, an old rival. Whatever the case, the mob then proceeded to massacre all the Jews living in the city.

Massacres by Muslims were rare, and usually spontaneous. Massacres carried out by Christians were much more common, and usually organised by the government, often as an exercise in control by terror, and sometimes to facilitate the expropriation of the Muslims' or Jews' property.

This is eerily mirrored in the Civil War, with the Republican civilians acting spontaneously and the Nationalist (Fascist) forces working towards a definite policy aim.

Chapter Ten

The Palace Hotel

The Palace Hotel still exists, and anyone with a fair number of euros in his or her pocket can enjoy the experience of taking tea or drinking a beer under that same cupola.

Chapter Eleven

Kay Francis

Kay Francis is one of the more obscure Hollywood players nowadays, but between 1930 and 1936 she was the number one star, appearing on more movie magazine covers than any other actress (with the exception of Shirley Temple). In 1935, for example, she earned $115,000, while Bette Davis, who is now much better known, earned a paltry $18,000. *Give Me Your Heart*, based on a play by Joyce Cary, also starred George Brent (who?)

Chapter Seventeen

Guardia de Asalto

A paramilitary constabulary founded by the Republican government in 1931. It was made up of men considered to be especially loyal to the Republic, and was meant to be a counterbalance to the Guardia Civil, which the government did not entirely trust.

Chapter Eighteen

Toledo steel

Toledo is seventy kilometres from Madrid, and was once the

capital of Spain. It has been famous for its steel since early Roman times. Hannibal had all his weapons made there during the Second Punic War (218 BCE), and the Romans learned from him, and had all their swords made there. In the Middle Ages, kings from all over the known western world commissioned their weapons from Toledo, and though many other places tried to imitate the steel, they always failed.

Today, tourists buy paper knives and swords made of Toledo steel with delicate patterns in filigree picked out on the blades.

Toledo was also the home of El Greco, and many of his works can be seen there.

Chapter Twenty-Seven

Señoritos of Seville
The term means 'young gentlemen' or 'young masters', but is more often used in a pejorative way, to mean 'spoiled brats'. Among the rich families of Seville, there were many señoritos.

Chapter Twenty-Eight

Zarajos and morteruelo
Zarajos are the marinated intestines of suckling lambs, wrapped around vine shoots. They can be fried, roasted or grilled, and are usually served with a sprinkle of salt and a drizzle of lemon juice.

Morteruelo is a pork liver-based pâté. The pork liver is ground up, then combined in a pan with spices, other meats – quail, partridge and hare are typical – bread crumbs and either broth or milk.

Suggested Reading

This is a list of books the general reader may find interesting. I have given a brief description of each one. They are in no particular order.

The Story of Spain *by Mark Williams – Mirador Publications, 1992*
A concise, amusing, and easy-to-read history, from pre-historical times to the post-Franco era.

The Clash *by Arturo Barea – Flamingo, 1984*
Barea was born in poverty in Madrid. He had a varied career, being at one time the head of the patent bureau, and, during the Civil War, the chief censor in the press office. Having fled to England, he worked for the BBC during World War Two. This book is the third part of his autobiography, and covers his time in Madrid during the siege.

The Face of War *by Martha Gellhorn – Granta Books 2016*
As well as a beautifully written section on her time in Madrid during the siege, this marvellous book also has accounts of the many other wars Gellhorn covered.

El Hambre en el Madrid de la Guerra Civil 1936–39 *by Carmen Gutiérrez Rueda and Laura Gutiérrez Rueda – Ediciones de Librería 2015*

An excellent account of the hunger in Madrid, based on eyewitness accounts, and written by sisters who were young children at the time. Unfortunately, it is only available in Spanish.

The Spanish Civil War *by Hugh Thomas – Pelican Books, 1968*

A dense, detailed, scholarly work on the whole of the war. Mainly for reference and dipping into.

Death in the Afternoon *by Ernest Hemingway Arrow Books, 2004*

Everything you always wanted to know about bullfights – and probably a few things you didn't!

Frontline Madrid *by David Mathieson – Signal Books, 2014*

An excellent account of the siege of Madrid, with several carefully worked out itineraries.

Blood of Spain *by Robert Fraser – Penguin, 1981*

Eye-witness accounts, some of them pretty harrowing.

Hotel Florida *by Amanda Vaill – Bloomsbury 2015*

Tells the story of several famous people – including Hemingway and Dos Passos – who spent some time in the hotel. Very readable.

CPSIA information can be obtained
at www.ICGtesting.com
Printed in the USA
LVHW110457130522
718633LV00006B/229